San Mateo's Axe

San Mateo's Axe

Terry Lee Fowler

Illustrated by Donald S. Fowler and Michel R. Henderson

LIST OF ILLUSTRATIONS

ACKNOWLEDGMENTS

It is often said that it takes a village to raise a child. In fact, it takes a village to do almost anything. Spanish would not exist in this book were it not for Ashlin Green, Beatriz Gonzales, Oscar Antonio Dozal-Gonzalez, and Adriana Viola. General proof readers/copy editors include Beatriz Gonzales, Elizabeth Darby Junkin, Catherine (Missey) Ritchie, Jill Henderson, and Ian Fowler. A very special thanks goes to my father who cried over this book and illustrated it. He died unexpectedly four days after completing the illustrations. The book contains his last drawings. A very special thanks also goes to Michel Henderson who edited and reformatted my father's artwork and whose drawings grace the covers.

On several occasions, I lost my way and nearly gave up. Ashlin Green (a true daughter), my father, Jill, Mike, Beatriz, Darby, Pat Pinzler, and Missey made sure I did not. Thank you!

Sometimes it almost feels a formality to thank one's wife and family. It is not. Every minute (week, month, year) spent on this project was time I did not spend with them. Missey and Trevor, thanks for tolerating my time away.

Para Ticha, siempre una amiga

"And the Lord God planted a garden eastward in Eden; and there he put the man whom he formed." Genesis 2.8

Prologue: The Llano Estacado

The Llano hides it all. Fifteen or twenty miles east of the snow-capped Sangre de Cristo Mountains, not too far from present day Las Vegas, New Mexico, lies the remnant of the village of San Mateo. Perched on a small hill on the most northern edge of the barren and treeless Llano Estacado, San Mateo once marked the boundary of the lands controlled by the Spanish kings and later Mexican governors. Only reachable over a faintly traceable jeep track, San Mateo now fades into the dust from which it came.

Below the mound that was once la iglesia de San Mateo, the outline of the plaza and the fallen walls of the fortified village protrude through leafless brush and scrub oak. To the north, down a steep embankment, a small partially frozen creek meanders through the barren winter-gray cottonwoods and the skeletal remains of fallen apple trees. Piles of decayed and chewed timber laced with sparkling ice suggest that beaver ponds once lined the streambed.

Further north, on a slight incline well beyond the creek, wheel-carved tracings of the Santa Fe Trail fade into the chicory blue of sky set off by the snow-covered mountains above Ratón one hundred miles away. In the flat, vast, emptiness to the east and south, the untamed Llano Estacado, checkered in winter white, slopes imperceptibly downward toward what is now Oklahoma and Texas.

La Llorona, the crying woman of myth and nightmare killed her children then wailed in remorse, but the Llano hides her dead, and is unrepentant. Not so long ago bursts of human and animal activity interrupted the hissing wind. Now, all of it, the stomping buffalo feet, the hushed voices of hunters, the battle cries of Cumanchis and Presidio lanceros, and the later frenetic locomotive noise have all been swallowed repeatedly by the vast emptiness and numbing wind that rattles through the grass.

After 1730, there were only two peoples here, the Cumanchi and

11

those they displaced. Embracing Spanish cavalry tactics, the Cumanchi, a former foot-bound people of the faraway Great Basin conquered the Llano and warred deep into Mexico. For the hard-pressed Nuevo Mexicano families of the Llano, the only rule was to survive and do it mostly without the support of King or Church. Cumanchis stole their horses, children, and women and burned their homes. In turn, the Nuevo Mexicanos bought stolen horses, stole children and women, and enslaved them. The history of the guerras de los Cumanchis, like so much of the past, now lies hidden beneath the knee-deep grass and a century of summers and harsh seasons of grinding wind and snow.

A faded red and yellow historic marker attempts to tell what happened here:

In 1770, the king granted land to the Griego family. In exchange for his gift, the family built a torreon and a walled village to stop the French from trespassing into Spanish lands. After the massacre of General Villasurs and his army by the French-allied Pawnee along the Platte in 1720, everyone in the kingdom was fearful that the French would swoop into Santa Fe. However, it was not the French but the Caballeros of the Cumanchis (los indios bárbaros) riding their Spanish horses, secured by Spanish saddles, armed with short Turkish-style Spanish Cavalry bows and metal-tipped lances, using light cavalry tactics that defeated Spanish efforts to tame and control the Llano. Often better armed than Presidio troops, the Cumanchis controlled the plains and trade from Nuevo México to Kansas and deep into the Mexican heartland for more than 150 years.

In 1790, several families joined the Griegos in the new walled village of San Mateo. Every family who lived in the village was required to own a firearm. Families that initially could not afford a firearm were given a dispensation to use a good bow for two years. If after two years, a family could not buy and maintain a firearm, the family had no choice but to return to a safer village in the interior.

When first built, perhaps 60 or 70 people lived in the village. Soon many died fighting los indios bárbaros. Children died from cholera and smallpox. Exhausted by the harsh conditions and poor chances of survival, most people left. By 1830, fewer than 20 souls remained. This remnant served to protect the Yanqui and Mexican traders on the new Santa Fe Trail. When Fort Union was built, San Mateo was abandoned for there was no longer the need for a presidio town.

In the end, the historic marker does not tell the full story. In Spanish, among thieves and robbers the saying goes: *Los muertos no hablan—The dead do not speak.* Few of us would disagree with the general premise, except for my family. In my family, the dead have spoken for years. We have a peculiar and fortunate knack for writing down, saving, and enhancing ancient familial stories.

Staring at the worn historical marker in 1970, I muse quietly to myself. I struggle to remember any Spanish. "Polvo eres, y en polvo te has de convertir. Dust thou art, and unto dust thou shalt return."

Memory is painfully short and the Llano unforgiving, still I know all about this place. I know the intimate details of the lives of Victoria Griego and Thomas Trent, my great-great grandparents. My grandmother, Victoria María Josefa Rincón y Trent known to her family and friends as Josefa, carefully recorded their story during the winter of 1891.

Overexposed to the ruinous Catholic missionary zeal of Archbishop Lamy and gray Anglo-Presbyterian stodginess, my mother was embarrassed by Josefa's colorful stories about two young lovers and their dear friend. For most of her life, mother hid grandmother Josefa's papers in an old wooden box with delicate hand-carved interlinking hearts beneath the tin roof in our attic. Just before her death, mother asked me to bring the box to her.

"Hijo, son, tengo un secreto, perdóname. You will need estos cuentos. Read these stories. They are about your long ago ancestors." Caressing them carefully, she removed the thick, black braids of a mysterious young woman.

"Josefa's stories will tell you all about Victoria, Tomás, and María." She gently caressed the hair and then carefully handed me a stack of papers bound with leather strings.

"Do not be too ashamed of our family. Es una buena familia."

My mother's assessment of our family (and the hidden papers) led me to believe the documents would expose some criminal act, a murderer or horse thief. In fact, they contained a tender love story that was perhaps too graphic and honest for my rigid Calvinist mother who now lay in her bed with her worn quilt pulled to her chin and her face turned to the wall.

"I have tried to be a good woman, and I am proud of my family." She whispered struggling to breathe.

If able to stand, she would have said this with her hands firmly placed on her hips, but now she fixed her eyes on the faded, light-green paint covering the rough stucco wall. She spoke in co-mingled English and Spanish.

"Estos cuentos I have read munchas veces. I know my great-grandmother well. Live as well as she did and you will die a proud man," she reassured me in her heavy accent.

She spoke with an earnestness tinged with a dying woman's regret. Having embraced the gray facade of Presbyterianism, she never toasted a saint's fiesta with a glass of fine New Mexican red wine. She never wore a bright fiesta dress with multicolored petticoats and low-cut blouse. She lived hidden behind a black dress buttoned to her neck.

"Go, celebrate life. Búscate una bella señorita."

She turned to me and smiled as she quietly closed her eyes. Dried sunflower blossoms rattled in the cold fall wind, and a warm piñón fire burned in her fireplace when she died. That was a long time ago. Now, I have read Josefa's stories many times. I know the beginning by heart:

Victoria de la Cruz de Dios Griego y Lucero was la única hija, the only daughter, of Manuel and Ana María Consuelo Griego. When she was a little girl, Victoria, exhausted by terror, longed for a faraway safe place. She wanted to live in España, but she was a child of San Mateo and a determined father who did not intend to give up familial lands to seek safety in Santa Fe, let alone move to a place so encumbered by civilization as Spain. Victoria's father, don Manuel Griego, inherited the land, homes, and village of San Mateo. He wished to defend and keep them in a brutal land, but he could not do it alone. If he did not keep the village occupied and its walls repaired to defend against Cumanchi raids, the government would repossess it and re-grant it to someone more capable. Don Manuel needed help. He found it when a tired, wet stranger stopped in San Mateo to pray.

Chapter 1: 1829—A Marriage Proposal

Victoria

This is how Tomás came to me. On a dark, rainy August afternoon in 1829, when I was eleven, Robert Trent stopped in our village of San Mateo. With mild curiosity, I watched the stranger sitting on his horse shivering in his rain-soaked oilskin coat. His long blond hair hung in stringy clumps from beneath his soggy, drooping hat. I watched from the shelter of the zaguán, by our heavy wooden gate, as the extranjero, the stranger, went into la iglesia. Perhaps he went in to pray or to find a dry place. Pero, no Anglo ever went into the church before. En verdad, in truth, very few of the aldeanos, the villagers, entered the church except to bury someone. When the rain stopped, the extranjero left the church. He carefully picked his way through the mud toward our house.

I did not know then that this stranger would bring his son to me, la persona lo más importante en toda mi vida—the most important person in my life. I did not care to know this Anglo man. I had no interest in making new friends. I did not want to know that the Anglo had a son named Tomás. At eleven, yo sabía—I knew everybody died. In the Llano, people suddenly appeared and were just as quickly gone. Cholera, smallpox, blizzards, hunger, and indios bárbaros, stalked the living. God forsook this place as soon as he created it.

Glad to meet anyone new, Papá walked out briskly to greet the extranjero. Papá's traditional single long braid slapped against his back with each firm step.

"¡Buenas tardes!" Papá called out. "Seigo don Manuel Griego. Esta es mi única hija, Victoria. I am don Manuel. This is my only daughter." Papá pointed at me half-hiding behind the gate.

"I am Robert Trent." The newcomer did not smile or wave.

As a trader along the Santa Fe Trail, papá spoke fair English. The extranjero spoke some Spanish. With slow stilted language and large hand gestures, the two managed to understand each other. Papá translated for me.

"He is alone," papá explained. "He is from Missouri."

They talked about the Cumanchi and life in the wilderness.

15

"Muy peligroso, dangerous, dangerous. ¡Bárbaros, Bárbaros!" Papá warned.

"You mean the Comanche." Robert Trent scratched his head struggling to understand.

"Sí, sí, los Cumanchis. They have killed munchos and scared more away."

"Cumanchis?" Robert Trent pulled a blade of grass, chewed it, and drawled, "I see nothing but knee-high grass and far-away snow-covered mountains. I hear only the wind and distant thunder." Beneath the broad brim of his water-stained leather hat, with eyes as blue and distant as the sky, Robert Trent gazed into the green Llano that stretched eternally eastward.

Señor Trent suffered. I sensed it. He was trying hard to forget something. He had the same lost look as mamá who drank heavily to forget her dead children.

"Would God call a man in need of peace to a place that was not peaceful?" Señor Trent spoke to no one in particular.

"Él piensa que este es un lugar seguro. He thinks this is a safe place," papá whispered to me in surprise.

"If you were called here, now that would be a milagro, a miracle," Papá half chuckled, half growled. "As to the Llano, your eyes and heart deceive you. There is no peace here—just danger. The grass will burn soon enough and los indios bárbaros will come for your scalp."

"Danger?" Señor Trent's coat suddenly seemed heavy. His shoulders sagged. "What is danger? My wife is dead. My son is far away. I need a place to stay."

Papá's eyes suddenly brightened. He pointed to the lifeless, empty houses surrounding the plaza.

"¡Hay munchos lugares aquí! There are many places here. Pick one!"

Papá was not generous. He would have offered an empty house to any man who had a rifle and a horse.

Robert Trent sighed in relief. "In return for the house, I will help you in any way I can."

Mouth open in wild disbelief, I stared at señor Trent. In San Mateo, when a man's wife died, he took his children and left for the safety of Santa Fe, Durango, or Monterey. He did not hide in the Llano pretending to be Juan el Bautista.

"Assure me that you are no criminal, señor Trent. Stay five years, serve as a soldado, work in the fields and flour mill, and help me in trading with the merchants on the Santa Fe Trail, and the house will be yours."

Papá happily bartered with the man he thought was safely on his hook, but señor Trent turned and walked slowly back toward la iglesia. Discouraged, papá shook his head and whispered to me.

16

"Él no se quedará, he won't stay."

Señor Trent stopped and looked intently at the church.

"I have to know something," he almost pleaded. "Who carved the crucifix above the altar? Christ's hands have veins and wrinkles. His eyes look right into my heart."

"¿Quién esculpió el crucifijo de la iglesia de San Mateo?" Papá repeated in surprise. "Paula Teresa, mi cuñada, my sister-in-law is the woodcarver and santera here. She is very good with her knife. She sells her work in Chihuahua and St. Louis."

"Then she is a religious woman?" Señor Trent asked struggling to understand papá.

"She denies the existence of God and carves saints. Some would say she is a bruja, a witch, but as long as she stays here on the Llano and shoots the Cumanchis, people let her alone." In those days, papá still fancied himself a matchmaker. As an afterthought he added, "She thinks the Llano is a peaceful place too. She is a señorita—unmarried!"

"She carves saints and is a non-believer?" Señor Trent questioned half-frowning. He squinted, shook his head, and ignored the comment regarding tía Paula's single state. His long hair, now dried, sparkled in the cool afternoon sun. He walked briskly along the muddy path toward the thick, buttressed adobe of La Iglesia de San Mateo. Papá grasped my hand as we followed. Our feet crunched loudly on the gravel path. Uncomfortable with silence, papá took the opportunity to describe tía Paula's qualities in detail.

"Señor Trent, she is a non-believer and a lover of life. She is a good woman."

Señor Trent agreed. "Her carvings show her love of beauty." He drew an outline of the crucifix in the air. ¡Está loco! He is mad, I thought. Peor, worse, they are both mad.

"Sí, sí, she loves to make beautiful things." Papá spoke while watching señor Trent's hands. "Some think she is dark and homely. In truth, she is exquisite like her carvings. She is a rarity on the Llano. She has a good education. She studied Latin, English, and French," he added. Papá was horse-trading. He hoped to persuade señor Trent to stay with promises of a new home and an educated wife.

¿A quién le importa? Who cares, I thought. Accuracy with a rifle is all that matters here. Formal education by itself just got a person killed. What made papá think strong-minded tía Paula wanted to marry anyway, I wondered?

Papá and the extranjero did not go into the church, but meandered into the plaza overgrown with hip-high weeds and littered with broken wagon parts left by hunters, traders, and trappers over the last twenty years. Señor Trent suddenly stopped in front of an abandoned one-room house facing the back of the church. Dark red and pink hollyhocks bloomed in front of its narrow, short door. Tightly closed, faded blue shutters hid its interior from the summer heat and curious eyes. The outside adobe walls desperately needed a new coat of mud plaster.

"This was the Barela house. The señora was a good cook," Papá explained.

Although not a sentimental man, papá's eyes reddened as he described señora Barela. He cleared his throat and stammered. He gulped air and turned his head away from us. He did not mention that the children who once lived in the house died from cholera or that their broken-hearted parents fled to the safety of Santa Fe. He did not mention that the house was abandoned long before I was born.

Papá abruptly shook his head. His long braid swung wildly. He dealt with the Barela's leaving in the way I had come to expect.

"Cobardes, cowards," he said. "They could not deal with the hardships of living here, but you, señor, you can. I can see you are strong."

Hombres de armas, mannish strength was all that papá cared about. He wanted to keep his lands. Men and women with rifles made it possible.

Pushing open the door and ducking under the low, faded-blue wooden lintel, papá motioned señor Trent to follow. Soon both men stood in the dark, cool house. I slipped in after them. The house smelled like a stagnant pond. A fine layer of adobe dust covered everything including the muddy floor. Papá opened the cobweb-laced shutters. Sunlight and flying insects rushed in through the glassless window.

"This is a sturdy house. You will like living here." Papá spoke firmly but quietly. His calm face and voice suggested he knew he had finally closed the bargain and he did not wish to do anything that might change señor Trent's mind. Señor Trent brushed his hand over the cracked and water-streaked plaster. It had been white once. Sunlight trickling through the roof sparkled in the pools of water left on the floor from the earlier rain.

"The roof should be repaired first," señor Trent said. Sunbeams filtering from above danced on his face.

"Bueno, you are staying then. Sí, el techo, the roof, yes it should be fixed first," papá approved.

Señor Trent nodded, but said nothing.

"There is no one here to help you repair the house but my jita," Papá squeezed my arm, "and my sister-in-law, Paula."

"The offer of help is kind, but I have learned to work alone." Robert Trent stepped back, rubbing the front of his neck and chin.

"Ah," papá said. He walked out and left señor Trent and me standing in the middle of the worn and empty house. I shuddered. As far as I was concerned, the Llano had collected another foolish soul.

* * * * *

20

Before breakfast the next morning, Robert Trent found a rickety ladder and climbed up to examine the roof. Tía Paula Teresa and I watched him as we approached. She shouted up to him.

"¡Hola solitario! You have been taught poorly. Don't you know that building houses is women's work?"

Señor Trent stepped back in surprise as tía Paula bounced up the ladder. Although twenty-seven, her uncut hair was tied in one thick braid that fell well below her waist signaling she was unmarried. She wore no hat or scarf. Her low-cut cotton blouse barely clung to her thin shoulders. Her bare feet were toughened and hardened by three months of summer. Her full skirt swished just above her knees. Soft black hair pleasantly accented her legs. From her forehead to the top of her barely-covered breasts, her light chocolate skin glistened with fine sweat.

As she climbed the ladder, I looked up then turned away blushing. She wore nothing under her dress. I stared at the ground until I heard her happily chattering. Curious, I had to look. She was safe at the edge of the roof with her dress pulled snugly around her legs. She stretched her hand toward the extranjero.

"If you are a gentleman, you will help me," she called out cheerfully.

"Perdóname, señorita." Señor Roberto quickly grasped her hand.

"Gracias." She stood beside him pondering the worn roof. "You have no idea what to do, do you?" she said. "Solitario, I am Paula Teresa, I am known as 'la Fea, the ugly one.'" Her laugh made it clear that she did not believe she was ugly at all.

"They say my skin is too dark. ¿Qué te parece? What do you think?"

Señor Trent chuckled but he did not answer. I could see tía Paula put him at ease. Tía Paula Teresa knew it too. She flirted with him.

"Solitario, don't you know that building houses is women's work?" She repeated.

"Señorita, I did not." Señor Trent spoke crisply. I thought he seemed angry, but he smiled.

"Then, señor, I will teach you what every good woman knows—how to make a strong roof. Come out into the Llano and we will cut straw." She dashed agilely down the ladder. This time, she wrapped her skirts tightly about her legs. Señor Trent followed. Tía clasped my hand and led us out the village gate into the meadows. She alternately sang and gave instructions as we pulled clumps of tall grass and stacked them.

"Now, Solitario, weave the grass into ropelike strands."

She showed us how to twist the grass into long, stiff, and thick pigtails. We bundled the woven straw and carried it up the ladder to the roof. There, tía carefully stuffed the tight ropes of straw into the spaces between the latías, the small cottonwood slats that supported the clay

21

covering the roof. We laid new sod over the straw and packed it, first with our feet, then with wooden mallets. Later, tía showed us how to plaster the inside walls with yeso. At the end of the week, the house was again livable.

"Señor Trent," tía Paula said, "I hope you are as satisfied with the work as my sobrina and I are." She squeezed my hand. "You have a warm dry place to spend the winter."

As we walked away, she whispered to me, "He will not spend the winter alone." Her dark eyes sparkled and she sang.

* * * * *

El otoño, autumn, came quickly. Señor Trent, tía Paula, papá, y los otros arose early and went into the fields to pick corn and cut wheat. Tía Paula and señor Trent worked side by side. I watched them from the top of the wall as they chased each other through the dried corn stalks.

Inside the pueblo walls, mounds of wheat filled the churchyard that served as a threshing floor. Dos viejos, two old men, drove their goats in circles over the straw and chaff. One called for me to come down from the rooftop.

"Niña, ven para aca. Come here. Sing for us."

I hid. The old men chuckled.

"La niña con ojos negros y sin fondo. The girl with bottomless black eyes." I heard them worry. "She has no one. She hides. That is what she does."

At the end of October, it snowed.

In late November, my mother, Ana María, officially introduced señor Trent to tía Paula as a prospective husband. My mother spoke cautiously.

"Hermana, you have no god-mother to arrange a marriage. Forgive me if I help you?" She half-said and half-pleaded while nervously pulling at her fingertips.

Paula Teresa chuckled. "My forgiving you depends on who you propose I marry."

Mamá carefully studied señor Trent. "There are not many good women here. She has an education and property. She is old at 27, but you are not young anymore either."

"So, you think I am old," Paula Teresa teased mamá. "Then perhaps, at 40, you are ancient." Paula Teresa smiled gently at her older sister.

Mamá blushed with the frustration of a timid woman who was trying to do her duty and not doing it very well. She ignored tía Paula's comments.

"Marrying him would be practical." Mamá tried again. "He

22

makes good money working with my husband."

For a few minutes, no one spoke. Señor Trent and tía Paula examined each other carefully in silence. I watched them since they first met. I watched them repair the roof and chase each other through the fields. I knew they cared deeply about each other. Now, both hid their feelings from mamá.

"My husband promised that certain fields and the house would be yours, señor Trent, if you stayed for five years. He will keep this promise. Even if you live with Paula Teresa, which I recommend since her house is more comfortable."

Señor Trent raised his eyebrows in complete confusion, and looked to tía Paula. Tía smiled at señor Trent, and then smiled at mamá.

"Ana María, sweet sister, you are a tongue-tied woman. Let me help you," she paused then spoke to señor Trent. "It is the custom that god-parents arrange a marriage. Since we have no god-parents, my sister has bravely taken on these duties." Before he could speak, tía abruptly turned back to her sister and said, "He is not interested. Adiós."

Tía left our house singing. Señor Trent followed her with a puzzled look. A week later, papá invited them both to dinner. Mamá and her servant Bárbara set the table with silver and candles. She brought out the best wine. Papá now made the proposal to tía on Mr. Trent's behalf.

"Paula Teresa, I remind you that you will not lose your property by marrying. A good marriage will help you keep it. Señor Trent is a good businessman as you say. This is why I have asked him to stay here. He is good with a rifle. He also has a son who is fast becoming a young man. He has agreed to send for his son, and his son will help us. Your marrying señor Trent will benefit us all."

Tía listened quietly to papá's reasoning. She turned to señor Trent and clasped his hand.

"I am a woman of property, but I have no slave help. I rely on the goodness of my sister and her husband to help me bring in my crops. However, I can afford to pay for help in the spring planting season and for the fall harvest. I own a musket and I can shoot. I own horses. I have worked with you in the fields and I helped you repair your house. You are a good trader and merchant and earn good money, but how much money have you saved since your arrival? You *do* have horses and a rifle." She weighed her options. "I must think about this."

She turned toward señor Trent and winked so that only he and I could see. At that moment, I remembered tía whispering to me that señor Trent would not spend the winter alone. I bit my tongue trying not to laugh.

Papá spoke again. "Paula, as you know life here is very dangerous. It is noble and right, perhaps your duty, to accept help. You must think about this seriously."

"Does señor Trent know it is the custom that he buy the bride's wedding trousseau? Does he have the money for this?" tía Paula asked.

Papá stepped back in surprise, but said nothing.

"And the trousseau?" Paula insisted.

"You either drive a hard bargain or jest. I will pay for it out of my own pocket. When was the last time you gave a fig for fine clothes?" Papá asked in exasperation.

He turned to señor Trent. "Roberto, it is appropriate to plead your case."

Señor Trent smiled. "Paula Teresa, I have watched you for many months as you have come and gone. As you say, we have worked in the fields and you have helped me repair my house. We have always dealt with each other fairly. If you agree to marry me, trust that I will always treat you with respect and kindness." He did not mention love.

"Paula Teresa, he is a good man. You are a good woman. Marry as soon as possible. Since I am the alcalde, I will perform the ceremony. If a priest comes, he will bless it. The governor is my good friend and he will not worry that you marry the extranjero. Señor Trent es un buen católico. He is a religious man. He prays more than I do. This will please the priest. I will vouch for you both," papá insisted.

Paula Teresa sat quietly for a few moments. "I could go home and sleep on this marriage proposal, but what is the point? I do not intend to live the life of a nun. I am not suited for the religious life." She turned to señor Trent and smiled. "You need a woman who knows what to do with the yeso. I can help you. You may pray for us both, but do not ask me to pray with you."

Señor Trent laughed. "That you are called, 'bruja y hereje, a witch and heretic,' is not a problem. You will always have my respect." Then he teased, "I can afford a yeso trousseau. If I apply it, I can guarantee it will fit you perfectly. I am now good with the yeso too!"

"Then you have met your responsibilities and I must say yes!" Tía Paula laughed until her ribs hurt.

Mamá blushed and grew flustered. Papá pounced on the opportunity to close the transaction.

"It is settled then. She has her trousseau!"

They were married a month later. In early spring, señor Trent sent for his son. After a six-week journey by wagon from St. Joseph, Missouri, Thomas arrived in San Mateo.

Chapter 2: 1830—Inocente—Victoria de la Cruz de Dios Griego y Lucero

Victoria

One hot June afternoon, after Tomás arrived, smoke blew in across the Llano. The men of the village went to investigate. My brother, Patricio, who lived with us in the village, went along. Patricio was a cabo of the lanceros assigned to the Presidio in Santa Fe, but to make my father happy, the governor stationed him with five other men in our village. Then, in order to avoid paying their wages, the penniless governor carefully forgot about them. As a matter of honor, the men served on without pay. Papá made up for the governor's forgetfulness by providing each man a house and land to farm.

My father joined Patricio and the lanceros, as they rode out toward the fire. The lanceros dressed in heavy leather armor cueras, carried lances, assorted flintlock rifles and pistols as well as bows and arrows. Leather shields, still decorated with the royal coat of arms of Spain, dangled at their horses' flanks.

The men of the village often rode out on patrol, but I remember that day in June because my new tío joined them. With the help of his wife and his practical nature, tío Roberto quickly adapted to local customs. Only his blue eyes marked him as out of place. He dressed in a heavy cuera and carried a rifle, and, for good measure, a lance. He wore his light-brown hair in a single, long braid down the middle of his back. Tanned by many years of riding in the sun, his skin still blistered and peeled easily. To prevent sunburn, he kept mud on his nose.

I often rode with mi papá y mis hermanos. Although not the best shot, I knew how to shoot a mosquete. Still, I did not like the taste that gunpowder left on my lips from biting open los cartouches. I did not like holding the lead ball in my mouth to load either, but my life depended on these skills.

Today father and Patricio forbade me to ride with them. "Es muy peligroso," they said. It was too dangerous--not because I was a chica, a little girl, pero porque yo era demasiado joven, but because I was a young woman. No one spoke it, but everyone understood that at twelve, I was old enough to marry and have children. I had become someone worth protecting.

For most of my life, papá ignored the fact that I was a girl. He made no effort to hide the fact that he wished I had been a son. It angered him that during the summer I wore a dress. He said that leather pantalones protected a person from cactus, snakes, and arrows. Today, he looked me up and down. Clicking his tongue in disappointment, he forbade me to go.

"You are too young to fight los indios bárbaros."

"I can ride and shoot as well as Patricio," I angrily exaggerated, but I didn't want to go and he knew it.

"Un hombre no se pone falda," he muttered. "A man in a dress, a man in a dress. What kind of son is this?"

"¡Yo soy la mejor de sus hijos, ya!" I challenged him.

My lips trembled and my hands shook. I wanted him to notice I was a girl and yet, I was telling him that I was his best son! I pushed my hair back in frustration and stared sadly at the ground. Still annoyed, papá shrugged his shoulders, wheeled his horse, and trotted off. Nearby, Patricio mounted and sitting in his saddle laughed.

"Jita, querida. Creo que estás loca. You are crazy. Nevertheless, for a young woman you are not a bad man, not a bad man at all. Next time, if you want to come, dress in leather. Put a little mud on your face. Smell like dried blood. Father will mistake you for a cibolero, a buffalo hunter, and take you along." Patricio chuckled again. "Of course, if you die like a man you will never marry or have children."

"But there is no one here for me to marry so what difference would it make? This is such a lonely place!" I glared at him.

"Querida, you don't want to go. We don't want you to go. Today it is too dangerous. That is all anyone needs to know."

He reached down and pulled me onto the saddle in front of him. "Ahead there is another little man who needs your company." He dropped me gently on the ground, but I tripped and tumbled at the feet of a surprised Tomás Trent. Embarrassed, I sat at his feet trembling and clutching my dress over my knees.

"Standup jita," Patricio teased. "You give the sad impression that you cannot walk. Two little men," he chuckled, shrugged his shoulders, and then grew thoughtful. "Chica querida, forgive me if I have been cruel, aquí está tu príncipe. Take care of your primo, your cousin. He is lonely like you."

Patricio recognized the obvious. He tipped his wide brimmed leather hat and dipped his lance to Tomás and me in a playful salute. He then spurred his horse and galloped off to catch up with papá. I often watched my brothers and father leave the safety of the village. Pero ahora, today, I said a little prayer.

Without speaking, tío Roberto's son, Tomás helped me stand.

26

Together, we waved sadly as the men rode off. In his paleness, Tomás, like his father, looked ill. I never wanted an Anglo cousin. Since his arrival several weeks before, I avoided speaking to him. Now, dropped right in front of him, I had no choice. I grabbed his hand. He squeezed it, but did not look at me. He pulled me after him to the top of a small hill. Still holding hands, we watched the men disappear into the Llano.

He mumbled in English that I did not understand. Then he said, "¿Eres Victoria?"

"Sí, yo seigo. ¡Y tú eres Tomás!" The words barely came out of my mouth and my voice shook.

He grinned and laughed. "We have met before. You had trouble speaking then too. You were afraid!"

"What makes you think I was afraid?" I challenged still firmly grasping his hand.

"I just do," he insisted with a broad, full smile and comforting laugh.

With his free hand, he softly brushed my cheek. I talked and talking made him happy. I blushed and felt warm. Soon we were chasing each other back and forth through the high grass near our pueblo, éramos niños. We were children.

Thomas

The day my father rode off, I watched from the edge of the village. To me, the village was a grim and uninhabitable fortress of a few desperate, rundown houses, most of them abandoned. The outside walls facing the Llano had no windows or doors—just openings at the top for firing muskets and arrows. Roads entered the village only at the corners. Seen from a distance, the brown adobe walls tarnished an otherwise perfect sea of lush, green grass.

The desperate houses and walls surrounded a desolate plaza used only during the occasional fall trade fairs with the Cumanchis and as the annual fall gathering place of buffalo hunters heading into the Llano. The rest of the year, no one walked in the plaza. Few children played in it. Abandoned traders' wagons cluttered it. Except for the few worn paths between the inhabited houses and the church, grass and high weeds grew everywhere.

I did not understand why my father brought me to this broken, failed place. My friends lived in the faraway country that father forced me to leave behind. Alone, I did not care if the entire prairie, town and all, went up in smoke. Then suddenly, I had a new friend.

Dropped at my feet, as if by a miracle from the sky, Victoria, a small, lost hummingbird with trembling wings, stood up, shook the dust from her thin cotton dress, and placed her gently shaking hand in mine. I

27

had no choice but to notice Victoria de la Cruz de Dios. Born on Easter day, March 22, 1818, like Christ's resurrection, her parents hoped her birth signified the victory of life over death. Victoria's mother prayed desperately that her daughter would simply survive on the Llano, but her father expected her to do more than survive. He expected her to prevail. Although I had seen her before, we had never spoken.

Shortly after I arrived, I helped my father in the fields along the río. I led the horse team while he plowed. Victoria, Paula Teresa, and the other village women followed behind the plow. With their hoes and long sticks, they knocked holes in the fresh furrows and planted corn. Victoria ignored me. My father said we were cousins.

After that day of planting, I thought of her as thin, frail, and shy or, maybe, arrogant. As lonely as I was, it never occurred to me that either of us would ever speak. She seemed permanently part of a foreign way of life I could never understand. Today forever changed how I thought of her. She would always be frail, but I would never again think of her as shy or arrogant.

Her hair and eyes were jet black. Her eyes were so black her pupils were impossible to see. She knew this. She knew that others could not make out where she gazed. She hid behind her impenetrable eyes and kept secrets. She seldom spoke. She watched and studied. If others mistook her silent studious nature for shyness, it suited her. She did not need to reveal herself to such people. She had no need to reveal herself to anyone.

She wore her hair in long braids, dowsed in buffalo tallow. Like heavy thick ropes, her braids looped out from the sides of her head and back upon her ears. Signifying innocence and purity, her hair had never been cut. Her long braids gently framed an angular jaw and a smooth pale-brown face accented by forever-cracked lips. Her face, braids, and head appeared exquisitely designed by the maker of expensive double-handled china. Her nose was elegantly dusted with fine black freckles. At four feet six inches, she was as tall as she would ever be. As the sun and wind danced through her thin dress, it blew the salty perfume of her sweaty hips and legs across my nose and lips. From this moment until the day she died, her scent would linger in my head and heart. Later, when I missed her, I easily recalled her taste and smell by touching my tongue to my lips. Her dress, no more than a threadbare chemise, mirrored her in its frailty. By summer's end, it would fray to nothing. Now, behind the flapping, faded pink gauze, danced a pleasing, smooth, sun-baked shadow of light brown skin scarred with occasional scratches, rough elbows and scraped knees.

On a small hillside, bound by our new friendship in a manner we still did not understand, we were no longer alone. Hand in hand, we watched our fathers ride straight toward what looked like the burning fires of hell. The wind-whipped flames now danced fifty feet above the horizon. The men disappeared into the cornfields on the outskirts of the village, and then reappeared in the tall grass prairie. They skirted a copse of trees and then disappeared again when the dark, thick smoke finally swallowed them.

We stared. Two delighted souls. What unlikely fate finally brought us together? Her dark eyes sparkled. She laughed. Her laughter soon turned into a broad, warm smile. With open arms, both palms up, she grabbed my hands and pulled me toward her causing me to stumble. We danced and twirled. For a dizzying moment, we lost the ability to speak. Soon enough, she shared her secrets. Soon enough, I would understand she wrestled with the serpent of despair and loneliness. In time, I would be her peace, a strange sort of confessor with whom she gladly shared forbidden fruit, a confessor with whom she suffered, lived, and loved openly. Spinning in expectant delight, she finally broke the silence.

"Seigo Victoria de la Cruz, la única hija de Manuel Griego. I am Victoria, the only daughter of Manuel Griego. Oh, my father, he wanted another son. He loves me, but he wanted another son. If I wear a dress, he ignores me. If I wear leather pantalones, he lets me ride with him. Today, I chose to wear a dress and he left me behind. I don't know why I made this decision, but I did and I am happy." She talked on, "Your accent is funny, but now I like you, no? ¿Tú eres mi primo?"

Victoria's every other sentence was a question. She examined me closely and curiously. Her face said, "I am sorry that I hid the last time I saw you. Forgive me." She introduced herself with a deluge of pent-up words that spilled from her mouth like a springtime flood following a rapid snowmelt. Like an inexperienced opera singer briefly interrupting a solo to catch her breath, she paused then furiously chattered on.

"My brother, Patricio, your papá y los otros went to see who set the fire. Two of my brothers went to the Río Mora to herd sheep for the summer. They go every summer. Your father has told you we have many sheep, no? Pascual y Felipe, they are the ones who stay with the sheep. They are the ones who take the herds up the mountains in the spring. They spend the summer in a small, fortified house. It is beautiful, ¡sí! My Patricio, he is a Presidio soldier since he was eighteen. Un soldado de cuera, but the governor has not paid him in many years. Patricio is my favorito. He is the youngest brother, but he is still much older than I am. He does what he wants. Sometimes he is a lancero, y otras veces un cibolero o Cumanchero, a buffalo hunter and a trader with the Cumanchi."

She never mentioned her mother, but I had heard that the Satan of the Llano and the deaths of many of her children had long ago defeated tía Ana. Sad and lonely, tía drank too much wine and hid in her room much of the day.

Before, Victoria hardly spoke, but now she could not speak fast enough. She spoke like one who knew herself well—if she did not say what she needed to say right now, right away, she might never speak again. On and on she went, emptying herself of words and emotions.

"My father married your aunt!" I finally interrupted. "My father said you were quiet. My father said you would be my friend. My father said I would like you. My father said you would be my cousin."

Each of us in turn spoke in desperate barrages laying bare our hearts and souls. Patricio was right. We were both desperately lonely.

Victoria peered at me with her head cocked to her left. Her thick doubled black braid brushed her shoulder. I knew then that hiding behind her dark eyes, she gazed deep into other's souls. I studied her eyes carefully. Startled, she squinted until only jet black was exposed. Except for Patricio and the family servant, no one else had ever tried to find her eyes and meet her gaze. Driven by some unseen spirit, I was compelled to search her out. She knew and rejoiced. Her furrowed brow and thoughtful face responded, "Finally someone sees me!" She squeezed my hands tighter. She spoke solemnly.

"I had other brothers once. They are dead now. Not even their names matter. We never speak of them. God takes everything here. Many men and many women working in the fields have been killed. Las niñas arrebataron, seized as slaves. Death surrounds us here and only God knows the reason. Now God brought you and your father here. Only He knows why!"

She panted and pressed her nose close to mine. She squinted at me, her black eyes searching for my soul.

She whispered, "I must speak to God about all this."

Suddenly she grew pale and drops of sweat erupted on her forehead.

"I am sorry." Her voice was soft and sad. "I think about these things too much. I think how lonely it is. I hear the frogs on late summer nights. They frighten me yet their singing brings me peace. Their deep, droning voices lull me to sleep. I know that when they sing they are both brave and foolish. Their singing brings coyotes, yet they sing, 'life goes on, life goes on.' When I am too frightened, I sleep in a secret place. I hide. I do not sing like the frogs."

Victoria's jaw gently trembled. She paused and looked at me again as though I were the first person she had ever seen. For a moment, she seemed lost. Suddenly, she plunged her hands into my hair. Then, surprised at her uncontrolled impulse, she jumped back nearly falling. Red-faced, she stared at the dusty ground. With her barefoot, she pushed up small mounds of dirt and kicked at clumps of grass until she had scraped a spot of earth bare. She rocked from foot to foot as the east wind tumbled through her dress. A whiff of smoke and a sprinkling of ashen grass sprigs blown from the distant fire drifted over us like gently falling snow. She sneezed. I waited for her to speak again.

"Enough talk of God and fear." Still, she prayed just loud enough for me to hear. "Dios te salve, María, llena eres de gracia—hail Mary full of grace."

She pulled on my hands and then let them go. She backed away watching me carefully. A tear slid gently from her right eye. I tried to brush it away but only managed to smear her face with falling ash. Struggling to control emotions she never intended to reveal, she lifted her dress to wipe the tears from her eyes. Her brown body radiated the warmth of the sun. It did not occur to her that she was exposing herself. She was not ashamed or embarrassed. Her body brought her both happiness and pain. These contradictory gifts often confused her. Soon covered again by a worn dress now smudged with ash and tears, she smiled the broadest of smiles, her face filling with brilliant joy.

She ran toward the grass and weed-choked plaza, stopping only long enough to be sure that I would follow. For hours, we chased each other back and forth through the overgrowth. We jumped off the broken-down wagons. Nearby our mothers chatted. My stepmother quietly carved while her sister talked in hushed tones. We were too far away to hear, but Ana María spoke quite seriously. Paula Teresa smiled and waved from time to time, but her sister did not seem to notice that we were there. Near noon, suffocating smoke borne by a stiff east wind billowed into the plaza leaving us exhausted and choking. We hid beneath one of the wagons.

"Why are you here?" Victoria narrowed her eyes and shook her head gently as she struggled with this profound mystery.

"Because this is where my father is, I don't have a choice," I answered overwhelmed with sadness, but she immediately grew cheerful.

"Good, then you will stay. I will not lose anyone else." I was trapped and she was pleased!

"Let's go," she said. "Merienda, merienda. Come for lunch. Come for lunch. Our genízara servant makes the best chili stew with dried antelope, beans, and peppers. She makes good bread too." She talked again without taking a breath. Stepping backwards, she pulled nervously at the sides of her dress stretching it tightly across the bones of her pelvis and thighs. Looking repeatedly over her shoulders and still fussing with her dress, she slowly walked toward her mother and announced that I would have lunch with her.

"Bien, I will talk some more to tía. You both go. Bárbara will look out for you. I will come soon." Ana María approved.

My stepmother whispered to me. "Be polite, be careful. Te quiero."

"He can come?" With a soft questioning voice, Victoria looked to my stepmother.

"Sí, go, go," stepmother agreed. Victoria half-ran and half-walked home. Sneaking frequent, nervous backward glances, she reassured herself that I followed.

"¡Sí, sí, ya voy! I am coming," I said in the best Spanish that I could muster. She ran. I chased her, caught her, briefly held her, and then set her free. When I touched her, my heart raced in a strange way that I had never before experienced.

The Griego hacienda was on the northeast and highest side of the town's dusty plaza. From its hillside, its heavy adobe walls dominated the village and the Llano. From its roof, one could see far out onto the eastern plain. The house itself was L-shaped. Three-foot thick adobe walls completed a square protecting the open side of the house. The walls facing the Llano had no windows, but in the central courtyard, floor-length windows with solid pine shutters lined the portal. Two fortified wooden gates opened from the plaza into a kitchen garden surrounding the well. In the courtyard, the yeasty smell of baking bread, the scents of chopped basil and cilantro mingled with the coarse earthy incense of ripening cabbages, and still buried onions and garlic.

Hungry, I followed Victoria through the mixture of plush smells to the back of the garden. There, in the middle of her outdoor summer kitchen, a short, round woman prepared lunch over a small cooking fire.

"¿Conoces a Tomás?" Using informal Spanish, Victoria excitedly reintroduced me to Bárbara the family servant.

"Sí querida. I know him." Bárbara assured Victoria and then turned to me.

"Bienvenido."

"Gracias," I said.

I met señora Griego and her servant Bárbara when I first arrived. They helped my new mother unpack my things. Victoria refused to come. She refused to meet new people until she was sure they would stay and survive.

"¿Tienes hambre? You are hungry," Bárbara said reading my face.

" Muy—very," I shook my head in agreement.

Suddenly, a ghostly Ana María Griego appeared at a door behind me. Although forty, Señora Griego appeared closer to fifty. Her tired, pockmarked, and furrowed face reflected her hard life and her resignation to tragedy. Despite flawed and worn skin, shades of her past beauty reappeared in her rare smiles. Elegant, yet emotionally exhausted, she depended on Bárbara to run her household and care for Victoria. The only family member she had not given to her genízara's care was her husband.

Tía had her first child when she was only fifteen, her second at sixteen, and her third at seventeen. Victoria was born when Señora Griego was twenty-eight. Three children born between Patricio and Victoria died, but tía Ana María was unable to describe any of them. A permanent haze of wine driven forgetfulness numbed and protected her from the painful loss of so many children. She tried hard to recall their faces and the years they died, but she could not. She knew one died at birth and two died later of cholera. She remembered vaguely there were two boys and possibly a girl, or maybe it was three boys. She was not sure, for she often described herself as a woman who only gave birth to boys. Manuel Greigo indulged his wife's confusion about the gender of her children. He often treated Victoria as his youngest son.

"Sobrino, I am glad you came. There are not many children here. Victoria has no friends." Tía Griego spoke to no one in particular.

Her gaze fixed on a crack in the outside wall. Her breath smelled faintly of red wine.

"It is lonely here but we do our best," she smiled half-heartedly.

To Bárbara, her slave and confidant, she whispered, "I prayed that the children would find each other."

"They have." Bárbara gently touched señora Griego's shoulder to reassure her.

Señora Griego stared blankly about the kitchen. She stared through me and then through Victoria. She drifted into some hidden place. She prayed often and hard. It was not surprising that Victoria also prayed in the same way, but Bárbara also influenced Victoria. Bárbara did not care much for el Señor y Jesús. The two, Father and Son, were unreliable. They never showed up when needed the most. Bárbara often reminded Señora Griego that the busy Christian God never listened. In response, Señora Griego drank wine and slept many days until noon. She slipped further and further away from her family. When anxious, she pushed nervously with her feet against the floor just like Victoria. Bárbara soon learned talk of God caused señora Griego to grow remote and frightened. She carefully avoided religious discussions.

"Dios, espero que los niños se cuiden el uno al otro. God, I hope the children take good care of each other," señora Griego prayed as though alone. After she said "amén," she distractedly begged me to forgive her.

"Joven, sobrino, con mi preocupación, me había olvidado de ti. In my worry, I forgot you. ¡Perdóname hijo, perdóname!"

Nervous, I smiled and nodded, but did not speak.

"Ayúdeme Tomás," Bárbara whispered. "Help me cut the peppers."

With an understanding smile, Bárbara rescued me from señora Griego.

Chapter 3: Voices Not Heard

Victoria

 I *am* mamá's only daughter, a girl among brothers, and mamá's last child. She worries too much about me. She worries about everything. She drinks too much wine. She shows her worry by ignoring me or treating me like the youngest of her sons. In this way, she is like my father.

 Growing up on the edge of the Llano, I learned to ride a horse, shoot a mosquete, and defend myself like a man. Mamá never allowed me to wear a dress beyond the walls. She feared that if anyone recognized I was a niña, I would be kidnapped and sold or worse! Mamá frequently told stories about the unfortunate girls who ignored their mothers' warnings.

 "Strong men die on the Llano. Do not go into the Cumancheria. If lucky, a captured niña is raped, and enslaved or sold to a stranger for his wife," mamá scolded. "Young women bring a good price in the slave markets." She would nod her head sadly. "An unfortunate niña is raped, her heel tendons cut, her breasts slashed, and she is left to suffer death in the mouths of hungry coyotes. All this as a warning to trespassers in the Llano."

 Having frightened even herself with her gruesome stories, she shrugged her shoulders in despair and quietly slipped into her room where she kept her best red wine. She thought of me as un chico. Quizá, perhaps she thought I would be safer if she pretended I was a boy. ¿Quién sabe?

 Hiding in her wine, she left me alone to deal with her vivid and grisly imagination. Fears of slashing and torture terrified me night after night. Many nights I slept in a secret hidden room, but many more nights I did not sleep. Bárbara warned mamá her stories were too bloody and too cruel.

 Mamá would answer, "He must know. He must know."

 Bárbara gently corrected her, "*Ella*, ella es tu hija. You mean, 'her.' Victoria is your daughter."

 "Sí, sí," mamá agreed covering her face with her hands.

 Today, for a few minutes mamá was different. Sometimes I

brought home stray dogs, turtles, and frogs, pero, ahora un chico, a friend, and a new cousin. ¿Qué sorpresa? To bring a playmate, that surprised and pleased her. She hoped that her sister's stepson and I would be friends. Perhaps, she needed a new friend too.

* * * * *

Even at eleven, I knew that mamá did not understand her sister even a little, at least not that she would admit. For mamá, her sister was one more person ruined by the Llano. Mamá drank her wine, hid, and slept. In her better moments, she prayed relentlessly for the souls of her servant, her sister, and me. She left her sons and husband to their own devices.

"Querida," she often said to me, "if you survive your childhood, you must marry before you are too old like my sister. She is like Sara. She is too old to bear children. God will never make a miracle for her. She will be punished for her blasphemy."

She would then shake her head, "You see how unhappy she is. She will die without children. God will send her to the inferno." She sighed with deep sadness, and then added, "She must be unhappy, I know it. Es la verdad. It is true."

Mamá and her sister, tía Paula, looked like twins, but tía was chocolate and mamá pale. The villagers were certain that neither sister was truly Spanish. Perhaps Ana María was Basque or a descendant of the Visigoths and Paula Teresa was una Morisca? Rumor held that they did not have the same father. Attempts to correct the rumors were pointless.

The villagers traditionally gave nicknames. Ana María, a pale pelicastaña with green eyes, was called "la Irlandesa." The darker Paula Teresa was called "la Fea" or ugly. All agreed it was fortunate Paula Teresa had an education since her prospects of marrying were poor. It surprised everyone when a foreigner agreed to marry the "dark woman." "The Anglo was certainly down on his luck!"

For mamá, the myths about her ancestors' lost fortunes explained her present unhappy situation. Had her ancestors hung on to the familial wealth, she would never have lived in this god-forsaken place. The wealth of her husband rescued her family from poverty and restored its honor. She married well. Her marriage made good business sense, but the marriage left her stranded more deeply in the wilderness she despised. She often wondered aloud to her sister, "Would lost honor have been better?"

Tía Paula Teresa never considered leaving the wilderness. She loved it. It gave her independence she could not have anywhere else. Still, she was a single woman and custom dictated she rely on a man for her occasional business transactions. Pero ella seguía la costumbre a medias. Tía met the custom halfway. Papá added the weight of manly authority by accompanying her on business, but tía did all the speaking.

Tía distinguished herself from mamá whom she regarded as hopelessly dependent on her husband. Because tía lived on the land and farmed it for the required five years, she owned her property outright. Although tía enjoyed her freedom, she understood the dangers of living in San Mateo. Because life was precarious, disagreements and even infidelities were excused so long as one made an honest effort to reconcile and remained committed to staying. Tía Paula Teresa thrived in what she described as "Este ambiente peligroso y compasivo—this dangerous and compassionate environment."

As the youngest daughter with few marital prospects, tía Paula Teresa was sent to a Durango convent school to learn Latin, English, and French to improve her life situation. Her mother prayed she would become a nun. Her father said "no," and tía Paula Teresa rebelled with his encouragement. She soon read Latin, English, and French philosophers, and she proudly spoke all three languages even when no one understood. Cuando mis abuelos died in a Cumanchi attack, papá Manuel paid her way home from Durango. Tía did not mourn the loss of her parents for too long. She blamed no one for their deaths.

Tía doubted the existence of God, but she carved reredos and other church goods because she enjoyed working with wood.

"I like the smell of fresh-cut wood, and I like to see the chips fly," she said. "The spirits of the wood are released by my hands. I have a duty to free them."

Her marriage to an Anglo, encouraged by papá, was a conscious and good business decision that satisfied everyone. Everyone understood, "El amor es muy tonto." Love was foolish. It was as dangerous as anger. Both emotions caused a person to lose self-control.

Tía's well-arranged marriage guaranteed that she and señor Trent would stay in San Mateo, and that San Mateo had two more sets of hands capable of carrying mosquetes. Her marriage let her continue living safely at the edge of the wilderness away from prying eyes. When the occasional visiting priest complained about San Mateo's lax moral standards, she pointedly wore an extra low-cut blouse.

Other than offending the occasional itinerant priest, Tía's lack of faith was ignored or forgiven. Under Spanish rule, no one from San Mateo ever took the Inquisition seriously. After the revolution, there was no Inquisition, and of course, tía was now a married woman. With a husband bound to protect her honor, tía acquired complete independence. From all but her husband, she carefully guarded the fact that she was deeply in love.

Unlike tía, who blossomed in the dangerous wilderness, mamá hated and feared the Llano. Mamá often dreamed of her childhood. When other families gave up and returned to the safety of Santa Fe, the village of her birth, she longed to leave with them. Every evening she watched the sun set over the distant western mountains that hid her childhood home. She pulled herself away from the windows only when it was completely dark and her tears had dried.

Mamá sometimes cooked, but her servant Bárbara, did most of the work on hot summer days. Bárbara said that she was Tewa, perhaps from Nambé, but she barely remembered her early childhood on the Río Arriba south of Taos. Captured in a raid as a little girl, she lived with the Cumanchi most of her life. She did not know her exact age. When her elderly warrior husband died fighting the Osage, she found herself old, toothless, and for sale. Cumancheros bought her for two blankets. The blankets were a bargain to the Cumanchis who no longer cared to feed her. The governor required that captives be returned to their families or villages, but Bárbara did not wish to go home, and the men who bought her wished to make a profit by selling her.

Mamá said that she bought Bárbara because she was too old and too tired to continue traveling with horsemen of any kind. Grateful for any unexpected kindness in the harsh land, Bárbara worked hard for mamá. Mamá promised she would set Bárbara free one day, but she never did for fear she would lose her only friend.

Mamá bought Bárbara on December 5 (Santa Bárbara's feast day) and renamed her in the Saint's honor. I never knew Bárbara's Cumanchi name. Neither she nor my mamá ever spoke it. Bárbara laughed at the Christian God. As far as she could tell, God had done nothing to stop smallpox or cholera. Like mamá, she had many nameless children buried in shallow graves across the Llano.

Mamá never understood Bárbara's feelings about the Christian God. She hoped that naming Bárbara after a saint would encourage the genízara to save her eternal soul by confessing and taking communion before her death. Mamá may have thought that Bárbara's life with the indios enemigos was terrible, but Bárbara often pulled me aside and reassured me that her life among the Cumanchis was a good one.

"They are a good people," she said.

Bárbara cared for me and loved me like her own. When I awakened at night with terrifying nightmares, she rocked me and comforted me until I slept. Sometimes she attempted to correct my mother's horrible stories, but her words were not reassuring.

"Do not be too much afraid," she said. "Los indios no son los únicos bárbaros en la guerra, todos son bárbaros. Your mother describes the terror of war, but who is innocent? I have killed many enemies myself. We maimed the dead and left their naked, torn bodies behind to strike fear into our enemies. An enemy who does not fight but runs in fear is the best kind."

After lunch, tía Anna Maria wandered off into her garden. She did not excuse herself. She forgot we were still there. While we ate, Victoria grew dark and remote. With her mother gone, she smiled and laughed. She jumped up from her chair and ran down a darkened hallway with her gauze dress bouncing at the back of her knees and thighs.

"¡Sígueme! Follow me." She called.

She stopped abruptly at a set of worn double-doors decorated with intricate carvings of the apostles. Faint light flickered through the jamb. A cool earthy smell mixed with sweet incense and the stench of decay rushed over us when Victoria opened the door. She took my hand and led me into a small, dark windowless chapel. Smoke shrouded tallow candles and incense flickered and glowed. The unsteady light gave life to demonic shadows that haunted the holy space. Although Bárbara dusted daily, fine spider webs and soot misted the altar and the reredos. The ceiling, a latticework of small aspen latías overlaying rough-hewn pine beams, left me feeling hopelessly trapped and caged.

A heavy, hand-carved crucifix of a suffering Christ dangled above the altar. His sad, hand-painted blank eyes and contorted face stared downward into some unspeakable hell. With my eyes closed, I easily imagined his half-opened lips moaning in agony. The wrists, ribs, and ankles dripped with bright blood. He was the Christ of the Llano—a Christ of hard lives who did not look toward heaven. The intricate carving reflected tía's somber sensibilities.

The chapel, a reliquary for bones, was dedicated to San Diego—Saint James—a proper Spanish martyr. Just the mention of the Saint served to remind those who entered the chapel of the bones of many children long buried in the floor. Victoria gagged with nausea and then recoiled with horror at the ever-present faint smell of rotting flesh barely disguised by wafting incense and candle smoke. The sight of a bloodied, crucified Christ terrified her. She trembled ever so slightly in its presence.

"To mock our God, los indios bárbaros strip captives and hang them on trees. I do not want to be tortured and hung like that." She shuddered and her teeth chattered. The possibility of rising to heaven after such a brutal death did not appeal to her. She fell back against me, and I wrapped my arms around her. Shaking and soaked in cold sweat, she led me deeper into the grim, dark room.

"I never come here alone. I do not like this place, but I wanted you to see it. Los muertos están enterrados aquí. The family dead are buried in the floor. Mamá says that God lives here. She says that He lives on the cross, ahora, pero no lo sé. No lo sé. I do not know. This is not a holy place! The smell of death comes up through the floor. This is not a holy place," she moaned.

She pulled from my arms and turned to face me. In the dim light, I could see her eyes glaze with tears. She stared at the floor and whispered a prayer for the forever-unnamed brothers and sisters lying beneath its hard-packed clay. God confused her. She needed him, yet she recoiled in horror at so much unexplained blood and death. She did not believe in Satan, because she knew that God could not have created such evil.

I did not tell Victoria that I liked the haunted Christ and the gold, red, and blue reredos of the last supper and Christ ascending. The room, filled with candlelight and haze from thick incense, unexpectedly mesmerized me. The sensation that I was trapped in a cage gave way to a feeling that I was floating on a sea of amber light. Confused and breathless, I quietly crossed myself.

"¡Apúrate, vámonos!" Victoria's urgent high-pitched voice made it clear that she had enough of the chapel. I stood still until she grabbed my hand and led me down another hallway through a heavy wooden door and up steep adobe stairs to the roof. The roof was flat and covered with a layer of hard-packed clay. On the Llano side, the castle-like wall extended three feet above the roof. There were slots for muskets placed at four feet intervals along the top of the wall.

From the roof, we could see that the smoke and flames had grown to a huge billowing and flashing cloud that both gobbled up and hid the distant eastern plain. Whatever the cause, the uncontrolled prairie fire raced towards us at great speed. In front of the fire, silhouetted riders of the morning patrol trotted along at a brisk enough pace to assure they kept a good distance in front of the fire. They stopped from time to time to measure the speed of the fire and watch for any change in the fire's direction.

"Tomás, they are so close, and you must soon go, but before you do, I must show you a special place." Victoria led me down the stairs and into a dark passageway through another heavy hand-carved door.

"Este es mi cuarto." She pulled me into a bright room with a canopy bed made of rough lumber. Buffalo skins and a large Navajo blanket completely hid the hard cotton-packed mattress. A blue-trimmed window faced south into the central garden. We did not stop.

"Mañana," she said. She pulled me into her closet. "Shush," she said as she reached down beneath the floor to find a hidden oak lever. She put my hands on it.

"¡Jala! Pull the lever!" she abruptly commanded.

"I am pulling!" I said, but nothing happened.

We both pulled. The heavy back panel of the closet slowly creaked open and we slipped into a hidden room. Victoria took a candle down from a niche on the wall and lit it with the clay oil lamp always left burning in her room. She closed the panel. The only dim light now came

from the smoky, tallow candle. A heavy, unpainted, and bloodless, carved wooden crucifix hung on the wall. She held the flickering candle up to it.

"This one I like," she said. Her Christ mysteriously hung, but was not nailed to the cross. "He opens his arms to embrace me," she whispered reverently. "Even in death, He smiles and looks to the night skies. I like to watch the night skies." She tilted her head and with her eyes traced His upward gaze into the darkness that hid the ceiling. "Your stepmother made this."

"My stepmother's carvings are everywhere."

"She will teach me to carve some day," Victoria spoke earnestly.

My eyes adjusted to the dim light, I could see strips of dried meats hanging from the walls, water in clay jugs, and Navajo blankets stacked in the dark corners. Pistols, powder horns, and lead balls lay on a low wooden table. From the outside, no one would ever know the room existed. In surprised disbelief, I shook my head and whispered.

"A secret place!"

"Sí, es la verdad. This is my hiding place," Victoria replied softly. "It is my secret room. Only mamá, papá, and my brothers know where it is. We can hide here, safe from los indios bárbaros. They will not steal me from this place," she said with confidence. "I come here to be alone. When I am afraid and I cannot sleep, I come here. It is always dark and quiet. Even in the summer, as you can see, it is cool."

Victoria danced and twirled, sending her dress flying above her waist. Beneath her floating dress, the silhouettes of her bare legs and hips cast eerie umbrella like shadows across the walls. She was Eve before God invented the serpent. She spun, danced, and delighted in sharing her secrets.

"Es un secreto! You must never tell anyone." She spread the blankets out on the floor. "When I am afraid I sleep here," she said snuggling into their warmth. In the glow of the candlelight, she held out her hands. "I am scared. Abrázame. Hold me."

I sat down on the edge of the blankets and put my arms around her, avoiding getting too close.

"What are you afraid of?" I asked her.

She slumped against me in the dark. Then suddenly she shouted, "Basta, enough," and jumped to her feet. "¡Sígueme! Follow me!"

She struggled to lift a heavy wooden grate on the wall that opened into a small child-sized escape tunnel. We crawled on hands and knees through the pitch dark. Spider webs caught our faces. I heard mice scurrying in front of us. I bumped into her repeatedly in the dark. I grabbed her thighs at first by mistake. Then I grabbed her feet, ankles, and thighs because I had to touch her. To my relief, she laughed. Suddenly she stopped. In the darkness, I plunged headlong into her bottom. I nearly bit my tongue.

"¿Te encuentras bien? Are you okay?" Her worried voice echoed in the dark.

"My head hurts a little, but you are soft. Tell me when you are going to stop the next time."

"I will cure you." She fumbled in the darkness until she found my face. In complete blackness, she traced my eyes, lips, ears, and chin. She combed my hair with her fingers. Repeatedly, she ran both hands through my hair, over my face, and across my ears. She pressed her lips into mine. She ran her tongue along my ears and chin. She felt my chest and arms. She pressed her nose against me.

"You are permanently carved in all of my senses. I will never forget you. Now I will make you remember me. Tócame. Tócame otra vez. Touch me again! Touch me like I have touched you!"

She put my hands on her face. I carefully ran my fingers over her thin, cracked lips. Her bottom lip, scabbed and split in the middle, jutted away from her mouth. She puckered her lips in the dark. She stifled a sneeze when my fingers probed her sunburned nose. I pulled her smooth, heavy, and oiled braids gently back and forth. I felt her head rock in the dark. Beneath my fingers, her cheeks curled into a smile. She put my hands on her chest.

"Just use your finger tips," she said breathing softly.

She had large nipples and the faintest hint of new breasts. I traced her thighs and legs in the dark. With my tongue, I gently stroked her salty lips and ears. She pushed her chest and body into mine and broke the silent darkness with an earnest, pleading whisper.

"Ahora, no me olvides. Yo no te olvidaré. Do not forget me. I will not forget you. We have felt, tasted, and smelled each other even when we could not see. We cannot forget, promise me!"

"¡Yo nunca te olvidaré! I will never forget you, and you must never forget me," I said.

She agreed, "Nunca, nunca. I will never forget."

In the dark, tears ran down our faces. Caught by some unfathomable spell, we had spent our morning and afternoon together and pledged an unbreakable bond in utter darkness. I closed my eyes and breathed deeply through my nose. The early morning scent of her salty hips and thighs now mingled with the sweet taste of her mouth. She gently touched my lips one last time. I trembled. The smell of her hands immediately brought back the pleasing roughness of her cracked lips and soft tongue. I pulled her face to mine.

I would have been content to sit in the dark with her forever, but her dress rustled slightly, and I felt her moving again in the dark. This time I rested my head on the middle of her back and wrapped my arms around her warm belly beneath her dress. Entwined, we crawled to the end of the dark tunnel where streaming sunlight burned our eyes. With one hand shading her face, Victoria pushed open a hidden wooden grill and dragged me onto the stable floor behind her. The heavy door hiding the tunnel slammed shut with a solid thunk.

"You can get out, but you cannot get back in unless someone lets you in," she said.

"Hurry, follow me." She directed me with her hands.

We ran through the zaguán, out the opened gate, and into the street in time to see the riders returning. In the west, the sun hung briefly over the montañas then finally slipped away. In the golden twilight, the tired men, caked in dust and covered with fine ash, dismounted and then led their tired horses toward us.

Chapter 4: Out of the Water

Thomas

Father dropped his horse's reins into my hands and bent from his saddle to hug me. In his heavily accented Spanish, he asked me about my day.

"Cuéntame de tu día."

"Father, father, this is Victoria, Victoria de la Cruz de Dios. She is the daughter of señor and señora Griego. She lives in the big house on the plaza. I was in the house. It has glass windows. It has glass windows! It has a church! Father, father, she has three brothers. Her servant is a very good cook. She let me help her." I rattled on just as Victoria had earlier in the morning. My father closed his eyes. He leaned his head against his horse and fell to sleep. I talked louder.

"They have their own well, and new corn, and new squash, and new beans. They have orchards. We have seen the orchards you and I, papa. None of the trees has fruit yet but they will. There are goats, cattle, and sheep. I have not seen them, but Victoria will show me when it is safe. The stables must hold twenty horses."

Startled awake, father peered at me with groggy eyes. "Sí, sí, yo lo sé, I know, but tell me more about this girl," he said struggling to follow my chatter. Next to me, Victoria nervously spun and pulled at her dress. Father, now fully awake, chuckled and watched her in curious amusement.

"Tell me about the señorita's brothers," he said. "What are their names? What do they do?"

"I don't know." I wrinkled my face and thought deeply.

About Victoria, I had learned a good deal more than I would ever share. I knew the thrilling taste of Victoria's mouth and her perfect hot, sweaty smell. I did not remember anything about her brothers except that some were buried under the chapel floor.

"I hoped that you might finally learn something about your new family," he scolded. "Well then, let me introduce you to one of her brothers. This is Patricio. He is older than Victoria but he is her youngest brother."

I tried hard not to yawn with tired indifference.

"Sí, yo lo conozco. I know him from this morning. He brought Victoria to the hill." I did not mention how he dropped her at my feet. "He is nice," I added.

Victoria squinted and cocked her head. She silently swayed from side to side, balancing first on her right foot then on her left. She carefully observed my father and me in a manner suggesting she was attempting to untangle some curious mystery.

Patricio chuckled. "Our other brothers are Felipe and Pascual. They tend sheep in the mountains."

"Mamá named us for saints and holy days. Mother picked the names hoping for our salvation," Victoria impatiently interrupted.

"Creo que nuestros nombres son una broma. Perhaps, our names were meant as a little joke since, as we know, God sometimes forgets the Llano," Patricio complained bitterly.

The cock crowed for the third time that day. I closed my eyes and shuddered. Had the Llano caused this much pain?

Victoria shifted her weight from her right foot to her left, rocking faster and faster. Trembling, she rested her left elbow on her ribs and her chin on the back of her left hand.

"Mis padres me nombraron por la Pascua también, I am named after Easter just like Pascual," she said quietly. "I am the risen one." She struggled to control her hands. She looked at me with a pained face and said, "No sé por qué. I don't know why," but she knew.

She knew she was somehow meant to replace and atone for the three dead children before her. She took a deep breath. Everyone waited for her to speak again.

"But my brother is wrong! It was not to play a joke. We are named for saints and holy days. This is important. It reminds us that God will save us," her voice faltered. Perhaps her brother was right. Her name was a horrible joke, but she continued, "Then there is Patricio. He is my favorite saint." She pushed into his arms, then slipped and fell to the stable floor. He quickly picked her up and threw her across his shoulder.

"It is time for dinner and then bed." Patricio spoke to no one in particular. Victoria pushed herself off her brother's shoulder and again fell to the stable floor. This time he ignored her.

At twenty-three, Patricio was eleven years older than Victoria, but the youngest of the brothers. Except for his dark features, he strongly resembled his mother. Like Victoria, he had a scattering of pleasing, dark freckles across his nose. He smiled indulgently when Victoria spoke. He held her. He hugged her. He spoiled her. He loved her dearly.

"El incendio, who had started the fire?" she asked ignoring his comments about dinner and sleep.

Patricio mused a bit and then said with complete indifference, "I am tired." He added lazily, "¿Quién sabe? Ciboleros, Cheyenne,

Cumanchis, Cumancheros? Who knows? No one was injured. No one was attacked."

Victoria looked at him with disappointment then stomped her bare foot. "You wasted your day then! I am glad I did not go." She said no more to him but whispered to me, "It was a very good day." Suddenly, she announced loudly to the others, "I am hungry."

Until she mentioned hunger, Victoria's father sat quietly on a tack box chewing on a piece of straw. Everyone had forgotten he was there. His spurs clanked as he reluctantly arose from his comfortable spot.

"Adiós, hombres," he called. "It was a good day, señor Roberto."

"It is good to come home seated in the saddle," agreed father.

"Mañana, por la mañana," Victoria called as she headed the procession consisting of horses, her father, and her brother into the stalls. We walked through the zaguán and back on to the dusty path that connected the village's few occupied houses.

With a screeching groan, the gates closed us out of the Griego's world. In the silent twilight, the magic day ended abruptly, more or less, where it had begun. I was standing on a weedy path by myself. Filled with sudden, inexplicable grief, I stared in wide-eyed alarm at the gates and walls that hid Victoria from me. I found myself overwhelmed by the odd fear that my new friend or I might suddenly die. I ran back to touch the heavy, windowless walls that locked Victoria out of my life. Fearful that I would never see her again, I pressed my hands against the adobe cocoon that surrounded her. I did not move until my father's sharp voice jolted me.

"Come along," he called out wearily as he waited with his horse far down the path that crossed by the church and took us home. Still not quite ready to leave, I lingered until called for me a second time.

"Come along, hijo!"

Absent-mindedly I followed, tripping over the smallest pebbles and twigs.

"Are you tired?" he called back to me.

I ran to catch up with him. I wanted him to know about my special day, my new friend, and my new fears. I said nothing. He handed me his lance. I carried it home. His poor horse, ears down, plodded tiredly after us.

"Father, you are all I have here. It scared me when you left. What will I do if something happens to you? What will I do?" I pondered quietly for a moment. He watched me, waiting for me to say more. "Father, I think Victoria will be a very good friend," I quietly added, then absent-mindedly pressed my face into my hands.

"We need friends, little man. However, Thomas, if something happens to me, you will go on living. When your mother died, I didn't know what to do. I left you behind, and I am very sorry for that. I was

49

wrong. I will never leave you behind again. That is a promise I can keep. I cannot promise that I will not die, but I will promise to be careful."

He knew I was worried, but I did not tell him what really concerned me. I did not tell him that I feared losing my newfound friend.

"Father, there are many widows here. Victoria and her mother say that children are buried all across the Llano. I have heard that los indios enemigos kidnap children and sell them as slaves."

He answered in a roundabout way.

"Thomas, I have found Paula. She is a very good woman. She is brave and, perhaps the villagers are correct when they say she is a bit eccentric. She wants only to be free. I want to be free. El Llano, mi esposa, y mi vida—all God's plan." He walked on quietly.

"And mother's death was part of this plan? Who is here for me now?" I demanded to know.

"Paula is here. I am here." He touched my shoulder.

"Victoria says that God takes away everything on the Llano, but she prays to the Virgin. Bárbara says the Christian God, our God, is not very good. She says he never comes when he is needed. Even Patricio says that naming children for saints was a family joke."

"You and Victoria are children," he said shrugging his shoulders. "Bárbara is an old india and Patricio is a soldier and buffalo hunter."

We did not discuss Paula Teresa's doubts about God's goodness, nor why she carved saints. We talked about other things.

We soon arrived at the small log shed that served as our stable. I helped father brush his horse, clean the bit, wipe down the saddle, and shake out the saddle blankets. Father filled a bucket with oats and brought in hay and water.

"Papa, can you imagine a house with so many rooms and a church? Can you imagine?" I did not mention the secret room or the escape tunnel that day or ever.

"Thomas, I can imagine many things, but I do not see how imagining them makes a man happy." He walked slowly into the house.

Three heavy clay bowls of hot soup waited for us on the table. Paula Teresa added her best pottery cups and dressed the table with a collection of flowers from her garden. She lived by the motto, "La vida es demasiado corta. ¡A celebrar!" Of course, it was living on the Llano that made life short, and so she added, "What is there to feel if one does not take risks?" I quickly grew to appreciate Paula Teresa's contradictory nature. She did her best to live honestly and that was all that mattered.

Even though she insisted she was not religious, Paula Teresa carefully heeded two Bible passages, "Let the dead bury the dead…" and "No man having put his hand to the plough, and looking back, is fit for the kingdom." Paula Teresa never mourned for too long and she never looked back in regret.

There were many mothers, fathers, and niños buried in the Llano, but the Llano had not buried Paula. Protected by its vastness, she flourished. She decorated the house and table with wild flowers and flowers from her garden. She sang to celebrate my coming to stay with her. She sang all the time. She even loved my father whom she claimed she married solely for business purposes, and so, with abandon, she joyfully celebrated the loss of her own good senses!

"Paula Teresa, tía Ana María cannot remember the faces of her dead children. She cannot even remember their names. I am afraid I will forget my mother's face."

Father's face reddened and he stood up, "Forgive me. I must wash and sleep."

"We will follow quickly," Paula assured him. With head down and drooping shoulders, he stood and dragged himself out of the room. She shook her head as she watched him leave. When he was gone, she looked at me and spoke quietly.

"Memorias, memorias give us such great pain, but the fear that we will forget is sometimes more painful than just forgetting."

I found myself stifling tears and struggling to remember my mother's face. Victoria smelled, touched, and tasted people she cared about, but I had never done this. Using every sense, she kept her sacred memories alive. I looked at my stepmother and sobbed.

"I can barely remember my mother's face. She is slipping away from me."

Paula Teresa grabbed a block of wood and charcoal from the fire.

"Describe her to me," she whispered.

I closed my eyes. "Her hair was light and her eyes were blue. Her left ear stuck out between the strands of her long thin hair. She had a very straight and even nose. She had space between her two upper front teeth."

As I spoke, she scratched a face out on the block of wood.

"Querido, ¿qué más recuerdas? What more do you remember? Was she tall?"

"When you are little, everything seems big," I sighed in frustration. "She is slipping away."

Paula showed me her drawing.

"I cannot know if this drawing is even close to what your mother looked like. You must tell me what is wrong or right and I will fix it." The picture was as close a likeness one could have drawn without actually seeing the model.

"It is perfect." Relieved, I took a deep breath. "How did you know?"

Smiling, she leaned toward me and gently took my hand.

"Querido, you must look at yourself in the mirror. Your mother's reflection is there. I drew what you described and I looked carefully at you. You have not lost your mother at all."

I had not thought of myself as a reflection of my mother.

"Paula Teresa!" I wanted to say more but nothing came. She hugged me.

"Then you will keep this drawing on the mantle. You will not forget your mother. It will help your father too."

I carefully took the drawing from her and placed it above the fireplace where I could see it every day. I sat back down beside her and lay my head against her shoulder.

"Hombrecito," she studied me carefully. "Querido, life ends. Promise yourself to find joy every day, then joy will be the path of your life no matter how long your life lasts."

I sighed, "I think I am too tired to understand joy, but I want to tell you about someone special."

"Sí, querido, who is this special person?"

"It is Victoria."

"Ah, sí, te entiendo. Yes, I know. I understand. Then you must be kind to her always, and you must be kind to yourself."

"If she dies, will I forget her?"

"She brought you joy today, did she not? Then you will never forget her."

I struggled to keep my eyes opened. She put me to bed. Victoria's scent still clung to my hands and hair. The flavor of her salty sweat drifted back across my lips and tongue. I fell asleep, with the smoothness of her legs, belly, and face still tingling in my fingertips. I slept and dreamed the strangest dreams. I saw Victoria, undressed and spinning. I crawled to her, grabbed her thighs, and touched her bare skin.

Sunlight filtering around the solid wooden shutters awakened me. From my loft bed above the fireplace, I watched as hand-carved chairs and tables, and worn red and gray Navajo rugs emerged from darkness. Soon pine beam ceilings, whitewashed walls, and brown, ox-blood-cured clay floors glowed warm amber.

Although smaller, our house was not much different from the Griego house or any other house in the village. Because we could not afford glass, shutters closed the high narrow windows of the house on summer nights. During the winter, even though it made the house dark, the windows were always shuttered to keep out the cold. The prairie side of the house was a windowless, three-foot-thick wall. In the front of our house, a fortified, narrow door opened from the main room onto the plaza. Used as a workshop, storeroom, and parlor, the main room also served as my sleeping room. In a small courtyard that adjoined the house, were a vegetable garden and a horno for baking bread. The kitchen end of the main room had a great adobe fireplace, a fogon compañia, with a mantle that also served as the family altar. Near the fire, my stepmother had a heavy table for food preparation that also served as our dinner table. Paula Teresa kept her recently completed carvings on the mantle.

"I can look at them while I am cooking and see the flaws," she said. "If I see they have flaws, I fix them."

The fireplace had an open hearth that was level with the floor. Paula swept the dust and her woodchips directly from the floor into the fire. Despencias for grain and food storage lined the outside walls of the kitchen. My parents' bedroom was to the left side of the large room. Crucifixes carved by my stepmother and hung by my father protected each doorway. The house was always warm and smelled pleasantly of rose water and my stepmother's hair.

"Call me by my first name," Paula reassured me. "Right now you think you have only one mother. She is dead. And, may God bless her," she added, "if he chooses." She shrugged her shoulders then concluded, "One day, I hope I will earn the right to be called mamá Paula or mamá. You will decide when this time comes."

Paula Teresa's hands smelled strongly of pine and piñon. Woodchips nestled in her long hair and apron, and littered the floor in front of the fireplace. The gentle rising and falling of her breasts, her calm beating heart, and her ever-present wood scent comforted me. I curled next to her and daydreamed of my mother and the thick, deep woods of my early childhood. Paula told me stories of her own childhood until her warmth and soft voice lulled me to sleep.

Of her carvings she said, "I agree with the late Governor Concha who said 'the rear ends of horses say a better mass than ignorant priests.' I carve carefully so that I do not spread more misunderstanding and superstition, but mostly I carve because I must." She frequently talked about her father and the hours he spent conversing with Governor Concha about Rousseau and Voltaire over dinner. Her father taught her that her life was her own. She carved her favorite line from Rousseau below a crucifix: "Every man has the right to risk his own life in order to preserve it."

Victoria

"The Anglo-Mexicano," mamá said laughing to papá. "She brought the Anglo home to play." She laughed but also seemed confused.

"He is her cousin," papá spoke impatiently to mamá.

In 1830, nine years after Mexican independence, and five years after the collapse of the First-Mexican Empire, she was still uncertain what it meant to be Mexican. Anglo-Mexican, this confused her even more. She sometimes said her nickname, "La Irlandesa," made more sense than being called Mexican or Spanish. "At least," she would say, "I have some idea what it means to be Irish."

She talked fondly and sadly of Tomás. "He is a good boy. He has good manners." She looked at me. "I can see he is lonely, like you, hija querida. He will be a good friend. His father and my sister have grown to love each other very much. My sister is a good woman who loves this place. Her love I do not understand. Nevertheless, I know this; she will stay, so her husband and new son will stay. Your father and I already know this! Our village has grown by two people in the last year. This is very good news." She grew quiet.

"Lo amo. I love him," I muttered to myself.

She did not hear me. I had not given away my heart's secrets. I now spoke aloud with deliberate indifference.

"Yo quiero que él se quede. I want him to stay. Pero, no lo sé. I don't know, but I think he will."

"Hija, he will stay," Papá assured me. "I am sure and he will be a good friend and loyal cousin." He rubbed his eyes, yawned, and studied me quietly.

"Papá, he will stay. Sí, él se quedará."

I sat on my hands to keep them still. My newfound love was safe. He would not leave me. Mamá did not need to know how I felt about him. I changed the subject.

"Papá, ¿encontraste la causa del incendio?" I asked. "Is it coming this way?"

"Nada, nada. We found nothing. Maybe buffalo hunters set the fire. Maybe Cumancheros? Days have passed since the last lightning storm. Of course, a lightning-caused fire can smolder many days before the wind fans it into flame. The cause was not found in the ashes. Pero no te preocupes. Do not worry, the winds will change, and the fire will not cross the Río Canada."

The Río was not a río at all, just a brook with steeply eroded banks. Everything having anything to do with water in New Mexico always had such an extravagant name! I liked the extravagance. I liked my extravagant day. I wanted to tell my father about my day, but could not. I wanted to talk about my new love, but who would believe me? Adults think children do not have the wisdom to love, but they are wrong, so this is why children keep secrets.

I wanted to say these things but could not, "Papá, tengo un amigo. Tengo un amigo. ¡Tomás! I want to touch Tomás. I want him to touch me." I wanted to ask papá, "Why can't I breathe when I am with Tomás?" These were strange new feelings for me, but I could never tell papá my feelings. Maybe I could tell Patricio, maybe.

"You stayed within the walls with your new amigo? You were safe." That was all he asked.

My heart raced. Papá would never know that the smell of Tomás caused my thighs to shake. Mis padres talked quietly and seriously for a while longer. I heard papá say,

"It is good we live on the Llano. Boys and girls who live in town cannot play with each other."

Mamá looked at him and shook her head in disbelief.

"¡Hay otras niñas en Santa Fe! If we lived in Santa Fe there would be other girls."

"We will never live in that place," he growled. "Mujer, por Dios, they are cousins." He added almost meanly, "You treat her like a boy." His voice softened. "No, we treat her like a boy. We think we are protecting her." He sighed hunching his shoulders. "What does it matter if they spend time together?"

"I guess it does not matter," mamá barely whispered.

She cradled her head in her hands. She never again wondered aloud if Tomás and I were proper playmates. Papá, suddenly aware that I was still there, spoke to me in a loud stern voice.

"You and Tomás may play together anytime, but you must never go into the orchard or fields without me."

"Papi, estás enojado? You sound so angry!"

"I am not angry. I am worried for your safety." He turned and left the room.

"Te van a matar. Te van a violar. You will be killed and raped," Mamá spoke anxiously. "Listen to your father. Play in the garden or plaza where it is safe."

Hah, what do they know? I thought to myself, Tomás would take care of me. We were already one as far as I was concerned. Mamá and papá would not understand this. I said nothing. I did not lie. I never promised to stay within the walls. Bárbara came in.

"Chica, hora de un baño, tu cena, y después a la camalta."

Time to bathe, eat, and prepare for bed. It was late. When I ignored Bárbara's wishes, she clutched at her heart, struggled to breathe, and protested as though in deep pain.

She often moaned, "Niña, I am getting too old to take care of you. You wear me out. Be careful of my old heart."

Sometimes when she moaned and held her chest so tightly, I felt certain my bad behavior had finally killed her, but she recovered as soon as I was asleep in bed. The few times my sleeping did not cure her, my good behavior at breakfast did.

What a heavy burden to be the cause of so much pain for the old woman. I tried very hard to be good, but in the end, yo era testaruda. I was headstrong. Still Bárbara knew more about me and cared more about me than anyone. She cleaned my cuts and skinned knees, bathed me, and put me to bed each night. Bárbara rescued me from mamá's incompetence with grace.

Before bed, Bárbara removed my clothes and stood me in a large

55

terracotta basin scrubbing every inch of me. When the water turned brown from the dirt, she pulled me out, wrapped me in a warm cotton blanket, and patted me dry with a satisfied grunt. In the summer, she carefully tucked me, desnuda, under the covers. She then washed and repaired one of my two dresses for the next day. By mid-summer, the tattered dresses were freshly re-patched with any scrap of cloth or thin leather that she could find.

This night as she blew out the candles she said, "Niña, ya tienes pelo de mujer, y senos de mujer. You are growing women's hair and breasts. I am too old to continue as your criada. You will soon need a husband. I think you love this Tomás already. Is this true?"

"¡Sí! I love him. He is perfect," I said. "You are the only one who knows me."

"Perhaps, one day he will know you even better then I, doncella. On that day, he will take care of you."

"Bárbara, he looks into my eyes just like you and Patricio. I cannot hide from you. I cannot hide from Patricio, and now I cannot hide from Tomás."

"Niñita querida, you must never hide from the one you love. Give everything and you will never have any regrets even if your life is cut short. Do not save yourself for some distant future. Here in the Llano, the future is uncertain. Live, chica, live. Make sure you have children who live. Life is good medicine. The women around you, all of us, married for business. For Paula Teresa, it is good. She is in love, but your madre is unhappy. My husband had many wives. He mostly ignored me. I did not choose him. He is dead now. Were it not for your madre, I would die a lonely old woman. So love, querida, love!"

"Gracias, gracias, Bárbara, gracias. I held him today. He touched my legs and face. He ran his hand down my legs. I am happy. He is mine, I know."

"Bueno, eres una chica con suerte. You are a lucky girl," she replied. "You are making a choice for love. You will be the first woman I know to do this. The romantics say el amor es una buena medicina. On the Llano, we say that love is a dangerous emotion. Pero ¿quién sabe?"

"Bárbara, meeting Tomás changed me, and I am older now. I am, I know I am."

She chuckled, "It is true. In one day, you grew very old." She quietly left the room.

In the next weeks and months, I found myself very happy one day and in deep despair the next. The Llano brought me Tomás, but I also knew the Llano eventually took everything away. Tía Paula said the Llano freed her. I began to understand why. I also began to understand mamá. The sisters balanced precariously between terror and the exhilaration of complete freedom.

The next day, I daydreamed of Victoria, of her smooth skin, her cracked lips, her heavily oiled hair, and her salty scent. My head had no room for anything else.

"Tomás, are you here?" My stepmother asked sharply. "I cannot teach you if you cannot be present."

"What?" Embarrassed, I looked at her stupidly.

"We agreed that I would teach you, but I cannot teach a boy who is so distracted by a new friend." She dismissed me in frustration. "Go enjoy her. Adiós hijo y cuidao."

I started to run off, but she called after me, "One more thing. You must see your father in the fields. He may need your help. So, talk to him before you do anything else."

"I will talk to him tonight," I said impatiently.

Stepmother threw up her hands and said nothing more. Turning back, I could see she was laughing. I ran past the church with its low, fortified adobe wall. I ran into the Griego's open zaguán.

"Victoria, Victoria, ¿donde estás?"

"Estoy en los establos. Come see my horse."

"You have a horse? Why didn't you show me before?"

"No había tiempo. There was no time." She patted her sturdy, old Spanish horse. "This is my Francisco."

"Victoria, can we ride him? Victoria?" I asked out of breath from my run and from excitement.

"Sí, sí, but not today. Tomás, as you can see, I am barefoot and wear my dress. I cannot ride. I want to show you something else. Ven pa'ca Tomás, ven pa'ca. ¡Ven al manzanar! Come to the apple orchard."

"Victoria, the orchards are outside the walls. Your father? Victoria, no, this is not safe," I protested.

"Tomás, no te preocupes. My father does not know what I do. I go all the time. They ring a bell if there is trouble. Mamá is happy that I have found a friend. We can do as we please. ¡Vamos! Let's go to the orchards."

Nervous and fearful, I followed Victoria through the courtyard gate. We ran along the portal and then out of the village toward the río. A guard on the top of the Griego wall waved and shouted.

"Cuidao, Niños. I will call out danger. Escuchen para la campana. If the bell rings you must return as fast as you can run."

We were soon alone in the wilderness.

"This is where the frogs sing at night. I have listened to them for years." She took my hand and held it to her heart. "My heart is singing now too."

"I will not let the coyotes ever eat your singing heart."

"I hope not," she chuckled nervously.

She was determined to overcome her terrors. She said she slept peacefully on the days she went outside the walls and returned unharmed. So, we determined to live as my stepmother recommended and "take risks!" Although, had she known how literally we took her instruction, stepmother would not have approved. The genízaro guard would look out for us. We ran to the cold brook just below the hill on the north side of the village. Victoria's dress flew behind her like a flag on a sailing ship. She careened barefoot down the embankment into the cool of the cottonwood forests growing along the río—hardly a river at all but a lazy, clear stream.

"The orchard is downstream, but let's go up instead. ¡Vamos corriente arriba!"

"Victoria?" I questioned, "The guard will not know where we are!"

"Niño, every day I struggle with terror," she challenged, "It is true, I do not want to lose my breasts to a barbarian. I do not want to be kidnapped and sold as a slave. Estoy cansada del miedo. Nevertheless, you see, I am tired, tired of fear. Ahora tengo una sorpresa para ti. You will like this surprise! We will survive! Te lo prometo."

Panting from running and talking, I followed her into the woods that clustered tightly along the riverbank. We followed a faint path through thorny thickets and over massive fallen trees. We crawled through knee-high grass, and scrambled under low-lying branches. We ran until the creek turned swift and both banks gave away to steep red-clay cliffs. We had no choice but to wade. I removed my worn boots and splashed with Victoria down the middle of the creek. Our clothing was soon soaked. Sharp rocks poked our feet.

"Victoria, where are we going? My feet hurt."

"It is worth it," she said.

After 10 minutes of painful wading, the cliffs opened into a meadow where the creek drifted gently from beaver pond to beaver pond. Victoria suddenly pulled off her wet dress.

"Este es mi lugar, this is my place" she said. "Swim with me."

"¡Estás desnuda!" I stammered.

"One does not swim with clothes!" She frowned at me.

When I first arrived in San Mateo, the young children playing naked on warm days surprised me. To Victoria swimming without clothing was normal. Blushing, I did not know what to do or say.

"Eres hermosa. You are beautiful." I stammered.

"Gracias. Good. I am so glad you think so." She pulled on my shirt. "Come on. Swim with me," she said, impatient with my shyness.

"I don't know how."

"I will teach you."

I trembled with embarrassment, anticipation, and excitement all at

58

once. Last night's dreams of her suddenly grew real. Her salty taste and sweaty perfume from yesterday again washed over me. Overcome, I craved the warmth of her bare skin against mine. I tingled with delight. I grew dizzy.

She jumped into the cold water and impatiently ordered, "Take your clothes off and join me unless you are going to wear wet clothing home. Come in now!"

"Don't let me drown. It would anger my father," I warned her sternly.

"Loco, if you die, I will deal with our padres. I will even help bury you myself. Look, the water is not deep."

She stood up. Her hips protruded fully above the water. For a moment she did not move.

"¡Ves! See, if you are quiet you can see the trout swim!"

I slowly pulled off my clothing while she giggled.

"You are hairless. My brothers have hair!" she taunted.

Embarrassed, my skin briefly prickled. Soon more tingled than just my skin. I jumped into the water to hide. The cold mountain stream water left me sputtering to catch my breath. We had met just the week before and today we were swimming—without clothing!

"You have fuzzy hair and no breasts," I taunted back. "You are not worth torturing. You should never be worried."

I felt my face flush as soon as I spoke. She looked down, examined herself carefully, and then blushed.

"¡Qué barbaridad chico!" she yelled and laughed all at once. "Still my nipples are bigger than yours!"

"They can be cut off!" I shot back.

"Por favor, no hables de tortura. No more about torture," she shuddered horrified. "I did not mean to start this!"

"Perdóname, forgive me?" I dropped my head.

"You are forgiven," she quietly replied. "Por un momentito, you sounded too much like mamá." She shook her head, "I do not like to joke about these things. The Llano is too cruel." She looked up at me and held out her arms. Her sadness quickly faded.

Relieved, I rushed toward her trying to push her head under the cold water. She dodged me, and then dunked me. Her brothers had trained her well. Worse, she could swim and I could not. I came up coughing and gasping for air.

"Now it is my turn to ask forgiveness. Let me teach you to swim. Déjame ayudarte. Let me help you! Let me help you! I will teach you to swim. Lie on my arms." She stretched out her arms and I floated across them.

"Kick your legs. Pull with your arms. I will let go, and you will swim away!" she said.

I kicked as hard as I could and pawed at the water with my arms. I splashed and made lots of noise. Water flew everywhere. She let me go, and I immediately sank to her feet. I stood up sputtering, eyes closed, and nose full of water.

Before I could speak, she shouted, "Again. Otra vez, otra vez." I floated across her arms. She let me go, and I sank.

"Again, again," she ordered.

This time I made it five feet from her before, exhausted and thrashing, I again sank to the bottom of the pond. Coughing, I found my footing and managed to stand.

"¡Mira, Mira! You are breathing water. Mira, hold your breath, like this. See, watch!"

She took a deep breath and slid under the water. She did not resurface for a minute. The pond around her cleared and grew still. She smiled and peered up through the reflection of my face on the silvery water. Her hand broke the surface, and she gently touched my chest. I took a deep breath and plunged below the water. She pulled herself beside me and looked gently into my eyes. We floated back to the surface. A blue velvet sky stretching to the green edges of the wilderness enveloped us. The weight of my body drained away and my feet slowly drifted up. She held my shoulders. I put my head against her chest, and closed my eyes, listening to her heart's gentle cadence.

"Mañana. Tomorrow we will do this again. We have all summer!" She stared off into the distance, her eyes tearing in the sun.

"Mañana," she said, "but today is a lifetime." She carefully pulled me to the water's edge. "Do not take your head from my shoulder. No, no, do not get up. Por favor, do not stand. Keep your ear on my breast. Hear me breathe. Hear my heart. I am yours."

When she finally stood, she pulled me tightly against her. For a moment, we were one. She spoke softly as though praying, "Tú eres mi corazón y mi milagro." She gently let me go. She crossed herself, and then like a dark and graceful swan she bowed her face toward the water. I stood silently next to her running my hand down her back.

She leaned back into the water, closed her eyes, and gently washed her braids without letting them down. Una donseya, a virgin, her hair had never been cut and so her braids were too long for her to redo by herself. Even when braided, her hair fell to the middle of her thighs.

"Help me?" she finally asked. I helped her loop the braids into double handles at both sides of her head. I touched her gently as I had in my dream. I pushed my chest against her back. She pressed her head against my shoulder. She stood and climbed from the water.

She held my hands and pulled me to a large flat sun-drenched boulder. She lay down on the hot rocks. I rubbed her stomach, and she fell asleep. I watched her gentle breathing—a small, delicate, breastless woman with skinned knees and elbows. I wanted to lay my head against her chest and sleep, but stayed awake to keep watch. I ran my hands over her budding breasts. She blinked and squinted at me through half-closed, sleepy eyes. I felt that I had known her forever, but I wanted more.

"Who are you?" I whispered, shaken and confused. She groaned in her half-sleep. I spoke louder and more forcefully, "¿Quién eres?"

"¿Qué quieres decir? What do you mean?" She asked.

I confused her as much as she confused me.

"Who are you? How did I find you in this wilderness?" I threw myself across her chest crying.

"I am the one who loves you forever, no matter what," she spoke quietly and earnestly.

I grew even more confused and distracted. What did she mean? Suddenly I shuddered at the prospect of Cheyenne or Cumanchis slipping into the bosque and taking us slaves. If this happened, I would lose her. Trembling, I abruptly stood up.

"It is time to leave," I said.

She raised herself on one elbow and, with tired eyes, looked at the sun. "We have been gone for three hours I think." A bird's whistle in the willows nearby startled her. "¿Indios?" She too grew nervous. She bundled up her dress and ran down the middle of the stream. Her braids slapped at her ears and back. I grabbed my clothing and chased her. We splashed through the narrow canyon. We reached the mouth of the narrows. She sat down at the water's edge. I sat down next to her to inspect my cut feet.

She began to laugh. "We scared ourselves. It is good practice. If there is ever trouble, we will know what to do!" Except for the many birds, the woods around us remained completely quiet. We were alone.

"I will be dressed first!" She put her dress on over her head, and then sat down with a smirk to watch me pull on socks, shirt, leather trousers, and boots.

"I beat you. You wear too much clothes."

"Shh," I signaled. We listened intently for sounds of danger. The deep, shadowy woods drooped and hissed gently in the afternoon heat. The whole world had grown silent except for the occasional cooing doves. The stream gently gurgled in its banks. The warm sun flickered on our faces through the cottonwood leaves. The clay and silt deposits from the spring floods still gave off the scent of fresh-plowed earth. Rested, our breathing slowed and so did our racing hearts. We held each other in the grass. She pulled dandelions and ate the leaves. If we died today, this would be the last moment and every second would have counted. A cowbell clanked in the distance. She pressed her nose gently into mine and held my eyes with hers.

She whispered, "Me conoces. Me conoces. You know me."

She did not turn away in fear, but with intense honesty she continued to caress my eyes with hers. I could not be the first to look away.

"We must go." She nudged me from her spell, and then rose quickly to her feet.

Shaking my head in disbelief, I looked at her. Time had stopped. What magic spell had she cast? Unperturbed by the fact it was now near three o'clock, she led us back down the river toward the apple orchard. Lost in confused emotions, I stumbled after her. We crossed a clearing, and in the distance, the sentinel waved to us from the village wall. We were soon in the cool of the orchard where a new crop of apples tugged gently at the trees.

"Bárbara and the guard will never let mamá and papá know where we were," Victoria said.

I did not tell my stepmother where I had been during the day and she did not ask. For the next few weeks, Victoria and I swam every day. Perhaps foolishly, I stopped worrying about the possibility of our being captured, tortured, and sold into slavery.

Open and playful with me, Victoria withdrew into her near impregnable shell around her parents. She discovered that her parents lied and expected honesty in return. She hid from them behind her deep impassable eyes.

Of her parents, she said with desperate urgency, "If they know me better, they will take away my soul. Our lives are our secret. We must swear it!"

"I swear it," I said in complete agreement with her. I kept all her secrets.

* * * * *

Victoria

Dropped at the feet of Tomás not by my own choice, I hoped and prayed for friendship. He lived among us for many weeks. I hid and watched him wander alone through the broken and fallen houses on the plaza. Certain that he would be killed or leave if I spoke to him, I contented myself peeking at him over windowsills and through cracked doors. Sometimes he kicked at the walls with his heavy boots. Sometimes he sobbed and asked, "God, what have I done that you put me here?" I hid from him and watched him for weeks. Me sacudí, I shook when I thought of meeting and talking to him. Me escondí, I hid and watched. The more I watched, the more I wanted to talk with him, and yet, when I tried, I trembled and suffered horrible nausea. He cursed and cried. Conocía sus secretos. I knew his secrets. He missed his home and the woods where he was raised. He wanted to go home, but now this was home. He had no place to go. He hid in the empty houses and cried. I hid and watched him, wanting so much to reach out and touch him, but I was afraid. I wanted to remember his face. I tried hard to capture and hold onto his image, but I could not. Every night I lay in bed with my eyes tightly closed and my fingers outstretched trying to touch him. Each night before I slept, I tried to remember what he looked like, but I never could. If the Llano took him, I would be saved from the pain of trying to forget another face.

Ayer, yesterday, on the hill, I had no choice. He hid his tears and worry for his father riding on the Llano. Nos tomaron de las manos. We held hands. I had a friend. Suddenly, I wanted to share everything I had with him. Hoy, today I waited too impatiently. Yo corrí, I ran back and forth from my room to the window. I paced. I was not hungry, but Bárbara made my breakfast and sat me down to eat. I painted corn meal designs on my plate. Finally, Bárbara chased me outside.

"If you must run back and forth, then run to his house! You are making this old woman dizzy," she said.

I stood outside quietly in the morning sun, not sure what to do. Where was this new friend? My hands shook. Me enojé conmigo misma. I was angry with myself. No one was there to see, but my shaking hands angered and embarrassed me. I pulled at the sides of my dress, trying to still them.

"Wait for hombrecito in the stable." Bárbara's voice startled me. "Hombrecito, hombrecito," she muttered. "¿Una chiquilla, un hombre? Una mujer, un chiquitito. ¿Quién sabe? Feed your horse Victoria, he grows hungry while you wait."

I dashed to feed my Francisco. My busy hands stopped shaking. The Cumanchis traded weary, old Francisco to my father for iron kettles. The Cumanchis thought we would eat him. My father had other plans. He had watched Francisco pass several mares and barely turn his ears. He knew Francisco would be a good horse for a young and inexperienced girl. Francisco and Bárbara had much in common. They were too old to follow the buffalo across the plains. My parents bought them from Cumanchis at a good price. They were part of our family.

When Tomás ran into the stable, my heart raced. My chest hurt, and I was sure he would see it beating though my ribs. I wanted to grab his hands and wrestle him to the ground. I wanted to pull his hair and call him names. I wanted to wrap my arms and legs around him. I wanted him to love me. I pretended he was a prince from Asturias, but my prince ran directly to old Francisco and threw his arms around his neck. I forgave Tomás and closed my eyes. He held my horse, but in my mind, he held me. Por hoy, eso era suficiente. Today it was enough to remember how gentle his hands and arms were as they wrapped around me the day before. Tomás looked at me and smiled. He wanted to ride, but I could not ride without my brothers or father, but we could sneak outside the walls unnoticed!

"Follow me," I called.

We raced out of the village. We would do this many times. Our parents were too busy to notice. There was always a guard on the wall. I knew he would warn us of any danger. Today I would live in the joyful manner of tía and Bárbara. I put aside mamá's fears for another day.

One never swims in clothing. One never butchers a lamb in one's only set of leather trousers. I took my clothes off and jumped into the water. In the secret room, I wanted to take off my dress and ask him to lie beside me, but there was no reason. We touched in the dark tunnel, but this was not enough. Jumping unclothed into the cold water was crazy. Pero yo tenía razón. Smooth, pale, and beautiful, he blushed beside the bank. He was my prince. He quickly jumped into the water.

"Victoria, Victoria, teach me to swim." He was impatient.

I held out my arms. I cradled him.

"Trust me. Lie across my arms. I will hold you. Kick your legs hard and you will swim," I assured him.

The afternoon heat, splashing water, and his scent intoxicated me. The yellow-green of the cottonwoods and the sunlight shimmering on the water mesmerized me. I daydreamed of a safe far-away Eden. God walked in the garden. Tomás stopped trying to swim. No longer ashamed, he turned over on his back and lay quietly in my arms. He bobbed on the water, looked into my eyes, and soon slept. Cradling Tomás carefully against my chest, I looked into his sleeping face and prayed to Santa María for guidance. God trusted her completely with another life as Tomás now trusted me.

"Se alegra mi espíritu…. My spirit rejoices." I whispered.

The next day we swam again. I held him in my arms. He kicked and splashed. He kicked and I let go. He sank. I pulled him up. I held him. He kicked and I let go. He sank. I pulled him up. I held him up yet again, and he kicked and he slowly swam away. Suddenly he put his feet down, slipped, regained his balance, then stood, and yelled with excitement and delight.

"I can do it! I can do it!" He hugged me and pulled my braids from side-to-side.

He ran naked along the stream bank shouting. I ran after him and jumped on his back. He ran with me until we fell in the mud. We wrestled and rolled in the grass. Tired, we slept covered with mud and twigs and did not care. We were indios bárbaros in the bosque. Suddenly the crows' calls scared us. Frightened, we ran for safety.

"Curré, curré, Tomás."

Breathless and reveling in fear, we grabbed up our clothes and ran until the pueblo came back into view. There had never been any danger.

The crows were chasing away a hawk. Laughing off our fear, we rinsed the coats of mud and grime from our skin, dressed, held hands, and walked quietly into the orchards. Last fall's pungent, half-rotted leaves were strewn across the ground. The earth gave off the vinegary scent of old cider. The apples grew larger as the happiest summer of my life slowly ebbed away along with my childhood.

"Tomás, Bárbara will have something for us to eat. Come home with me. Come home with me forever!"

We ran, yelled, and laughed through the empty village. Our voices and footsteps echoed in the plaza. The guard smiled. He never told my father of our dangerous adventures. Then maybe it was not too dangerous at all since from his place on the wall, he could see way into the plains even if he could not see along the río.

In the village, the sun's warmth soaked the adobe. Heat radiated off the walls. A short time before, we had been swimming and sleeping near the cool water. Now the afternoon heat suffocated us. Sweating and hot as though we had never been for a swim, we looked for shade.

The doors and windows of the house were carefully shuttered to keep out the summer heat. Bárbara had food prepared when we came through the door. There was goat cheese and smoked meat. She spread out dried apples and bread with honey. She made chocolate to drink. Even on a warm day chocolate was a special treat.

After our late lunch, I showed Tomás my father's books. I could not read them. Tomás picked up papá's Bible and read the first page aloud to me. He could read Spanish and I could not. His Spanish still had the accent of an Anglo, but he could read.

"Tomás, who has taught you this? Would you teach me?"

"Paula Teresa is teaching me. I am not good at it, but I am learning. Paula Teresa will teach you too." He grew very excited. "She will be our teacher, and we will study together. I will help you read, and you will help me swim."

"Pero, Tomás, tía tried to teach me before but mamá said, 'no.' Mamá said that education wasted everyone's time. Mamá said I would be captured and sold as a slave, or worse, I would be raped and left to die with my ankles cut."

Gripped by fear I suddenly dripped sweat and gagged. I struggled hard not to vomit. I could not hide my trembling hands.

"Por favor, abrázame. Don't let anyone hurt me," I pleaded.

"I will take care of you," he promised softly.

He held me. I put my head on his shoulder and closed my eyes.

Thomas

The next day Victoria knocked on our door. She announced boldly, "Voy a estudiar contigo." She had come to study. "There are Ladinos in the Indian pueblos who are better educated than I. You will help me!" She ordered Paula Teresa. Her voice softened and she grew desperate. She begged meekly, "I have come to learn. ¿Por favor?"

"Sobrina," stepmother spoke carefully, "Tomás told me that my good sister thinks learning is pointless since you will surely die on the Llano. ¡Ella tiene un gran sentido del drama! Her sense of drama! Queridísima sobrina, what are you going to do while you await this horrible death?"

"No lo sé." Victoria looked confused.

"I will die one day too, but I will die an educated lady," stepmother replied.

"Then I, too, will die an educated lady," Victoria agreed.

Pale and sweating, Victoria plowed furrows in the ground with her bare feet.

"Querida," stepmother held out her arms and pulled Victoria to her, "enough talk of death. The Llano is dangerous, but it is beautiful."

"She will teach you," I answered for stepmother.

"Señora," Victoria started to speak.

"There is no need to say more," stepmother interrupted her. "I will teach you both to read Spanish and English."

"Learn to read Spanish and English?" Victoria said dancing about the room. "How do I learn to do both at once?"

"By listening carefully to your teacher." My stepmother held up her hand, stopping the dance. "Here are the rules. I will teach you as long as you are willing to study and learn. If you do not pay attention, I will stop. There is one other rule. Jóvenes, you cannot play every day. You must also work in the fields. We cannot survive without your help."

My stepmother brightened with purpose. Teaching two would be easier than teaching one alone.

"A little friendly competition will help you both," she explained. "We will begin now."

She pulled a large blanket out and spread it on the ground in the shade of the garden wall.

"Sit down on each side of me," she instructed. She pulled us both to her and rocked us gently. She read to us softly for a few minutes then she put down her book and held us both tightly. "We learn better when we are not afraid. This is your first lesson."

On the edge of a far distant wilderness, at the edge of hope, Paula Teresa took in the lost and the abandoned. From my place in the garden, through the open door I could see the picture Paula had drawn of my

66

mother. I closed my eyes, sighed, and kissed my dead mother a final goodbye. From that day onward, I called my stepmother, "mamá Paula," or simply "mamá."

When I opened my eyes, señor Griego stood in the garden. Surprised, mamá Paula jumped up.

"Niños," she whispered, "I must speak to señor Manuel." She winked and smiled mischievously.

"Buenos dias, don Manuel," she called cheerfully. "Have you come for your daughter?"

"I have."

"Don Manuel, I have something to ask you. What is the point of extra hands if they cannot work? Since the fire, you have forbidden Victoria to go into the fields unless you or her brothers are with her. What's the point in this?"

"Los indios enemigos..." he started to say.

"Los indios had nothing to do with the fire. You said so. I have thought much about this. Victoria and Tomás will work in the fields. It will be safe if they work together. They will carry mosquetes."

"Ay cuñada, sister-in-law, Victoria must do her chores. Every woman must do her chores," he agreed. "Pero cuñada, a musket is too heavy and too long for Victoria to carry while she works."

"She will manage!" Mamá disagreed.

"She cannot work and carry a musket that is so much taller than she is. She is trained to shoot, but she is too small to carry a musket all day," don Manuel complained.

"Don Manuel, do you carry a musket while you work? Of course not! A musket would be heavy for you, too. No señor, you simply keep it loaded and close enough so that you can use it if you need it. Tomás and Victoria will take muskets to protect themselves in the fields, but they must work. Work is necessary." She turned to us, "Bien, it is settled. You will work in the fields."

"Wait," señor Griego began to speak. Mamá Paula stopped him.

"Tch, Tch," she clucked. "Manuel, you are a good man and well intended, but Victoria must do more than chores. She must be educated."

Señor Griego interrupted, "Victoria is educated. She can ride and shoot. Bárbara will teach her to sew and bake bread. She helps in the fields."

"Señor, you seem confused. First, you say my niece cannot do chores because it is too dangerous. Now you tell me she does many chores and you call that her education." She paused. Her eyes twinkled. "An educated person can read. Victoria is right. The Ladinos from the pueblos are better educated than she is. Educating a woman to read and act independently should be a father's goal." She clapped her hands sharply for emphasis.

"¡Si usted lo dice! If thou sayest!" He growled with sarcasm. His face flushed with anger and his lower lip twitched.

"I have made my point then. They will work in the fields together and they will learn to read together." Mamá Paula lifted her chin and calmly stood her ground.

"Mujer, you have made your point. Your sister nags me enough!"

Red faced and in a huff, he turned and stomped away. His leather boots clacked loudly over the hard garden path. He scuffed back through our house, into the plaza, and slammed the front door as he left. Mamá Paula smirked. She grabbed our hands and laughed.

"Mañana you start your chores and studies, now off. Go play!" Still chuckling, she chased us out the garden gate.

Chapter 5: La Cueva

Thomas

When mother told us to leave, it took no further encouragement. We ran past the church through the high weeds of the plaza. We slipped out the southern entrance of the village. Running at top speed, Victoria did not want to stop until we were out of our parents' sight.

"Victoria de la Cruz espérame. Wait, where are we going?" I yelled.

"Quiet," she ordered. She darted along the outside village wall circling first to the west and then back north. In a few minutes, we were yards from the back of my house and the northwest entrance to the plaza. Victoria slowed to a cautious walk. She dropped to her knees and peaked around the corner to see if the path was empty.

"No one is there. Come on. Follow me," she whispered.

We snuck past the gate and away from the village. Within minutes, we were at the edge of the barranca, the ravine that hid the beaver ponds and stream.

"What are you doing?" I asked.

"I want you for myself today. The guard always sees us coming and going. He cannot see us if we go this way."

"Victoria, this is dangerous! No one will know where we are."

"I don't want anyone to know where we are. We are going down to the stream."

"Victoria, you confuse me! Yesterday, it was pointless to learn because you might die. Today you are going to get us killed."

She did not stop, but breathlessly explained, "Before, it was pointless to learn because I did not know you!"

"Now because you know me is it pointless to live? You don't make sense," I complained.

"Because I love you, I will not die."

"Victoria, we cannot do this. It is too dangerous."

"Querido, we are doing this. See, you are following me! Stop worrying. If the guard sees trouble, he will still ring the bell. This is true even if he does not know we are here."

We dropped safely down the sides of the ravine into our private world.

"What would your father say if he knew?"

"Tomás, you fuss like an old woman. Are you going to tell him?"

Victoria pulled her dress over her head and dropped it on the bank. She plunged happily into the water. I stood cautiously on the bank scanning the woods.

"Mi amor," she laughed. "This reminds me of the first day we came here. Then you were too shy to swim. Now you are too worried."

Sunlight reflected off the water. She squinted. She held out her arms. I carefully pulled off my clothing and climbed into the cold water. She cocked her head and smiled at me. She reached out and grasped my hair.

"Estoy feliz. I am happy." She smiled and lay back in the water.

Half submerged, she drifted like a soft, white lily. Lost, I stared at her. My heart beat furiously in my chest.

"Victoria de la Cruz, will you marry me?" I blurted out.

"Sin duda. We have seen each other like Adam and Eve, and we are not ashamed. It is as if we are already married. Do not forget that from this day, we are betrothed," she pleaded with me.

"I will not forget," I said firmly.

"Bésame," she said, "A kiss will seal it."

She then surprised me by gently reaching between my legs. She touched me as a small curious child would have touched the nose or face of a strange adult. She touched me as thoughtfully and carefully as she first touched my face in the tunnel many weeks before.

"This part of a man I do not know. I will remember you."

She squinted and cocked her head. Content with her new knowledge, she jumped from the water onto our sun-soaked rock. I dropped down beside her. The afternoon heat dried us quickly.

"If we are to marry, we must have a house. Follow me," she ordered. We left our clothing on the bank and walked up the stream.

"Ven pa'ca." She reached for a small rock ledge above the creek. She was too short to climb to the top without my assistance.

"Con mis hermanos, I have been here before, but I needed their help. Now you will help me. Push me up." I pushed her onto the ledge and scrambled up after her.

"Victoria, the meadow is perfect from here. I can see into the Llano." I shook my head at the unexpected beauty and her newest surprise.

"We should live here. What do you think?" she asked.

We were on a two hundred square foot ledge about eight feet above the river. Behind the ledge, the wall of the ravine rose another twenty feet.

"Esposo, we can dig a cave home in the cliff wall and no one will

ever find us. We will be safe."

Someone had already carved a small hollow into the clay wall just big enough for one person.

"My brothers made this before I was born. We will make it bigger." She found several pieces of granite nearby and began to dig.

"Este es nuestro hogar. This is our home. We should raise our children here," she said.

Making a house was very hard work. After about two hours, we had chipped out enough clay to double the size of the cave. The shadows grew long. The ledge and cliff house were fully shaded. It was getting late. We climbed down from the ledge and with a quick swim washed away the dust from the afternoon's work.

"Tomás, tomorrow we irrigate the fields. When we are done we will come here." She looked at me hopefully. "We need a house."

She acted as though a house itself was the consummation of marriage. Without it, she would never be married, or perhaps worse, she would lose me.

"We must keep our promises to work hard," I said. "You must come to my house to study."

"Tomás, sí, we will study. We will water the crops, pero tomorrow and the next day, and the next day, we will come back and we will finish our house."

"If we had a shovel, an iron shovel, we could do this quickly. Tomorrow we will bring our fathers' shovels," I said. "They are needed for field work. It will be expected that we carry shovels."

We slipped back into the village the same way we left. No one missed us. We ran to the Griego house. Bárbara was prepared for our coming. Victoria spoke first.

"Bárbara, tenemos un secreto. Tomás has asked me to marry him. I said 'yes.'"

Bárbara chuckled.

"You are happy then at last?" she asked Victoria.

"Sí, por fin soy feliz," Victoria agreed, her hands trembling.

"Then señorita, since you now know how to be happy, you must always be happy. Never fail at happiness again," she warned.

"Bárbara, I don't think about happiness. I do not try to be happy or unhappy. I just feel."

"Chica, so you are dangerous then." She turned to me. "Señorito, ¿eres un caballero?" She answered herself, "Sí, sí, you are a gentleman, I am sure. You know the customs. Then you must have your father ask her father for her hand, but not today. There is plenty of time. Now we have warm bread and honey and celebrate with a feast." She chuckled to herself for the rest of the afternoon.

73

Victoria

Mi Vida, mi Vida. My life has changed so much. My love, I think about him every moment when I am not with him. I will marry him. He asked me! Today I spent the morning at his house learning how to read. We had lunch then left to work in the fields by the south road. When we passed la iglesia, I prayed to San Mateo y San Rafael that Tomás would know how much I loved him.

The wheat rocked gently in the sunny fields. A few men, their rifles and mosquetes stacked neatly nearby, hoed weeds in the corn. The summer passed so quickly. Weeks ago, I wanted to be alone with him. I wanted to touch him all day. I wanted my first kiss, and then suddenly he asked me to marry him. It was as though the saints heard my prayer. He is mine and he said he would be forever.

Mamá and papá did not notice us. Pero, Bárbara did. She called us, "cachorros, puppies." To her, our love was good medicine. Keeping our secrets was also good medicine, and easy since no one else paid attention. She called Tomás "el marido." Mamá thought we were playing a precious children's game. Bárbara knew this was no game.

Thomas

By the end of July, the lush community gardens outside the village were overgrown with pumpkins, squash, peppers, and corn. A section of the garden and the acequia that watered it were entrusted to our care. Early every morning armed with muskets and shovels, we waded along the ditches looking for leaks. Repairing ditches and working in the fields gave us more time together. Still, we took every opportunity to return to the cliff to work on our cave home above the beaver ponds. We found some old metal tools and chipped away at the hard cliff bank until we had created a room that was about five feet wide and five feet long. I could just stand underneath the low ceilings.

"Esposo, how will we heat our house? Fall will be here soon and we have no way to close the door. We have no place por un fuego. Let's build a fireplace and make a wooden door," she suggested.

Making a wooden door would not be easy. There was no leather or rope to waste binding small sticks together to make a play door. There was no leather or metal to waste for play hinges. There were no nails in the village. Anything made of wood was carefully held together with pegs and glue made from buffalo hoofs.

"Querida, a fireplace will be easy to make. We just need to cut a wide niche in the wall and make a small hole to the outside to let out the smoke. This we can do, but I don't know about a door."

"Querido, if we do not have a door the wolves, coyotes, and maybe even bears will move in during the winter. We must have a door."

We explored along the río for anything that might be useful to make a door. Victoria suddenly began to dance.

"We will weave a door of willows and reeds. It will be like a basket. Bárbara will show us how."

We carefully pulled bundles of soft willow switches and cattail reeds and ran with them to Victoria's house.

"Niños, you are early today. I have not made your lunch. This is such a fine surprise, but you will have to wait."

"Bárbara, we are not hungry. We can wait. Por favor ayudanos," Victoria begged.

Victoria excitedly chattered about a door, weaving, and reeds in an incomprehensible stream. Poor Bárbara threw up her hands and arms in dismay.

"Niña, you talk too fast. You make me too tired. I do not know what you want. Tomás, ¿qué dice la chica? What does she want? You must tell me so I can understand."

"Tía Bárbara, Victoria wants you to teach us to weave willows and reeds."

"Tía, tía, I am now family? Sí, sí you want something," chuckled Bárbara. "Do you have the willows and reeds?" She told us to sit. "Sientense. We will begin. These are very green and fresh. Bueno, bueno."

She removed a large cooking pot from the cupboard, filled it with water, and added the reeds.

"We must keep them all fresh. If the wood dries, it breaks. What are we making today?" she asked.

Victoria shuffled her feet and her hands trembled slightly. She did not want to give away our secret. To Victoria, the cave sheltered our souls and love. Its hard shell protected our very essence.

I spoke cautiously. "Señora Bárbara, it's a secret. We are making a door for our house." She looked at both of us curiously.

"Bueno. Then we must ask your God's special blessings on this door. I will keep your secret and a blessing will keep you safe. How big is this door?"

"It is about half my height and twice my width," I said.

"That is a small door. How will I visit for tea?" Bárbara wondered.

"When you visit we will have tea on the patio," replied Victoria excitedly, "and you will come, sí?"

Victoria did not mention that the "patio" was a small ledge the height of a tall man's reach above the riverbank.

For two days, Victoria and I did not go to the cave. We studied with mamá Paula. We worked in the fields, and learned to weave. Señora

Griego often came in to the kitchen to see what we were doing.

Bárbara explained, "The children are learning a useful skill—basket making." She kept our secret.

Señora Griego was curious, "What will you do with this large basket?"

She sometimes sat down with us and engaged in awkward talk.

"Niños," señora Griego thought a moment, "¿Se sienten solos a veces? I am lonely," she said. "The emptiness of this place! The emptiness of this place! It burns a hole in my soul."

Victoria and I stared nervously at each other. Pale and sweating, señora Griego looked to Bárbara for a sign of support or sympathy.

"Señora, the children are happy. I think this is what you want to know," Bárbara reflected. "They play together every day. ·I make them lunch. I patch Victoria's clothing and make sure she is clean." Bárbara quietly concluded, "Pero señora, it is true that you are not happy. What can we do?"

"As long as the children are happy, this makes me happy too." Señora Griego lied, stood wearily, and left for her room. Freed from her dark presence, all of us sighed.

At the end of our second day, we finished a large rectangle of woven willows to make our door. The weave was not tight, but Bárbara helped us block the holes and gaps with reeds.

When done, it was the size of a Roman legionnaire's shield. I created a lance and, like a legionnaire, I fought my way out of sight of the village. No one suspected the true purpose of the "shield." Victoria followed.

After putting up our new door, we worked on our fireplace. To make a hearth, I chipped a new hole into the cave wall about six inches off the floor. I chopped another small hole directly to the outside to make a chimney.

"Mañana we will bring coals from Bárbara's fire and we will try this out," I said.

"We can spend the days here in the winter." Victoria clapped her hands and smiled.

Content that the cave house was finished; Victoria let down her braids, undressed, and swam effortlessly across the pond. Her black hair radiated about her head like rays of light from a saint's halo. Her smooth, dark skin glistened in the sun. In the distance, heat shimmered above the Llano, and a blue cloudless sky stretched to every horizon. Birds and crickets hid silently in the cool, dark shade of the cottonwoods. Barely disturbing the water, she turned and floated quietly on her back. She somehow sensed that any noise risked ruining the stillness of the day. She drifted noiselessly awhile longer, then without a splash, she cautiously waded from the pool and climbed the rocks. Saying nothing, she lay down beside me. I put my arm around her. The sun bathed us in heat. I ran my hand down her spine and through the crease of her buttocks to the soft, sweaty skin of her inner thighs.

"We are safe here," I said.

"I pray so. Te quiero. I love you," she whispered as she drifted to sleep.

* * * * *

The next day Bárbara gave us hot coals in a broken clay pot.

"Do not burn the bosque," she warned Victoria. "Y cuidao con sus manos. Es muy caliente."

"We are always careful, Bárbara," Victoria assured her.

"You are off to play with fire," Bárbara warned. "You cannot be too careful."

We ran by the guard on the wall. He waved and smiled. We dashed into the bosque and down the stream. A faint trail of smoke drifted along behind us. Victoria carefully carried the coals until we reached the ledge.

"This is a woman's special responsibility," she said. She put the hot embers down at the base of the cliff.

"Push me up, then pass up the coals," she instructed. On top with her treasure of fire secured, she examined the ledge.

"Tomás, Tomás, we need wood."

I passed up dry grass, brittle cottonwood twigs, and large sticks, and then climbed up to her. The day was hot, but we lit a fire, and the fireplace worked.

"Stand with me, querido." Victoria commanded solemnly.

We stood. Victoria clasped her hands and said a prayer.

"En el nombre del Padre, del Hijo y del Espíritu Santo. Bless this house and our marriage."

We crossed ourselves.

"Soon it will be el otoño and our house will be warm. That will be blessing enough." She smiled and leaned to me for a kiss.

Seasons change. As it turned out, that was the summer of the cave and the pond. There would never be a summer or even a season quite like that one again. The cave became an empty memorial, almost a tomb. Victoria went there alone from time to time to seek solace. I returned to the cave only once. In later years, we still swam in the ponds, but the circumstances were never again so happy.

Victoria

Bárbara sometimes watched the slight tremble and shaking in my hands with concern and curiosity.

"Niñita?" she asked one day, "Do you know what spirit causes this shaking? ¿Es esto algo que tu sientes? Is this something you feel?"

I sighed and studied her carefully. Summer passed too quickly. I worried that when the grass dried, I would lose Tomás. What joy could winter possibly bring? Exhausted, I tried to answer.

"Bárbara, it is hard for me here. I never asked to live here. I never asked to live. Although I did not ask to live, I still do not want to die. Tomás makes my life so much happier and I sometimes feel safe. I tell him this. I always tell him we are safe, and he believes me but the spirits hunt me down. Sometimes they come out. Me siento loca. I think I am crazy. I think no matter what I do, I will always be afraid. Es la misma espíritu mala que persigue a mi madre. The same evil haunts mamá. She will die lonely—I cannot live the way she does."

"Jita, what will you do?"

"Me iré. ¡Me marcharé! I will go away."

Bárbara was silent. She did not smoke often, but today she took out her tobacco, rolled a small cigarillo, and sat down to think.

Finally she asked, "Where will you go? Will Tomás come with you?"

"No lo sé. I want him to come, but he will have to find me."

"Jita, this is a mystery. He can come, but he must find you? Since he has found you already, do you plan to lose him?"

"Estoy cansada." I stood to leave.

"Cuidao, querida. You are right. You are acting like your mother. This will only make you lonely."

Suddenly dizzy, I turned to see a most fearsome red face. What was it doing? Ah, the sun, just the sun and clouds making patterns on the wall.

"Why do I see these things, ¿Por qué, por qué?"

I gagged and ran for the door. I fell to my knees and vomited. Bárbara followed me and softly caressed my head and neck.

"¿Te sientes mejor?"

She asked me if I felt better, if I was sleeping well, and if I was pregnant. Her face blurred into the frightening vision I had just seen.

"What am I seeing? ¿Dónde está Dios? ¡Estoy buscando a Dios! I am looking for God!"

"But you have not answered me," Bárbara challenged.

"I am fine and I am not. I see terrifying visions, and I live wretchedly just like mamá. She is alone because she is always unhappy. Her dark moods drive everyone away. I will drive my love away too."

Bárbara carried me to a sunny spot in the garden and rocked me gently to sleep. I dreamed of the one I loved. He held my braids and rocked my head back and forth. He ran his fingers over my chest. We crawled through tunnels and caves. We hoed weeds, climbed tall trees, and sharp ledges. My own sighs awakened me. Bárbara had covered me. I lay still and watched the sun set behind the mountains. Its fading red light bounced off the walls and streamed warmly over my face.

"Ah mocita, you are awake. You needed to dream then. You were restless. You fought with the serape."

"I did not fight, but I swam with my love." I stretched contentedly.

"You will not leave him then?"

"Why would I leave him?" I looked at her cautiously. What did she know about my thoughts?

"Before you slept, you planned to run away. Perhaps you forgot." Bárbara studied me carefully then quietly added, "A woman who forgets her heart, a woman who lives in fear, always runs away."

Suddenly, my head was no longer part of me. It was a window, and a little girl stood behind it waving goodbye to everyone she knew and loved. Worse, she waved goodbye to everyone who loved her. Why would a little girl run away I wondered? Would I forget my heart? Had I already forgotten it?

Chapter 6: The Utmost Edge

Victoria

      In early October, I told tía Paula that I wanted to live in Santa Fe. She mused for a moment.

      "Sobrina, you may leave, but what will you learn in Santa Fe that you cannot learn here? Aquí, eres muy importante. Here you are important. Better, you are free."

      "Tía, how does fear free me? I am too much like mamá!"

      "Querida, fear cannot free you, but there is always something to fear. You will go to Santa Fe, and you will fear hunger or cold. Wherever you are, you will fear that no one will love you. Querida, your fears will kill you."

      "Does it matter what I die from?"

      "Querida, it matters how you die. It is better to die in battle fighting a named enemy than to die running from unnamed fears. My dear sobrina, what you do not understand is that we need you here. You are important to us. That is not a reason to stay I know, but what makes you think life will be better across the mountains?"

      "I don't know. La seguridad, security, is important to me." I suddenly felt selfish.

      "Ahora jita, tú y yo protegemos la frontera. We help the others to live their lives in safety. We are rewarded with a freedom they will never understand."

      Tía was right about the freedom. Here I could do many things, but to live the way of mamá was to lose everything. In the end, I did not have to choose the Llano or Santa Fe. Las hadas me ayudó. Fortune chose the Llano for me.

      During the buffalo hunt of 1830, the governor ordered 25 soldados with canon into the Llano to protect the hunters. Señor Trent, Patricio, and the five lanceros from San Mateo were sent on extended patrol. The village could not provide enough men for the hunt. Papá had no choice but to ask for las mujeres y las niñas to join in. Tía Paula volunteered. She loved the hunt and had gone many times before.

      "Sobrina, you and Tomás will come. Victoria, I told your father you would be my responsibility."

"Tía, you have decided for me," I moaned. "I will not go into the Llano!"

"As you wish, sobrina. Tomás will miss you, I am sure," she shrugged indifferently. "Go home then. I have work to do."

The Trent house had become my home. I was not prepared to leave. Lost and near tears, I stood in the doorway as Tomás walked in from the garden.

"Victoria, we will be ciboleros. Maybe we will even fight the Cumanchi."

His excitement irritated me. I looked at him, but said nothing.

"I will help you get your things." He assumed I was going.

"Gracias Tomás, gracias, I have too much to carry by myself." I lowered my head and rubbed my eyes in dismay. "¿Qué estoy pensando? What am I thinking?" I muttered in frustration.

"You will work hard, but this will be fun, I promise. Y Victoria, there is something special I have planned for you." Tía's eyes twinkled. She never doubted that I would go.

The evening before we left, Bárbara helped load the carretas.

"Niñita, I am too old to go," Bárbara apologized. "Pero, your mother needs me here. Nevertheless, I tell you, tía Paula is a good example. Do as she does. Listen to her. You tremble as the cat purrs, but unlike the cat, you purr with fear. Querida, put aside your fears. The Llano will feed and clothe you. It will bring you many blessings. You will be a lily." She hugged me goodbye.

"A lily? Bárbara, you confuse me," I felt quite puzzled.

"Sí, a lily," she said firmly.

Thomas

During the first week in October, the population of the village swelled by more than eighty frolicking, boisterous people, mostly men, joining for the hunt. The ciboleros filled the empty houses, and their oxen and horse carts cluttered the plaza. At night, they sang and danced to a worn-out violin. Their cooking fires layered the village with the thick, sweet incense of piñon smoke.

The arrival of carretas from Estancía carrying salt for meat preservation signaled it was time to go. We left the next day in the chill of a bright fall morning, half the carts loaded with saltboxes, copper rending kettles, and large clay storage jars for tallow. Empty carts intended to carry the newly dried meats, hides, horns, and tallow, made up the other half of the train. Ciboleros, men and a few women, all incredible riders, with strings of their fastest and best horses led the joyous parade as it headed southeast into the Llano.

82

The scent of steaming horses, horse urine, and horse droppings battered my nose. Dust burned my eyes and coated my lips and tongue. Creaking cartwheels screeched in my ears. Everyone was laughing and singing. For a moment, I thought briefly of the excitement I felt when I left Missouri for Mexico. This was better. I had a new home. I had a new mother. Thrilled, contented, and happy, I pushed into mamá Paula as she drove our cart. Her worn leather pantalones were blotched with old bloodstains, as were her leather blouse and jacket. She smelled pleasantly like damp doeskin gloves. She patted my leg, gave me a quick hug, smiled, and then joined the others in singing.

Victoria rode ahead of us. Through the dust, I watched her head bouncing from side to side with the motion of her father's cart. Often she turned and waved. When tired of riding, we walked together along side of the slowly moving carts. We held hands and sang. In the afternoon, we slept beneath the robes in mamá Paula's cart, while ahead of us, scouts searched for the buffalo.

At the end of the sixth day, and fourteen leagues southeast of home, scouts overtook a herd. Excited, they rode back to warn us.

"Silencio, silencio, quiet, hush," they whispered. Every person, every horse abruptly stopped. Only the wind whistled in the dried grass. Buffalo grazed just over the hills. No one wanted to frighten them away. We set up camp quietly. Mamá, Victoria, and I prepared a smokeless dinner while señor Griego met with the mayordomo, the chief of the hunt, to plan for the morning. Soon, señor Griego returned with our assignments.

"Escuchen, júntense. Tomorrow is a big day. Carniceros y renderizadores will follow with the carts. The carts will form a line following the hunters. For protection, en caso de los indios bárbaros, the woman and children will drive the center carts. Men who are good with rifles and muskets will stay on the outside. Paula Teresa, you are our best shot. Is your musket ready?"

"Sí, señor." She snapped to attention in mock salute. Victoria and I laughed. Señor Griego missed the humor and continued to hand down orders.

"Paula Teresa and I will butcher. Tomás and Victoria, you collect and salt the meat for drying. Stake the hides, save horns, tongues, and bones. This work is heavy work. Tomorrow we will show you what to do. You will learn quickly." He sent Victoria and me to bed.

Después del almuerzo, after breakfast, the ciboleros rode out.

"Don Manuel," one called, "Send Tomás up that hill. He will signal you to start the carretas." Before don Manuel gave his nod of approval, I was running to the top of the nearby hill. From there, I watched as ciboleros cut a small portion of the herd from the larger body and surround it. On signal, each man killed his first buffalo with his lance.

83

The confused buffalo did not run. Instead, with lowered heads they formed a circle to protect the young. Each man brought down another buffalo. At this, the smaller herd jolted into a desperate run arousing panic in the larger herd. Chaos followed. Horses, riders, and buffalo tangled in a dust-choked stampede that abruptly disappeared over a few nearby hills. I turned to waive the carteros forward. Mamá Paula, señor Griego, and Victoria drove their carts up the hill and stopped to pick me up. Dead and dying buffalo lay willy-nilly across the valley in front of us.

"Hombrecito, our work begins," mamá Paula called out in excitement.

The butchers and skinners headed down the hill. They quickly cut, slashed, and sliced the fallen animals in front of us. Mamá and tío pulled off their shirts and joined them. Soon blood soaked the ground and everyone. I looked at Victoria. Wide eyed and holding her breath, she stared back in horror. Neither of us had prepared for this madness.

"¡Dios mío!" she yelled, stunned and trembling. "¡Vamos! Bárbara said I would be a lily, but today I will be a blood-covered, mad dog." It was warm. She stripped off her clothing and entered the fray. I followed her example.

We helped mamá and tío pull the first animal onto its back. Tío cut the head away. Mamá slit the belly and the skin of the inner legs. Victoria and I peeled the hide away. Mamá showed us how to stake the hide to dry. Tío moved on to the next animal.

Mamá called out, "Niños, ¡Aprendan de mí! We do not have much time. We must work faster. Tomás, see how I am cutting away the carne? Do this." She gave one curt order after another.

"Tomás, in the cart there is a heavy oak pole. Bring it. Niños, brace the head on its face with the neck up." She rammed the stick through the base of the skull and began to pulverize the brain. Splashed with blood and brains, Victoria started to pull away, but mamá ordered her back.

"Victoria, we need you. This is not a time for fear. It is a time for action. Dump the mash on the hide. This will start the tanning process and keep the hide soft."

Holding her breath, Victoria stiffly poured out the meaty pink pudding. With a small iron scraper, mamá cleaned the last drop of brain from the bloody skull. Dropping to her knees, she spread the foul mash over the inside of the outstretched hide.

"Victoria, ayúdame." In a few minutes, the hide was covered. Paralyzed by disgust and fascination, I watched.

"Chico, you waste so much time!" mamá Paula chastised me. I quickly returned to cutting flesh from the bone. Mamá now stopped us both.

"Do you know what to do now? Victoria and Tomás, after the hide is removed, you will stretch and stake it. Tío and I will butcher the

84

buffalo and put the carne on the hides. Victoria, you will smash the brains into paste. Tomás, you will help butcher. You will salt the meat and put it into the chests in the cart, then spread the brain mash over the hides. You will get better at this and we will go faster. Then bring up the cart and move forward."

As an afterthought she emphasized, "You are both very important here. We need you. We love you. Te queremos."

Completely blood-soaked from hair to calf-length leather trousers, and down to her feet, she marched ahead. Victoria began to laugh. Mamá looked back and laughed too.

"Niños, estamos cubiertos de sangre. Solo vamos a empeorar. We are a mess and we will only get worse. We can have fun. We can sing." She deliberately smeared more blood on her face and went off happily. Behind us, other women from the village started fires to boil bones and entrails into tallow and broth. In two short days, enough buffalo had been killed to fill our carts.

The following week, we worked from first light until after sunset salting strips of meat and whole tongues. We hung the salted strips to dry on ropes strung between the carts. Hides scraped of hair and with hair intact dried in the sun. We boiled the bones and poured the jelled marrow into clay jars. Tallow filled large copper vats. Sliced sinews dried into leather ropes and straps.

The cool mid-October days kept the flies away, but coyotes and wolves watched hungrily at a safe distance. At night, they slipped into camp to eat their fill of unattended scraps and lap up the dried pools of blood. We grew accustomed to the stench of splayed open buffalo intestines, rendering vats, and our own foul smelling, blood-caked bodies. After three weeks of travel and hard work, we readied to return home.

As we packed, riders appeared in the distance. It was the Presidio patrol. Two riders came forward while the others hung back. It was papá and Patricio. Victoria and I ran to meet them. Suddenly they lowered their lances preparing to charge. Frightened, Victoria and I stopped.

Patricio called out, "What savages are you, and what is that horrible smell? Your smell has offended our noses for days. By order of the governor, you must bathe before coming nearer." He began to laugh. "Niños, ¿les gustó la caza del cíbolo? Did you like the buffalo hunt?"

Victoria responded in her deepest voice, "Caballeros, den las gracias a los grandes cazadores que los alimentarán este invierno." Victoria continued in a grand, dramatic voice, "As you can see, we are the great hunters who will feed you this winter. Bow before us, caballeros, or we will throw ourselves on you."

Patricio holstered his lance, jumped from his horse, and fell to his knees.

"Ah, Diana desnuda, cubierta de sangre y apestosa. Me da gusto conocerte. Naked, bloody, and foul smelling Diana, it is good to meet you."

"Sí, seigo Diana con el arco y las flechas. It is time you pay the goddess respect! Why is your servant still mounted?" Victoria looked at my father.

Patricio continued, "Caballero, desmonta tu caballo, por favor. Obedece a la diosa." Surprised, I watched my father dismount. However, he did not bow. Instead, he covered his eyes and nose.

"What goddess smells and looks like this, señor Corporal? I don't like to question your authority, but this one time I think you are mistaken. I think we should run."

"Soldado, I think you are right. I will follow you." The two men pretended to run from us. We caught Patricio without difficulty and tackled him, and all of us fell in a smelly pile of dust. Patricio extracted himself as mamá Paula and don Manuel ran up.

Father looked at mamá and don Manuel.

"I have never seen a more smelly group of people." He put his hands to his head and staggered back to his horse. From a safe distance, he yelled to Paula Teresa.

"You must be the mother of the smelly boy. You two have much in common!"

Mamá grabbed my hand. "Sí señor, I am the mother of this fine young man. We have nothing but good traits in common." She whispered to me, "Hombrecito, recuerda, we should have fun." She signaled with her eyes that I was to follow her. Singing, we slowly walked toward father. When closer, we charged papá, knocked him down, and piled on top of him. Laughing, mamá grabbed his face and kissed him passionately.

Don Manuel grabbed the startled horse's reins. "It is good we are all safe," he said. "I hope the festivities and greetings are done soon so that we can head home. I am a tired old man who wants to bathe and sleep in his own bed."

"Cuñado," mamá teased him, "Since when are you too old to celebrate?" Still she agreed, "It is time to head home." She jumped up and pulled father and me after her.

"Señor, we are done with partying," Patricio nodded in agreement with his father. Patricio was official again. "Please tell the mayordomo to lead out. The troop will follow behind." None of the old-timers remembered ever having a military escort with canon. After stopping at the first stream to resupply our water barrels and bathe, we went home in the best of moods singing boisterously.

Victoria

"We are not all lilies. Some of us are dogs, coyotes, wolves,

88

hunters, farmers, and perhaps woodcarvers," Paula responded when I told her what Bárbara said to me before we left.

"And God takes care of them all, the coyotes and the woodcarvers?" I asked.

"Only if it pleases you," she said.

"Tía, you make me think too hard. It hurts."

"Jovencita, thinking is something you do poorly. This is no insult. It is simply true. You are a feeling person."

The first chilly night of the hunt Tomás, tía and I snuggled closely by the fire. She abruptly stood up and went to her cart. She pulled out her carving knife, a tooled leather pouch, and a thick piece of soft cottonwood.

"Sobrina, this pouch contains the surprise I promised you. Open it carefully."

I cautiously untied the leather cords. Inside was a shinny new carving knife.

"Tía," I shook my head with excitement and fear. "I don't know how to use this!"

"Sobrina, silly, of course you don't. Sit beside me, and I will show you how to carve your feelings in wood."

Paula Teresa taught me to carve santos. I quickly learned that when I carved my hands stopped trembling. Sitting by the fire listening to the others tell stories and sing, we carved something new every night.

At the end of the three weeks tía said, "As you can see, you are good at this, and it is good for you."

"I do not see that I am good, but it keeps my hands still."

"Then you must trust me," she warned. "You are good carver. You have an excellent eye and now a very steady hand. You carve naturally with the ease of an old santero who has carved his entire life."

The first week of November, as the weather turned cold, we returned home with a military escort. I had learned to live on the Llano covered in blood. Pero lo más importante, I learned to carve wood and how to keep my trembling hands still.

"¡Yo puedo hacer esto! I can do this. I can live here. I will carve a statue of San Mateo para la iglesia," I told tía. She smiled.

Chapter 7: Winter 1831—Doña

Thomas

A week after we returned home, it snowed. The crops had long been harvested. Dried chili and squash hung in ristras on the inside walls of the houses. Wheat, corn, and beans were stored in large clay jars or tight wooden chests. Meat was cured and hanging in the smokehouses. Tallow from the hunt had been molded into candles, shipped to Santa Fe, and exchanged for cotton cloth.

Christmas came and went quickly. January 18, 1831 was my fourteenth birthday. We celebrated with music and a fiesta. Most of the village came. It was cold. Father and mamá surprised me with the gifts of a horse and my own rifle. I could now ride on the Llano with Victoria.

"¿Un fusil y el caballo te hacen un hombre? Do a rifle and horse make a man?" Patricio congratulated me and mused aloud.

"No," I said, "but it is a start."

"It is true a rifle and a horse can be a start, maybe a bad one. Can you even shoot a rifle?" he chuckled.

"I know how to shoot my father's muskets."

"But can you hit anything?" he teased. "With your father's permission, I will teach you to shoot so you can actually hit something."

"Por favor, let me join you!" Victoria begged.

"Jita, jita. We will see. Now Tomás, you must talk with your father."

Finished with the conversation, Patricio turned and smiled at a young woman warming herself by the fire. With a peculiar urgency, he walked toward her pulling Victoria and me along with him.

"Come along, hurry," he commanded. "Niños, I would like you to meet Doña María Josefa Chávez." Patricio introduced us to a regal young woman of eighteen or nineteen. Thin but taller than many men, she had deep brown eyes and, like Patricio, an easy smile. She wore sand-cast silver Navajo combs at the base of her thick long braids. As was the custom, she carefully smoothed chalk over her face until her skin appeared a perfect ghostly pale. She painted her lips deep red. Accented by a heavy turquoise necklace, her low-cut purple velvet blouse exposed the tops of her breasts. She wore a long, embroidered, and tooled leather riding skirt with a carefully matched vest. Her knee-high riding boots were exquisitely carved and decorated with engraved silver medallions and leather tassels at the top. Her rebozo, carefully edged in white lace, matched her blouse. She wore it decoratively over her right shoulder in a manner calculated to accentuate her breasts. She smoked a tightly rolled shuck cigarillo. She looked every bit a lady of the court.

Doña María was the daughter of a wealthy sheep rancher who lived in the Mora Valley. When Doña was eight years old, her mother gave birth to a stillborn daughter, and died a month later of a breast infection. María Josefa, the sole surviving child, then assumed the role of woman of the house and insisted that others address her as Doña. Thus, she was Doña María from the moment of her mother's death, and she was indisputably in charge. If mistakenly addressed by doñella, donseya or by her name alone, she sternly corrected the offender. If an individual repeated the offense, she ignored them completely.

Until now, Victoria simply thought of Doña María as a pretentious young woman who accompanied her father, señor Chávez, when he visited. Victoria regarded Doña María as stiff and aloof. She was a good deal older than Victoria. The two had little in common. Now they could not ignore each other even if they wanted to. Victoria immediately understood Doña María was more than a friend of Patricio's. Doña had taken Patricio without Victoria's permission. Victoria turned sullen and glared angrily at Doña.

Doña María caught Victoria's scowl and softly commented, "Conozco esa mirada enojada. I will take care of Patricio, and he will always be your brother. Always, niña!" In a manner befitting a noble matron or grandmother, behavior that was both unnerving and reassuring, she gently put her hands on Victoria's shoulders. Victoria's eyes filled with tears and she hugged Doña María.

"Gracias, perdóname, Doña. Perdóname."

"No te preocupes, chica." Doña gently held Victoria for a few minutes, mothering her quietly and staring into space. Suddenly, she looked at me with a kindness and an intensity that left me emotionally undressed. For a moment, I thought that I could love her. I turned away ashamed and full of guilt.

Doña had a strange impact on all of us. Victoria, who had been angry, was now suddenly contrite. I felt guilty for briefly desiring a beautiful woman other than Victoria. Patricio was in love and completely lost. Doña looked first at Victoria, then Patricio, and then gazed slowly back at me.

Doña quickly understood she had confused all of us. She touched and calmed Victoria. She smiled gently at me mouthing the words, "Yo sé. Perdóname. I know. Your face gives you away." She knew that I could love her. I tensed. As she turned, she brushed my shoulder with her breast. With her eyes, she assured me she would not reveal what she knew.

As to Patricio, he could love her all he wished, but Doña firmly held the customary view of love, that once unleashed, it blunted one's ability to make thoughtful life decisions. Above all else, she was a businesswoman. She was a survivor. If she married Patricio, with hard practice, she would learn to care about him. More importantly, by combining her land with his, the two would gain in power and stature.

Patricio hugged Doña at the waist, lifted her off the floor, and twirled her around the room. He treated her in the same tender and teasing manner he treated Victoria. Doña showed her appreciation of his tender playfulness with an indifferent, crooked half-smile. Failing to notice Doña's lack of enthusiasm, Patricio dropped her back to her feet.

"Vamos a bailar la cuna con los demás. Let's dance." Patricio went happily off while Doña dutifully joined him and the other dancers gathered around the fiddle player.

I looked at Victoria. She shook her head at me, uncertain of what had just happened.

"Ella es una hada buena, una bruja, o una señorita desesperada--a good fairy, a witch, or desperate woman," Victoria cautiously whispered.

"Witches do not smile with such gentleness. She is a fairy enchantress. Desesperada, ¿qué quieres decir? What do you mean by desperate? Isn't everyone desperate here?" I sighed.

"You don't know her well enough. She seems kind, but she has killed many men. I will tell you one day," Victoria huffed.

"A good fairy or a witch?" I wondered to myself. "She has killed many men! Surely, if she killed any man, she did so by breaking his heart." Caught in her spell, I knew that only time would reveal the true nature of Doña María Josefa Chávez.

* * * * *

True to his word, the day after my birthday, Patricio met with my father and me on the Llano to practice loading and shooting. My father warned, "Train carefully." He cautioned that he could little afford to waste more than fifteen or twenty rounds. Patricio nodded in agreement that powder and lead were expensive.

Father took the time to teach me to take the rifle apart and put it back together.

"Be careful and keep your rifle clean. The powder will rot and rust out the barrel if you do not clean it. Always clean out smoldering powder from the last shot before you reload. Burning powder from the last shot can cause an accidental discharge. It will kill you." Father completed the first day of lessons, and then left with don Manuel for Taos.

The next day, Patricio continued my instruction. I cautiously fired, cleaned, and reloaded, fired, cleaned, and reloaded under his watchful eye. I never hit the target—a large block of wood set out at about fifty paces. Still, Patricio assured me that I had learned the most important lesson.

"You have not been injured. Tomorrow will be better."

The next several days were cold and snowy, and so I neither rode nor practiced firing. When it finally cleared, Doña María joined Patricio and me. Dressed in a cuera, Doña María carried two rifles with her. On the Llano, she always carried two rifles as well as her bow. The expense of shot and powder did not concern her.

"I will supply all the powder you need," she said. "Lo barato sale caro. Saving on powder comes at a high price. Life is expensive. Powder is cheap. Learn to protect yourself."

"Tomás, I promised your father that you would learn to shoot," Patricio laughed. "This I know. I am not always the best teacher. Doña María is the best. She agreed to help you."

She wasted no time. "Mira, hombre. Watch me carefully. Do not load your rifle. Do not shoot. ¡Pero mira! Look, watch!"

She suddenly darted five steps to her right and knelt in the grass. She took a deep breath, braced her elbow on her left thigh, raised her rifle, and counted. "Uno, dos, tres. Respira y dispara, breathe then shoot." She then jumped up and pretended to remount her horse. "Now do it with me. You must pretend you are killing un caballo de un Cumanchi. We do not hunt here. We kill to protect ourselves first. Hunting is a luxury you can afford only if you can first save your own skin. ¿Comprendes, mi cuñao?"

She called me "hombre y cuñao." I was a man and her protégé. She never treated me as a child. Childishness was a foreign concept to her. She had been a woman all her life. The Llano was not a place for children. Even so, in her presence, I felt small. My rifle was too heavy. I lifted it and watched her dart to the left and drop to her knee. I followed her example. In my mind, I imitated her exactly, but still she scolded.

"Hombre, two deep breaths. The first when you raise the rifle and the second just before you shoot. And, you see I didn't let my second breath out until after I fired. You must then prepare to quickly mount your horse and ride like the wind for safety. A man on foot against los indios enemigos charging on horses is a dead man. Again hombre, again."

We drilled and drilled. My arms and back hurt. My right knee throbbed. My elbow left a deep, excruciating bruise in my thigh.

"Hombre, you can hardly lift this rifle. You will die. You need to lift it above your head every day ten times. Tomorrow we will practice loading and firing. Now, we are going home," Doña scolded.

Barely able to carry my rifle on my shoulder, I dragged myself home accompanied by Doña María and Patricio. Victoria waited for us. She had spent the afternoon reading and carving with mamá Paula.

Doña María and Patricio said polite "hellos" to mamá and Victoria, then arm in arm they left for the Griego home. I hung my rifle on the wall and dropped to the floor. Victoria sat down beside me.

"I have a Doña María story to tell you, remember? You will understand her better if you know this story," Victoria assured me. "Bruja, hada, o una señorita desesperada que vive sola en el Llano como yo. Whether witch, good fairy, or desperate maid, she lives a lonely life on the Llano just like me."

"When will you know you are not alone?" I scolded Victoria. I did not care to hear about Doña if Victoria was unhappy. "Tell me any story you wish, but also show me you can be happy."

"Bueno, I am happy now! I will tell you about Doña and you will listen." Irritated with me, she began:

"Her mother is long dead. Her father taught her to read, write, ride, and shoot. Other than her father, Doña María is the last surviving family member. With little help from her father, she now runs the family estates. Because she is alone and the last, it is, of course, most important to her father that she have many children!

"When Doña María was sixteen, she intercepted mi hermano, Cabo Patricio, leading a patrol of cinco *Dragones de Cuera*, dragoons wearing heavy leather armor, chasing Cumanchi raiders into the Llano. She appeared from nowhere leading a string of her five fastest horses. Like a man, she wore her hair in a single, uncut chongo or uncut braid wrapped in leather. She carried a sturdy, hardened leather shield embossed with the king's coat of arms and wore a thick, many-layered leather cuera for her armor. At first, the soldiers did not recognize that she was a woman. When they finally did, she had dismounted and was changing her saddle to her last and fastest horse. Then, she was off again at a full gallop. The young men did their best to keep up with her. Siete dragones de cuera eran mejor de seis they thought, seven were stronger than six, and the seventh could ride! She gained quickly on the loot-burdened raiders. At seventy-five paces, she pulled her rifle from its holster, jumped to the ground, took a deep breath, counted to three, and fired off a shot, dropping a horse with its rider. Spread out six abreast to clear their line of fire, the soldados rode past her, dismounted, and fired. Two more horses and riders fell. She remounted and pulled out her bow and arrows. The dragones also armed themselves with bows. The race was on in earnest. As Doña rode past the unhorsed enemigos, she shot them with arrows. No side ever took prisoners.

"To distract their pursuers, the raider's set some of their stolen horses free, then scattered in three directions. Doña charged after the largest group of riders. She put four arrows apiece in rapid succession into each of last three stragglers. Her horse, excited by the hunt and danger, picked up his pace. Pulling away from the other dragones, she gained on the seven remaining Cumanchis.

"'I was never in danger,' she later said. She had already killed four of the enemy and now the numbers on both sides matched at seven. She also could see the dust of distant reinforcements behind her on the western horizon. She overtook and killed two more. 'Seven verses five,' she counted aloud. Everyone's horses were tiring. The small party of raiders left in front still had one extra horse apiece. The dragones were riding their last horses. She had no idea where the other indios bárbaros had gone. They might be preparing to attack. Cursing, she realized the remaining Cumanchis would escape. Today the Presidial troop claimed a rare victory without an injury. She let her horse slow to a walk. The other men soon caught up to her.

"'Hurra, Hurra,' they cheered. 'Bien hecho muchacha. Bien hecho. Well done.' They each tapped her with their lances, then quickly returned their full attention to their duties. They scanned the horizon for signs of a counterattack. None came. The battle over and no enemigos in sight, the men turned homeward to collect their horses, but Doña María was not done. She knelt by the dying indios, cut off their eyelids and testicles, stuffed them in their mouths, and finally slashed each man's throat. Patricio watched from a distance. He rode to her.

"'It is what the Cumanchis do,' she said defensively. 'Además, it is merciful. They die at my hand or in the teeth of coyotes.' She further excused her behavior, 'they killed one of my shepherds. They flayed him to death with willow switches.'

"Patricio had no concern for how the dead or those who would die were treated. He shrugged his shoulders and ignored her comments.

"'Señorita, ¿quién eres?' Then he recognized her. 'Ah, Doña, la hija de señor Chávez. I have seen nothing but your back all day. What are you doing here?'

"'They killed and tortured some of my servants. The indios took my horses. I came to take my horses back and punish them.' She was coldly matter of fact.

"'¿Pero, sola? But, by yourself?' he asked.

"'Sí, sola. Why not Cabo?' She wiped her bloody hands clean on the prairie grass, pulled a corn shuck and tobacco from her pouch, rolled a tight cigarillo, and lit it. 'I expect you to do your job well. I knew you would be here soon enough. See, even the men of the village are coming. They picked up the horses we left behind.' Biting her cigarillo carefully between her teeth, she shielded her eyes and stared into the distant horizon.

"'Señorita, you have too much faith. Had we not come, you would have been one against many. Surely, you do not wish to be raped and sold as a slave. Think of the pain your loss would cause your lonely father. You are the only family he has.' Then as an after-thought he added, 'I'm sorry about the shepherd and the others that the Cumanchis killed.'

"'Soy una mujer de acción, no de la fe. I have no time for sorrow. I trust in my skills with my rifle and my bow. I would never be a slave. Rape is a risk I take every day. The king put my family here to deal with indios bárbaros. I am carrying out the king's wishes. ¡Viva el Rey!'

"'Señorita, you well know there has been no Spanish or Mexican King for the last seven or eight years.'

"'Ah, so that is why no one pays your salary!' she snickered. 'The king gave my father the land. My father refuses to do his duty to pay for it so I do the hard work. That is why I am here, and as you can see, señor Cabo Griego, I have done *all* the work here. As for my father, if I were to die he might finally remarry—someone young—he could have more children. He relies on me too much!'

"My Patricio just shook his head. She had killed six raiders and mutilated their bodies to instill fear into her enemies. He helped her collect the horses left behind by the Cumanchis. Not all the recaptured stolen horses were hers. Some had brands indicating the Cumanchis had taken them from Durango. She lost a slave, but took home fourteen horses as her reward for protecting the borderlands. It was a profitable day in which she added to her own fearful reputation and gained a new admirer. Patricio fell in love with her, but he also slightly feared her. On horseback, she is as dangerous as any Cumanchi warrior."

Victoria concluded her tale with a shudder adding, "I am sure, Doña will marry him only because she thinks it is practical. If she ever loves anyone, it will be because she concludes it is practical. She is not an emotional woman. She makes both dead and living men tremble."

Thomas

The next day, Victoria came to watch target practice. Patricio watched seated comfortably on a sunny rock. Doña was not surprised that Victoria joined us.

"Hombre," cautioned Doña María squinting at Victoria, "this has become like an old-fashioned joust. Your lady watches you. Do not be distracted by her. One day your life or hers will depend on everything you learn today. There I see it, you are blushing. You are now a dead man. You must choose to live. Look at me!" she demanded. "Do not blush, do not fight in anger, or run in fear—not if you expect to live. Kill your enemy calmly and thoughtfully. Killing your enemy with deliberate calm, terrifies him and protects you. You must train yourself to shoot carefully." Staring at me, she quietly added, "and always think."

I wanted to say I was not blushing, but there was no point in that. Embarrassed, my forehead and hands dripped with cold sweat.

"Sweat from shame or fear is no good," she said. "You must overcome it. Pronto, pronto, lift your rifle ten times over your head. Now drop, breathe, count, breathe, and hold your breath, fire. Mount your horse."

She turned to Victoria and spoke sharply, "So you pretend this is a joust, and you are a lady-in-waiting, but the truth is that you came in jealousy. Now, like a stupid girl you are sitting here waiting to be killed. Here, take my rifle. You will practice with us. Lift it over your head ten times."

Shaken, Victoria sarcastically replied, "No seigo una soldada. I am not like you."

"No, you are weak! Ah, así estás muerta. A dead woman can never be a soldier. This is a good decision for you to make," Doña spat out her words. Victoria shook in fear and rage. Doña María continued, "You are like your hombre, Tomás. You want to improve your shooting but you are afraid and shake with anger. We will see then. This is good practice."

"Patricio!" Victoria pleaded with her brother.

"Hermana, I did not make you come here today. That was your decision. I now think it was a good one." He studied her thoughtfully.

I watched Victoria's eyes blaze with rage. Doña fanned the fire.

"Una mujer enojada es una mujer muerta. Anger will kill you." She abruptly knocked Victoria down. "I suppose you think the carved saint will come to your rescue? Fool," she scoffed and then quickly pulled Victoria back to her feet.

"Doña, what are you doing?" I yelled. Patricio smiled sympathetically at Doña. He held his hand signaling me to stand still.

"Señorita, take my rifle. Next time you must bring your own." Doña turned to both of us. "Escúchame bien. Listen carefully. What I am showing you today will work only if you are chasing the Cumanchis, and they are running from you. If they turn and attack you on the ground, you will die ten times before you reload your rifle. If attacked, mount your horse and defend yourself first with your bow and then your lance. Since neither of you know how to handle a lance or bow, you must learn."

Quiet and thoughtful for a moment, she turned to Victoria. "You came because you are jealous. You are jealous of the time I spend with your men. You are now over this, no? You are now a proper lady, no? Come tomorrow and I will teach you so you will live. Never think for a moment that I do not care about you. ¡Adiós!"

Victoria and I dragged home. "She knows everything about us," I said. "She knows we are in love. She knows we are afraid. She knows that I am a bad shot. She knows that we cannot defend ourselves."

"Una bruja, a witch," Victoria said, and then she reddened. "Doña cares about us. She cares as much as our fathers do. Maybe she cares more. She now does what they have not done, she teaches us to defend ourselves. I regret that I wasted her time and concern with my jealousy. I am ashamed."

Chastened, Victoria and I agreed that it was time we learned to care for ourselves on the Llano. Victoria looked at me sheepishly and managed a laugh.

"Now you have your own Doña story."

"And you have another," I sighed.

* * * * *

On warm winter days Victoria, Doña and I would ride. I named my new horse Viejo, or "old." He had been ridden hard and in many battles for he bore lance scars along both flanks. I soon learned that Viejo was extraordinarily well trained. He could be ridden without guidance from reins or a bit. He turned in response to pressure from the right or left knee. When he ran his gait was smooth and his head carefully down. He expected me to carry a lance or to shoot a bow. With an old estradiota, a Spanish saddle, I remained safely on his back no matter what turn he made. He knew his way home from every place we visited. If fed, he would go anywhere.

We passed the winter riding wildly across the snowy Llano. We filled the cold, blue emptiness of the place with laughter and shouts of joy. Doña always carried a bow and quiver of arrows on her back and kept her rifles holstered on both flanks of her horse. She taught us how to use lances and shoot our bows from beneath the necks and bellies of our horses.

On occasion, I found myself staring at her transfixed, with my heart racing. She often looked carefully at me expecting, perhaps demanding, that I should be watching her. Her glances and stares burrowed deeply into my soul. She glanced or stared with thoughtful, sometimes sad eyes, squinting from her narrow face. She rode with her head tilted slightly to the left as though her braids were heavier on that side than on her right. Doña's regal beauty was mesmerizing. Victoria knew it. She joked, "Doña arouses even half-dead men."

With warm weather approaching, Doña's father sent one of his genízaros to inquire as to her plans for summer planting. He was instructed to accompany her home. When they left for home, Patricio went along.

Three days after they left, a heavy, wet spring snow fell across the Llano. The wind howled for days and the snow drifted four feet deep along the walls. Victoria paced nervously. March 22 was her thirteenth birthday and everyone was snowbound. Where was Patricio? Her other brothers were too busy with spring lambing to celebrate, but Patricio was expected.

On the 22nd, plans for her party went ahead. Bárbara supervised the roasting of a lamb. Mamá Paula and I helped. As we finished dinner,

Patricio came through the door covered in mud. He brought Victoria a special gift from Doña—a worn leather book of the writings of Teresa de Avila. In the book, Doña inscribed, "Amamos con el mismo corazón—We love with the same heart."

Chapter 8: On the Mora

Thomas

Suddenly it was June again. Saying "Junio" now seemed natural and "June" foreign. Victoria and I worked hard reinforcing the acequias. In the orchard, we trimmed the trees and cleared away the branches killed by winter frost and snow. Work took up most of our time. We seldom had the opportunity to swim or play. Our time for childish things had passed. Still, we did not forget the promises of love and marriage we made the prior summer.

In July, Patricio returned to the mountain valleys above the Río Mora to assist his brothers herding sheep. He invited Victoria and me to accompany him on the first part of his journey. We went with him to the place where the Río Mora left the mountains for the Llano. The distance was about seven leagues. It was a comfortable day's ride to the Río and another day's ride to return.

"There will be a surprise when we get to the Mora," Patricio teased.

"Tell us ahora," Victoria demanded. Patricio laughed but said nothing more. We left as the sun rose in the midst of a scudding swirl of faraway clouds, early morning rainbows, and reflected light that made the distant horizon look painted above the dark grassland. In the damp of the early morning, everything smelled of leather--leather jackets, hats, boots, chaps—or horse. We holstered our rifles on the horses' flanks. Clay canteens, protected by hardened leather, hung from our saddles. We packed a two-day supply of dried bread and meats in our saddlebags. Patricio led a pack mule. Although mid-July, the animals' nostrils steamed in the cold, damp morning. Mud left from the prior evening's rain flipped off the horses' hooves. We rode three abreast until the trail narrowed to a single track.

Given free rein, Viejo forced himself to the front. At first he trotted, but soon he tired and then slowed to a casual walk. The other horses deferred to him. Mindlessly, we let him set the pace. The day rapidly grew hot. When we were tired of riding we walked. Walking with horses and a mule plodding along behind us suited the mood of July—a month of long days in which summer itself grew tired in the heat.

Near noon, we stopped in a cluster of piñon trees to eat bread and sheep's milk cheese. Over the high peaks, thunderstorms gathered. I fell asleep in Victoria's lap, reassured by the smell of horse, leather, and her sweat. After lunch, again alternately walking and riding, we continued at a slower pace. A thunderstorm caught up with us and drenched us, leaving us suddenly wet, cold, and miserable.

As the rain slowed, Patricio eyed the breaking clouds. "Hum, Cinco leguas hasta este punto. Se trata de dos leguas más y dos horas más. Five leagues traveled and two leagues to go, two more hours," he mused. "We must make it to the Mora before the sun sets."

Neither Victoria nor I answered him. We had no doubt we would make it, but now we were tired, wet, and cold. Fortunately, the afternoon rain had been spotty. In a short time, the trail again grew dry and dusty, and the late afternoon heat warmed and reinvigorated us.

Before we could see or hear the Río Mora, our thirsty horses smelled the water and quickened their pace. At the stream's edge, the horses took a short drink, and then Patricio quickly ordered us on. Leading his horse, he crossed the north side of the bank and then followed a faint path into the cottonwoods. Five minutes later, we followed him into a lush meadow still warmed by the last rays of the retreating July sun.

Near a spring hidden by a clump of trees on the meadow's faraway edge, a pitched camp awaited us. Doña stood in the middle of it looking every bit the fierce Cumanchero, but sprinkled with a few feminine twists. Heavy leather trousers, secured by a sand-cast silver belt, covered her thin frame. She kept a flintlock pistol and a knife holstered at the small of her back. A bow hung loosely over her left shoulder. She cradled a rifle in her arms. A gray, shaggy sheep dog eyed us cautiously from her side. Spurs jangled from her ornate, engraved boots. From pelvis to mid-breasts, she wore a bodice of layered, quilted leather armor. Above her armor, a carefully hand-embroidered, low-cut cotton blouse exposed the tops of her breasts. Shell combs decorated the two long, handle-like braids springing from the sides of her head. Despite her fierce reputation and appearance, today she clearly did not wish to be mistaken for a man!

With her dog, Perro, she had led a pack mule down from the mountains to meet us. Patricio whistled to her. Hiding behind a regal smile, Doña greeted us.

"Me da gusto que todos pudieran venir. Glad you made it. I have hot mint tea and soup for everyone."

Victoria did her best to look pleased by Patricio's surprise, but she was unhappy. When Doña returned home the fall before, Victoria worked hard to forgive Doña for knocking her down, and then she worked even harder to forget Doña existed. She hoped that Patricio would forget Doña too.

102

Now, Victoria hung back and seethed. She mumbled to me, "En el yermo nos vestimos iguales. ¡Pero no semos la misma! In the wilderness we dress alike, but we are not the same!" She caught herself and dropped her head in shame. "Jealousy," she mused and shook her head. "I am not a good sister to my brother. I am not even a good human being," she whispered to me. "Do not our women's hearts want the same thing? She cares about him. That should be good enough, but I will lose him. God demands too much." Victoria did not expect an answer from me. She was struggling with her own demons.

She called out to Doña, "Esta es la primera vez que te veo desde mi cumpleaños. Gracias por el libro de Teresa." Victoria thanked Doña for the book. "I know any book is precious. I have been very careful with it."

Doña dismissed Victoria's thanks with her distant, cool, practiced smile. "You are too careful. We will talk about the book after the sun sets."

With everyone's arrival, Doña felt safe enough to remove her leather armor and lay her bow and pistols aside. Without a leather bodice and bowstring to contain it, Doña's cotton blouse billowed in the breeze exposing her breasts. She did not attempt to cover herself. She relished the chance to confirm she was a woman.

She glanced at me. Before she could seal it in and wall it off, a dark shadow of hidden sadness flashed past the corners of her eyes and mouth. Her childhood had been painfully short. Unlike me, no grandparents rescued her. She had been in charge of her father's home and ranch from the moment of her mother's death. As her father's only child, only living relative, and only woman of the house, her father depended on her for almost everything. Out of necessity, she rode better than any man did. She shot a rifle better than any man did. She wore a chalked white face and painted red lips better than any woman did. She plowed, planted grapes, bought and sold slaves, traded with the Cumanchis, and ran her father's house so well it never occurred to him to re-marry.

She watched Victoria and me "playing at being in love," as she called it. Love was something for which she had no time. She was the last of her line. She was to have children—many of them with the right man as soon as possible. Her father had always spoken to her of the importance of this. She was the seed from which her dying family would sprout anew. Love was a luxury, "a children's game" her father would say. Still, if he so desperately felt the need for progeny, he should have made some effort himself.

In truth, Doña María was tired. Her extreme competence encouraged her father to do little more than continue to grieve the loss of his beloved wife. The same man who told her to forget love and marry for business remained hopelessly tied to a dead woman by unrequited love.

103

Had her father been a wise man, she might have assumed that he warned her about the dangers of love to protect her from the disaster that had befallen him, but he was not wise. He was selfish, thoughtless, and emotionally crippled. He let the wilderness destroy him just as Victoria's mother let it destroy her.

While small signs of hurt occasionally slipped through Doña's armor, she was far from bitter. Doña was firm with Victoria and me, but also gentle and kind, because one who shoots, rides, plows, and has the darkest red lips has also learned that practiced kindness masks the heart's deepest pain. Like the rest of us on the Llano, loneliness and danger haunted her. She cautiously revealed her hurt to me in brief, carefully directed half-smiles and short disconnected glances. She frequently whispered to no one or anyone who might be listening, "¡Basta, basta! Enough, enough." Like Victoria, she said, "God is cruel. He demands everything." Unlike Victoria, she attacked life and expected everyone else to do the same. Patricio was one more duty she would handle well. After watching Doña carefully, Victoria quietly came to me with a new understanding.

"Tomás, she is afraid. I can see it. For the first time I can see it. All of us are afraid all the time. What good is this?" As Victoria spoke, her lips and hands trembled.

"Perhaps how we respond to our fear is all that is important," I answered.

"You are beginning to sound like tía Paula," Victoria complained. She pulled her favorite knife from her saddlebags, sat by the fire, and delicately worked on a carving of San Mateo carrying the axe used in his own beheading. Her hands grew careful and still.

"This is my masterpiece," she said. "San Mateo is the right saint for our village. Each of us carries an axe every day waiting for the right moment to hand it to our executioner," Victoria mused loudly enough for all to hear.

"That is good then," I responded. "We each can sharpen our own axes. We can each choose our own time. We have no need of fear."

"Unless the executioner pulls it from our hands at a time of his choosing," she softly responded.

"I do not intend to turn the axe over to anyone. It must be pulled from me. I have a duty to live!" Doña added emphatically.

"Aquí, here, it is too hard to know how to live. You worry about duty as though doing one's duty was not living. Sometimes duty is a measure of living one's life well." Patricio stared carefully at Doña, and then continued, "Doña, we cannot see into your heart to know what you would do differently, but you seem to us to have lived well. The Cumanchis fear and respect you. All the people living at the northern edge of the Cumancheria know and respect you."

Doña cut Patricio off. "My father uses me! I am tired of this, to be bred like a horse to save the family." She looked at Patricio's hurt face. "Perdóname, mi amor. I love you," she said half-heartedly. To protect Patricio's feelings, she fell quickly back into the trap of duty. All of us were quiet for a long time. We watched the smoke meander into the warm evening sky and listened to the clicking of Victoria's carving knife. Patricio finally spoke.

"Querida Doña, marrying me will relieve you of some of your burdens."

"And add new ones," she responded too sharply.

In the growing darkness, Patricio changed the subject. He turned to Victoria, and asked as though he had read everyone else's mind, "You are carving San Mateo. What do you know about God? Tell me about God. You have been studying. Does God exist in this wilderness?"

"Hermano, God is a source of wisdom and a keeper of confidences. He is an old woman like Bárbara." Then she added, "He is not cruel intentionally, but he is cruel. God confuses me. I have no idea what he wants me to do."

She dropped her head and looked at me. She was silent for a few minutes. Then, she whispered.

"Dios es cruel. La tierra está llena de niños muertos. The earth is full of dead children. No matter how we try, we do not remember the names of the dead. There are so many." She thought for a moment, "Teresa tells us that God reaches out to all of us. She says that mercy is the law. As to mercy, I am not so sure. Here we kill or die. You, Patricio, are a man paid to kill. Doña, you cut up a dead man solely to terrify the living. You do these things to protect your old father and me. We say God wills this, and we say God is merciful. My heart hurts." She stopped carving and her hands shook fiercely. She quickly resumed carving to regain control of herself.

"I gave you Sor Teresa because, like you, I know there is no mercy in this wilderness. Hiding does not help us." Doña spoke thoughtfully.

"I know this," Victoria interrupted. "Doña, for the first time in my life, I know that you are like the rest of us. You are afraid. You kill and maim because this somehow makes you feel alive. It makes you happy."

"Victoria, you think too hard. Beauty matters, killing matters, and life matters. I do not enjoy killing and maiming. Killing keeps me alive. Maiming the dead and dying protects me by making my enemies fear me." She briefly gazed into the flames, and then added bitterly, "I am a practical woman. Nothing is supposed to make me happy!" She stood up and angrily circled the fire.

"I know that my father is very worried about children. He thinks that Patricio and I should be married. I think so too. What do you think?"

105

Uncomfortable with her loss of control and anger, Doña redirected the conversation to business and duty.

Victoria stared quietly at her exquisite rival. She wondered aloud, "How does a discussion of God lead to a discussion of marriage?" She did not wait for an answer. "Do you love Patricio?"

"He is a good man." Doña avoided the question about love. She complained about duty, but in the end, she did what she thought best for her family. To Doña and most families on the Llano, the business of marriage was more important to survival than love. Victoria knew it. Victoria did not ask about love again.

"I have many brothers, but he is my favorite and I will miss him. If you need my blessings, you have them. When do you plan to marry?"

"Gracias, en octubre," Doña narrowed her dark eyes, "Since you agree."

Doña negotiated with Patricio's little sister for her favorite brother's hand. I would not have been surprised had she traded a hundred sheep to seal the bargain. I had a new respect for Doña's business ability. All of us could ride and shoot because we had to. However, for Doña, riding and shooting were about her pride, her sense of dignity, and her personal worth. Her killing protected and continued the community. For the same reason, she needed a strong husband. Doña would never quite love Patricio, but she would be a good lover. Business was business. On the other hand, Patricio loved her and needed her love in return. He would never quite have it.

Victoria

The night swallowed us. Doña and I did not say it, but as women, we knew the truth. I had found love and she had found a good business partner. Only the wisdom of old age would tell us who made the best decision. I carefully chipped out the details of Mateo's axe until the fire burned out. Complete darkness sealed us in its protective envelope. If marauding humans were to find us, they would have to stumble upon us. Firelight would not give us away. Tired, Tomás and I crawled beneath our bed of buffalo robes. We lay quietly by the dying embers listening to the coyotes howl in the distance. Curled next to Doña on the other side of the fire, Perro responded to the howls with a low growl.

"¡Mira al cielo! Look at the sky," I said and pushed into Tomás' shoulder. "Y Dios. What does God do in this place? En este vacío? In this vast emptiness, the stars are too far away. El pueblo está demasiado lejos, y tú, Tomás, estás demasiado lejos. The Pueblo, my love, everything is too far away. Nothing is connected. Abrázame. Hold me so that I can sleep."

He pulled me on top of him. "Todo es hermoso y peligroso. Esa

106

es la forma en que está conectado. Everything is dangerous and beautiful; that is how it is connected. Pero Díos...but about...." He drifted to sleep mumbling about God. Life is too complicated—everything, everyone both beautiful and dangerous?

He started to describe the hidden terrible irony of true love, I thought, to hold one's lover tenderly in an embrace only to die giving birth to a child nine months later. A woman who dies as part of a business proposition hurts her husband less. However, I wanted love. I loved. I knew this. Others may have thought I was always afraid, but I was not. I was brave enough to love.

I nudged against Tomás. Would he awaken? When one is the only one awake, there is nothing so lonely as a dark night. I am sure this is what Jesus thought. I shivered from the cold. Even in summer, the Llano is cold at night. My querido, should I waken him? I let him sleep, but still he held me tight. His breath smelled of fresh wild strawberries. I buried my face in his long hair. His gentle, musky scent comforted me. Sí, foxes have warm holes and birds have cozy nests in which to sleep. I had Tomás. Entwined, entangled, and protected by him, I finally fell asleep.

At first light, the jubilant singing of robins and the loud calls of flickers awakened me. I lay still and watched as Patricio arose, dressed, and left to search and care for the horses. Soon Doña too crawled naked from her bed. At five feet eight inches, she was tall and well muscled but thin. Her ribs and hipbones protruded prominently, suggesting a hidden frailty. The delicate, soft black hair of her legs and her deep, thick black pubic hair sparkled and danced on her skin. Her pale gray abdomen and buttocks contrasted starkly with her sun-darkened arms, chest, and face. Her fierce image from the day before had softened during the night. Tomás was right. Life was both beautiful and dangerous. For a brief moment, she turned to face me with fully alert eyes and ears. Wolf-like, she sniffed the air for danger. I did not pretend to sleep. I stared and admired her. In the breaking dawn light, she smiled her faraway half-smile then turned away to dress without shame.

"Perro, ven pa'ca," she called her dog. He bounded from the woods. From her satchel, she pulled a piece of dried mutton. She held it out to him. He ate from her hand. After feeding her dog, she quietly prepared breakfast and packed up the camp.

"Tomás y Victoria, get up. Patricio and I must leave soon. I have made breakfast." Awake for a while, but unwilling to face the cold wet dew, we snuggled in the warmth of our buffalo robe bed for a few more minutes. When the sun finally warmed us, we quickly dressed and ate breakfast while Doña completed packing. When Patricio returned with the horses and mules, Doña was fully dressed, armed, armored, and ready to leave. Any suggestion or hint of Doña's thin frailty had long disappeared.

"Tenemos que irnos antes de que el día se vuelva demasiado viejo.

We must go before the day grows too old. Go in peace, beloved hermana," Patricio spoke, impatient to be on the way. He said a quiet prayer and waved the small crucifix of his rosary over us.

"You will always have my blessings," he said. "I will be gone until the mountain snows start falling in September. Watch for los indios. Do not linger here too long or you will not make it home before dark. Tomás, she loves you. You must take care of her. Take my knife. Protect her always." He pulled a belduque from his saddle and passed the long knife carefully to Tomás.

"Gracias, Patricio," Tomás thanked my brother, "but this is not necessary."

"My brothers have many knifes. I have only one sister who is forever married to you, though no one but Doña and I may understand this. God forbid it, but you will know what to do with the knife, Tomás." Patricio continued somberly, "Victoria, Tomás, you must take care of each other. Doña and I have done our part to prepare you for any danger. Victoria, take care of our mother. Tomás, I know your mother will be fine, but I cannot say this for your tía. Help Victoria and Bárbara take care of her."

"Patricio, hermano mío, te quiero. I will miss you. Come back to me whole. Come back to me soon. We will watch out for our mother and aunt," I cried and so did Patricio. He would be gone a long time. It felt like we would never see each other again.

Mounted and waiting on her horse behind him, Doña watched silently and shook her head softly. Ready to leave, she listened patiently as Patricio continued.

"You are strong. Adiós."

Doña, wearing her wide leather hat, a bow, and quiver on her back, and a pistol in her belt, leaned down from her horse and hugged us each in turn.

"Niño, tú eres lo más precioso." She held Tomás too long. Her eyes gently misted.

"It is the sunlight." She abruptly turned her horse, adjusted her canteen, and headed northwest into the mountains toward her home. It was halfway to the shepherd's camp. Patricio would spend the night with her and her father then continue on alone the next day. The two riders pulling their packhorses, with Perro in the lead, trotted along the stream and quickly disappeared into the bosque. An occasional bark in the distance marked their progress. Soon, except for the wind, it was quiet again.

It was time for us to go, but we lingered by the smoldering fire, sipping tea made from mint pulled from the stream bank. I put my arms around Tomás. Fine hair was growing on his face. It was too soft to scratch my cheek. I clasped his long, thick blond hair and then ran my hands down it to his mid-back. Through my shirt, Tomás held my breasts—he now had something small to hold.

Climbing toward mid-morning, the sun flickered across the top of the tallest cottonwood trees. The lush morning shade and a break in the deep green of the trees framed a far-off morning thunderstorm. The thunder, lightning, and trembling leaves added a somber melancholy to Patricio's departure. His leaving with Doña made the departure somehow seem final and ominous. We held each other and dozed by the now-dead fire. Suddenly awake, I turned to Tomás.

"Tomás, Doña is beautiful. Do you like her? She is very pretty. I watched her dressing. I know you saw her too."

"She is very pretty," Tomás interrupted me.

"My love, I can tell she cares about you in some special way. I can see it in her face. It is as though you remind her of some tragic event or place so many years ago. I wonder what she sees. I have watched you. I know you see it too."

"There is something about her which is a mystery. She seems sad to me. I want to reach out and touch her, to help her. This is the spell she casts." Tomás did not deny that I was right.

"Tomás, it is like you said, everything is beautiful and dangerous. I do not want her beauty to lure you to dangerous places."

"Victoria, is she so strong and beautiful that we think she does not need our help? We commend her for doing more than her duty, and we know that the duties she shoulders are finally her father's responsibility. She is exhausted. Sadness lurks in her eyes behind her careful smiles."

Victoria emptied out her saddlebags looking for her knife and San Mateo. Victoria carved and mused quietly beside the smoldering fire. Occasionally the fresh chips burst into flame and then quickly died out again. Mateo's axe grew sharper.

"Sí, es la verdad. She is proud and sad," I said. "She took my Patricio. Will this make her happy, or must I give her more?"

"Querida, Patricio is not Bárbara. You do not own him. You cannot keep him, but you can give him away."

Midmorning came so quickly. If we were not within the walls by dark or soon after, señor Trent and my father would come searching for us. We did not want to alarm our parents, nor did we want them to know too much about our lives. We picked raspberries and strawberries and packed them in moss and grass in our saddlebags, and headed home. We were not leading mules and our horses were well rested. We rode hard taking only a few short stops for water. A half league from home and with the sun dipping behind the mountains at our backs, we heard the guard on the wall ringing the bell to signal that we were safe. We dismounted our exhausted horses and walked them the rest of the way home.

"Querido, I am very tired, but I do not want this day to end. Come home with me for dinner. Let's watch the moon rise across the Llano from the top of wall." We walked to Tomás' house leading our tired horses. We left half the raspberries with tía Paula.

"Nice and fresh," she smiled.

"Tía, Tomás is coming over to eat with Bárbara and me, is that okay?" We did not stop to wait for her permission.

"Don't be home too late. Show me your carving of San Mateo tomorrow," she called after us as we ran with Viejo into the stable.

Thomas

As she watched me care for Viejo, Victoria prayed silently. I watched her lips move as she fussed with her rosary. Victoria did not wish me to hurry. She asked me to take "all the time in the world."

"Querido, why do days end?" she asked. She clearly did not expect an answer. I said nothing as I brushed Viejo. He fell asleep before he could be fed. I left oats and water for him in two wooden buckets.

"Querido, watching you is like watching a flower gently open. I could watch you and watch you." She unfolded her arms and reached toward me with both hands. "Ven pa'ca." She grasped my hand. We walked slowly to her house. Poor, drooping Francisco plodded along behind us. At the Griego's gate, the genízaro stable boy took Francisco.

"Come with me to see Bárbara. She will make us a dinner that we can eat up on the roof." Victoria pulled me after her to the kitchen.

"Bárbara, Bárbara, dónde estás?"

"Niña, calmase, calm down. Your papá has gone to San Miguel. The moment he left your mother went directly to bed. You know how she is. Now tell me quietly what you want."

"I want to sit on the roof with my beloved and have dinner!" Victoria said this with great flair and swish of her braids. In her drama, she stirred up a day's worth of trail dust that flew from her in all directions.

"¡Qué barbaridad, niños! You are filthy. I am not a fussy woman, you see, but if you plan to eat a fine dinner, you must remove at least one layer of dirt. Victoria, take Tomás out to the garden and wash by the well. Wash faces, hands, and shake the dust from your clothes. Then come back."

"Pero Bárbara, where is the romance in this?" Victoria moaned. We went into the garden. Victoria remained strangely animated as though she had done nothing but rest all day. She switched from a woman of the Llano to a child in her house. She tackled me and pulled my shirt off. She poured cold water over my head.

"I am cold and I will never get dry," I said with irritation, but she did not stop. She threw more water instead. Soon we were wrestling in the garden and dumping buckets of water over each other. Suddenly a candle flickered in señora Griego's window.

110

"Shh," whispered Victoria. We hid quietly behind the well watching the bouncing flame. Ana María Griego stared from her window, startled, awakened, and confused by the noise. She peered out the window and carefully studied her garden for several minutes. Perhaps satisfied that she had only been dreaming, she returned to her bed leaving her shutters open. As soon as her mother stepped away from the window, Victoria impishly resumed playing.

"Shh," she said. Then she pushed me over and fell on top of me kissing my entire face. "Querido, if mamá is watching I will show her how much I love you!" I watched the open window and nervously kissed her back.

"You are no fun," she teased jumping to her feet. "Come on!"

We snuck back into the kitchen. Bárbara took one look at us now covered from head to toe in mud and dirtier than before. She did the only thing she could do.

"Niños, take off your clothes right now. Do not move." I froze with embarrassment.

"Y Tomás," she said looking sternly at me, "I am an old woman. I have seen many naked children. I know how you both swim together. There are no secrets with me, and there will be no mud in my kitchen."

I started to say that I was now a man, but this would have been pointless. I knew that she would say, "Hombres o niños, men or boys, I am still an old woman. I have washed and buried too many dead men to count."

We undressed quickly and piled our mud-caked clothing by the door.

"Go into the garden and wash. This time come back clean."

"Pero Bárbara, what about mamá? We will be in trouble if she sees us like this!" Victoria stifled a laugh.

"Then you will be quiet, Niña." We slipped back out into the garden.

"Tomás, you have mud on your pito." She looked at me pretending to be in shock. I looked down at my mud-caked pubic hair.

"You can make plaster stick to anything," I teased. She laughed aloud. "Quiet, you will awaken your mother. Then we will be embarrassed," I warned.

"She drinks too much when papá is away. She will not awaken." She filled a bucket of fresh water, grabbed me, and giggling, scrubbed away her handiwork. I watched both the kitchen door and the bedroom windows. No one paid any attention.

"There," she whispered loudly. She poured cold water over both of us until we were blue and shaking. Mud-free, we went back in to the kitchen where Bárbara had lain out a clean, well-patched dress for Victoria. She also had found a pair of fresh leather trousers and a shirt for me.

113

"Stand by the fire to dry, then put these on," she ordered. We shivered briefly by the fire until dry then quickly dressed.

"I will make you a basket of sheep's cheese, bread and melons," Bárbara offered.

We accepted and with a basket of fresh food and warm blankets, we carefully climbed the narrow, rail-less staircase up to the roof. Tired, we sat down to eat. Victoria grew thoughtful. She looked into the black night sky.

"Where is the moon?"

"It will be up soon," I said, struggling to stay awake. She rested her chin on my shoulder, looked into my face, and gently chewed melon.

"Te quiero," she sighed softly. "In you I see the face of God. I know his face is like yours. I know he lives in the night sky.. The stars are so sharp tonight—so clear. You matter to me more than I can say. This is what I know. This moment is all I know. Oh, Dios mío. Hold my chest. Feel and touch my heart. It is yours."

"Te quiero. I love you, hummingbird." I placed my hands across her chest and felt her anxious beating heart. Her hands shook, but her breathing slowed as I held her. Soft and warm, she pressed into me. The stars grew sharper in her presence. The deep quiet of night set in. It felt as though all creation was holding its breath. Before I met Victoria, the silence and dark night would have been frightening. I thought aloud, "Victoria, I can never lose you."

In response she whispered, "Porque el Poderoso ha hecho obras grandes por mi. The Almighty has done great things for me."

I pressed my nose into her thick, black oiled hair. She held me quietly tracing my face. She whispered softly, "Tus cejas son hermosas. You have beautiful eyebrows."

Chapter 9: Fall 1831—No Hymns for the Dead

Victoria

At the end of our second summer, we watched the Llano again dry to brown. The tall grass rattled like so many skeletons in the wind.

"Tomás, every child buried there sprouts and then dies. They will all come back in the spring. Until then, we will only hear their bones clanking in the wind. This is why winter is not a happy season." I looked up from my carving to watch him read.

"We have become like abuelos," I chuckled.

"When Patricio dropped you at my feet, you did not run away," Tomás smiled.

"We have never fought," I said.

"My father will ask your father to arrange our marriage, if you agree."

"Sí, it is time." That seemed so simple, I thought. "Kiss me."

In late September, the village again bustled with ciboleros who stopped to rest and visit before heading into the Llano. There was also the last opportunidad por una feria, a trade fair, with the Cumanchis who arrived early one morning after the first October frost. Taoseños also came. The Cumanchi brought dried buffalo, buffalo robes, tanned leather, cattle, and livestock to trade for a winter supply of corn. Everyone knew the horses and cattle were stolen from the Presidio at San Antonio de Béjar or from Durango or Matamoros. If someone knew the brand, the governor might have the cattle returned, but mostly we kept the livestock. The fact that it was stolen from our fellow countrymen further south was ignored.

"What can we do about stolen horses and cattle driven hundreds of leagues from home?" Papá would shrug. "Seigo un hombre práctico. I am practical. We buy them or the Anglos do."

The fair began with an exchange of gifts between villagers and Cumanchis—tobacco for iron, a horse for two well-made saddles. The villagers and Taoseños then set out clay jars of hard breads, corn, and apples, locally made wool blankets, and bolts of cotton cloth to trade. The Cumanchi brought up horses, buffalo products, and slaves.

Trade fairs were dangerous. Many years before, Cumanchis,

thinking they had been cheated, attacked the towns of Pecos and Taos. Papá did not forget the dangers. So far, our village had escaped such an attack. Once allowed inside the walls of the Pueblo, the Cumanchis could easily overpower the other traders and kill them all without difficulty. Because of the danger, papá made me stay inside when San Mateo had a fair. Tomás stayed with me.

Papá did more than keep the women and children hidden to make the fairs safe. Together, my father and a Cumanchi capitán reviewed complaints about quality and weights of goods and enforced decisions regarding just exchanges. Over the years, the two gained the traders' respect and trust. As a result, when a fair was announced in San Mateo, people traveled several days to participate.

Thomas

Early Sunday afternoon when the fall fair was just about over, the guard on the wall frantically rang the warning bell. Startled, Victoria and I ran to the top of the wall. In the distance, two riders rapidly made their way from the Mora country to the north. It was Pascual pulling a packhorse behind him. Doña María accompanied him. Driven hard by their riders, the horses galloped relentlessly toward us.

"Tomás, where is Patricio?" Victoria stammered. "I don't see him. Dios mío, why would they leave him behind?" She paced nervously until she could wait no longer. She ran down the stairs and through the gates toward the frenzied riders. She screamed and pulled her hair.

"¿Dónde está Patricio? Where is Patricio? No, no, no!" she sobbed in panic. "¿Dónde está Patricio?"

"Patricio está muerto. He is dead," Pascual shouted as he and Doña galloped past Victoria and quickly entered the village. "¿Dónde está mamá? Where is mother? Where is mother?" he demanded. He jumped from his horse and stamped his feet like a hurt, small child.

"Patricio, Patricio," he sobbed. Tears tracked through the grime and dust on his face. "We have lost our Patricio. He is gone."

Alarmed, Bárbara ran into the courtyard. "Silencio, hombre. You will frighten your mother. ¡Apacíguate, apacíguate! Calm down!" She ordered. "Tell me what happened." She grabbed the reins of the packhorse and pulled it into the stable. Victoria and I ran after her. Doña María's lathered and dripping horse followed us on its own. Doña made no effort to dismount.

Dumbfounded and too tired to speak, she sat in her saddle muttering quietly.

"It was supposed to be all business. Anger and love—wasted emotions, wasted emotions." Hunched forward and unmoving, she stared into space.

116

Nothing in my life prepared me for that day. I could not recall the death of my own mother. Patricio was dead, and people bustled around me as though bustling would bring him back to life.

Victoria wailed inconsolably, "Se murió. He is dead. I will die too!" Her ear-shattering cries unnerved everyone. A stunned Pascual just looked at me.

"Lo siento, I am sorry," he said to no one in particular.

For a moment, Bárbara also lost her composure. She struggled to calm Victoria and care for Doña but failed at both. Victoria's screaming soon scared the exhausted horses. Their restless stomping worsened the confusion. Bárbara continued to give unheeded orders.

"Quiet child, as your good Lord has said—the dead care for themselves. Victoria, get Doña off her horse. Your screaming is not helping anyone."

Sobbing, Victoria reached toward Doña with both hands, but she was suddenly just a small child unable to help herself or Doña. Victoria collapsed to her knees. Mamá Paula suddenly appeared in the barn. She clapped her hands until everyone was quiet.

She immediately called to Doña, "¡Desmonta ahora, por el amor de Dios!" she ordered. Doña María did not move. Mamá Paula spoke louder but with a still controlled voice, "For the love of God, get off your horse. I will not repeat myself."

Mamá turned to me, "Jito, get her off her horse and take her inside."

I pulled Doña's arm. She stiffly slid from her horse. She made no effort to stand. I staggered as she collapsed onto the floor. Sobbing and panting for her breath, Victoria slumped down beside her. Mamá Paula spoke with her in a low voice.

"Sobrina, ¡escúchame! Listen to me. You must calm down. You upset the horses. Slow down your breathing. You will make yourself dizzy. Nothing will bring Patricio back."

Rolled in a Navajo blanket on the back of the packhorse, Patricio's rotting body filled the barn with an overwhelming stench. Mamá Paula and Bárbara carefully pulled the damp, oozing blanket from the packhorse. Overcome, Victoria vomited.

"Victoria, control yourself. Where is your mother? ¡Ándale! Hurry, get her now," Mamá Paula ordered.

"Tía, por favor, I am going. I am going now," wept Victoria. I grabbed her hand and led her into the house. We found señora Griego alone and in her room. She had no idea of the catastrophe unfolding in her barn. Victoria could not tell her. I had to.

"Tía Ana, come to the barn, Patricio is dead. Pascual and Doña brought his body home."

With a look of resignation, she slowly sipped the last of her wine.

117

She did not cry. She did not seem surprised. The bad news that she perpetually waited for had come again. This was not a false alarm. She was ready. She lived and acted out moments such as these many times in her dreams and nightmares. She sighed, crossed herself, got up, and slowly walked to the door in her wrinkled clothing. She paused by her mirror, straightened her dress, and adjusted the combs in her hair. For a fleeting moment, I saw why Patricio had fallen in love with Doña. His faded and worn mother still had some of the regal appearance that Doña possessed. Tía Ana wrapped her rebozo tightly around her shoulders, stepped out into the cool evening, and strolled distractedly toward the stables.

She turned to me and said, "Sobrino, this is what happens here. We cannot fix these things. We will walk to the barn with dignity. Nobody lives long in this wilderness." She re-straightened her dress and re-fixed her hair. She grabbed the wall to steady herself. She held her head high. Victoria and I followed her as she walked to her son's wrapped and oozing body. To block the stench, she held her rebozo to her nose and mouth. She pulled the blanket back just enough to reveal Patricio's face. She carefully patted his hair.

"Este es mi jito. This is my son." She stared into his grotesquely swollen and blackening face. Shaking her head, she said "Sí, sí. This is my son." She acted as though she had been called to resolve a controversy about his identity. Remaining cold and detached, she turned to Pascual.

"Dime. Tell me what happened."

"He was fishing and cut his foot on a rock. It got infected. He went so quickly."

"I see," she said. "Mejor, better than indios bárbaros. An accident, it could have happened in Santa Fe or Madrid." She turned back to her kitchen. "Bárbara, we will bury him in la iglesia de San Mateo right away. He is rotting before our eyes. Call for a few men to dig his grave tonight. Rápido, rápido. Bury him now and we pray over him tomorrow. The next time the priest comes, he will say mass."

Tía Ana gave her few orders. She sighed then walked to Doña and bent over her.

"Doña, querida, I'm sorry. He was a good man. You will miss him."

Doña turned her head away without speaking.

Ana María then called to Pascual.

"Hijo, you must tell your father. He is trading with the bárbaros." Tía Ana shuffled back toward the house. Before entering, she stood for a brief second at the door muttering.

"The floor of the capilla is full of my dead children. There is no more room." Then shaking her head, she commented, "Fishing barefoot in this cold weather. How careless. He could have caught a cold."

She then disappeared back to her solitary life of sleep and wine. She would not mourn Patricio, for she had mourned for him, for herself, and all her dead children every dreadful moment of her life.

Her apparent indifference to her son's death unexpectedly calmed everyone else. Everyone now knew what to do. Two men volunteered to dig a grave near the altar in the San Mateo church floor. When the grave was completed, the village women and children joined us to bury Patricio. Paula Teresa stood quietly in the back of the church. Doña, with muddy and tear-streaked face, still fully armed and dressed in her cuera, and mud-splattered, leather trousers stood beside her. Pascual, Victoria, and I stood at the graveside. Tía Ana did not come. The other men, including father and Tío Manuel, were also not there, for none could safely leave the fair without risking a riot.

Too decomposed to dress him in a proper shroud, the men pushed Patricio into his grave, wrapped in the ruined Navajo blanket he came home in. Except for a brief prayer, there was no ceremony.

> Dios te salve María, llena eres de gracia, el Señor es contigo, bendita eres entre todas las mujeres y bendito es el fruto de tu vientre, Jesús. Santa María Madre de Dios, ruega por nosotros los pecadores ahora y en la hora de nuestra muerte. Amén. Hail Mary, full of grace. ...

Pascual and the two other men filled the hole, stopping from time to time to pack the clay around Patricio's body with wooden mallets. An occasional gruesome snapping of bones echoed above the thudding hammers. Victoria moaned with each new blow. The floor was soon again hard and cold. The putrid stench of death, the last trace of Patricio, wafted throughout the church like sickly incense. Doña and Victoria marked Patricio's grave with a handful of pebbles.

In the smoky tallow candlelight, Victoria leaned against me, sobbing and shivering from cold, sadness, and despair. Her brother, whom she adored, now just rotting flesh, had been quickly disposed of, pounded into the soil to stop a foul smell and the possibility of infestation. Her lips moved in silent prayer. She struggled to cross herself with grotesquely shaking hands.

Finally, mamá Paula led us outside. Doña followed carrying a rifle in both hands. Her bow was strapped to her back. Her eyes had dried. She set her jaw. With mud-streaked face, she peered into the plaza just beyond the church wall where traders tussled in the fading twilight.

"Tendremos problemas. We are going to have trouble. You should go home and bar your door," she warned mamá Paula. Patricio, for the moment, had become part of her distant past. The new danger left her no time to mourn.

In the trampled plaza, angry voices haggled over the last few fair items—hard breads and rancid meats. I heard my father's voice, "¡Cálmense, hombres! ¡Cálmense, hombres! Calm down, men. Treat each other with respect!"

Señor Griego grew impatient and finally ordered the Cumanchi to leave. He prayed for a peaceful evening. His prayers would not be answered.

Mamá spoke briefly to Doña. "Stay away from the plaza. It is dangerous. You have lost too much today already ¡Cuídate! Go home. Nos oraremos por ti. We will pray for you."

"I do not need prayers. I am not ready to go home. Los indios bárbaros me tienen miedo. The Cumanchi are afraid of me. They will be careful." She put down her rifles, unslung her bow, and leaned against the churchyard wall that separated her from the plaza. She lay out powder, ramrod, and arrows. With an angry snicker, her eyes tightened. She bit off a cartridge, primed her firing pan, rammed a ball into her rifle, and watched the fair turn into a riot.

"¡La violencia me centra! Violence focuses me," she whispered harshly. Her sneer disappeared. Her face froze into a haunting mantle of serenity. Doña María Josefa Chávez's practiced serene exterior hid any hint of fear. Watching her, I again experienced the same strange confusion I felt when I first met her. Ella era La Virgen con un fusil. She was the Virgin with a rifle.

"Let's go home!" Mamá abruptly grabbed Victoria and me. We scurried to safety.

Behind us more shouting erupted, then a rifle shot, followed by a startled silence. I looked back to see Doña, silhouetted in shadows, aiming her second rifle above the heads of the retreating rioters.

"Apúrense niños, hurry, hurry." Mamá led us through the dim village. In the moonless, cold dark, our own shadows and the crunching gravel beneath our boots startled us. We safely reached our house and quickly went inside. We barred the doors and windows.

"Carguemos los mosquetes. We must load the muskets, hurry. Tomás, your rifle," Mamá Paula called out orders.

The three of us loaded the muskets and my rifle. I unsheathed the belduque Patricio had given me and laid it within my arm's reach on the floor. Mamá set out her bow and a quiver of arrows. We nervously listened for any strange noise in the night.

"Tía Paula, why am I here with you? It would be safer in the secret room at home." Victoria's voice meekly quivered in the darkness.

"Querida, it makes me sad to say, but my sister, your madre, is in no shape to help anyone. You will stay here until tomorrow. We are now ready for anything. The men will keep us safe. They will be on guard all night. You rest and sleep."

Mamá Paula lit a fire. Exhausted and unable to control her trembling, Victoria rested her head on my shoulder. The heat and flickering flames mesmerized us. Neither of us spoke. Finally, Victoria was still.

"Is she asleep?" Mamá whispered.

"She is," I nodded.

Mamá brought out buffalo robes and a cotton-filled pallet. She made us a soft bed by the fire. I pulled Victoria onto the pallet and curled up beside her. She did not move. Mamá pulled off our boots and gently covered us. She placed her hand on Victoria's head and prayed, "Dios, por favor, give Victoria's soul a rest." She kissed us goodnight, added wood to the fire, took her musket, and sat down behind us in her favorite chair.

Later, when father returned, he rechecked the wooden shutters and further reinforced the doors with our heaviest furniture. He took down his lance and adjusted the muskets and rifle. He spoke quietly but sternly with mamá, and then disappeared out the small garden window. Curled in buffalo robes on the floor, Victoria restlessly pushed against me. The house was pitch black except for a few glowing coals still smoldering in the fireplace. Victoria groaned in the darkness, but did not awaken. Somewhere behind me, mamá Paula sat quietly in her chair, a musket across her lap. I could not see her, and she said nothing.

Sleep was impossible. Visions of Patricio, dead, wrapped, and oozing from a blanket besieged me. The foul scent of rotting flesh and vomit clung to Victoria and me like an infestation of leeches. Desperate to filter out the horrors of the day, I placed my nose in Victoria's hair, but even her braids smelled of death. My own thudding heart brought back the pounding sounds of the heavy wooden hammers pulverizing Patricio. Terrified, I sat up. My weary eyes burned. I stared at the last glowing ember until it flickered out. Lost in complete blackness, I hugged my knees. Except for the gentle breathing of Victoria and mamá, the room was still. Death must be like this dreadful, lonely night, I thought. I lay back, found Victoria, and pushed my face into her armpit. Her musky, living smell only briefly extinguished the gruesome scents and sounds of the day.

Awake, asleep, awake again, the night exhausted me. What time was it? Attempts to sleep had become pointless. Where was father? A small ray of light flickered through the gun slits in the heavy shutters and suddenly disappeared as if blocked out by someone passing in front of the window. Father? Mother? Where were they? I grasped Victoria's hands. They were ice cold, sweaty, and shaking. Her breathing was shallow. Somehow, she had pulled off her sweat-soaked shirt, but her sodden leather trousers still clung to her repulsively. Her exposed breasts and arms were as cold as her hands, but her forehead burned.

She is ill. Maybe dying, I worried. "Stop it, stop it," I moaned quietly to myself. The shutters rattled. It is just the wind! On hands and knees, I felt in the darkness for my knife.

In the blackness behind me, I heard muffled rustling and the sound of a pistol being cocked. I heard the same sound repeated outside. Suddenly a spark of flint, a flash of light and the sulfur smell of black powder filled the dark room. Outside another explosion followed. The heavy thud of leather boots crunched over the gravel path outside our door. I heard mamá Paula and Doña whispering but could not make out what they were saying. Victoria moaned and trembled. Finally, mamá made her way to me.

"Tomás, we are safe."

"I know," I whispered. "Victoria is still asleep."

Mamá disappeared. It was quiet again. There were no sounds from inside or outside. Victoria's shaking worsened, but she did not awaken. I pressed my eyes into her face. Her eyelids remained closed. Otherwise, every inch of her body trembled. I held her and warmed her, but she still shuddered. I spoke to her quietly, but she did not respond. She slept and shook in my arms. I nodded off. Suddenly, screaming in wide-eyed terror, she jolted me awake. She sat up.

"Patricio, Patricio, ¿dónde estás? Ah Tomás, it is you. I was dreaming," she mumbled. "Sí, sí he is safe in the mountains." Her shaking worsened. She dripped with sweat until we were both soaked and shivering in the cold. Soon again light entered through the gun slits. This time the light was brighter and permanent. It was early morning—the village was silent. Mamá had already gone out.

No one came to see who fired the shots during the night. No one stirred on the dirt streets. After a night of fear, morning should have been joyful, but it was not. Shirtless and shivering, Victoria crawled to the window, stood on a chair, and looked out through the cracks in the shutters. She climbed down, collapsed against the wall, and began to cry softly.

"Patricio, come here," she called to me. I crawled to her. She was confused. "Ah, Tomás, it is you. Take me home. My brother wants me to go home."

"Victoria, querida, Patricio está muerto. He is not at home." I peered into the street. In the early dawn, I could see one empty house across the plaza still smoldering from a fire set during the night, but I could see little else. The narrow gun slits in the shutters blocked my view.

"Who are you?" Victoria's teeth chattered. I struggled to understand her.

"Seigo Tomás, I am Tomás, querida. Patricio is dead."

"Ah, ¿Tomás?" The room slowly grew lighter. Half naked, she curled on the floor. I pulled her into my arms and carried her back to bed. As I struggled with her, her legs and feet limply swung back and forth.

122

She made no effort to help. She did not even try to hold her head up. I carefully lay her back on our bed by the fire. She did not move but looked at me intently as though trying to remember something important.

"Ah ¿Tomás?" She called softly. I wrapped her in warm blankets and added wood to the fire.

"Querida, I will make you hot tea."

"I want to go home. ¿Dónde está tu papá, mi tío?" She whispered and wept through chattering teeth. I had no idea. In the terror of the night, I had lost track of everything and everyone.

"Querida, we are alone. I don't know where anyone is. You are running a fever." Victoria was clearly not well. She wanted to go home. I would take her myself if I had to.

Soon again, there were voices on the street. It was mamá Paula and father whispering to a third person. Doña, I thought. Then it was quiet again. The wind shifted and whiffs of smoke drifted through the shutters. The whispering began again. Then it grew deathly quiet. I crawled to the shutters and carefully opened them. Several empty houses in the village were still burning. I could not see anyone on the street. The night began with the arrival of Patricio's body. Mysterious shooting and house fires followed. Now, my parents whispered from some hidden place.

I found Victoria's leather jacket and tried to put it on her. She made no effort to help. Her arms were useless. She collapsed back into bed.

"Querida, help me so I can take you home." She did not move. I propped her up and brought her mint tea. She tried to hold it with her shaking hands, but tea flew everywhere. She dropped and shattered the cup.

"Dios mío, Dios, perdóname," she sobbed and lay back down by the fire. I pulled the buffalo robe over her. She did not speak. We held each other quietly until she briefly fell back to sleep.

"I want to go home," she reawakened sobbing. "Mi hermano, mi hermano. My favorito está muerto. My brother is dead."

"Querida, it is not safe to take you home."

"Por favor, I must go home, Tomás," she begged.

"¡Qué tonta!" I worried aloud and angrily. "I will take you home." I wrapped her coat around her and buttoned it without putting her arms in the sleeves. I pulled on her boots. I gathered up my rifle and powder.

"Our fathers would expect us to stay here where I can protect you. Even Patricio was clear to me in his instruction last summer—'protect my only sister.'" She stared vacantly into the fire as though I was not there.

"Querida, can you walk?" I asked.

"Sí, sí, I can walk. You will help me," she spoke in a toneless, flat voice.

123

"I will help you," I assured her.

I put my arm around her and quickly found that I was supporting most of her weight. I pulled her hip against mine to brace her, but I could not support her and carry a rifle. We stumbled out the door and she fell onto the gravel walk. Helpless with her arms trapped inside her tightly buttoned jacket, she lay on the cold gravel path unable to move staring up at me with a terror-filled face.

"You are too weak to walk. I will carry you," I panted.

Strapping the rifle over my shoulder, I picked her up. Her black pleading eyes fixed on me, she whimpered.

"I am cold. Take me home."

I carried her up the path until we reached the safety of the churchyard wall. I put her down and rested. On the south side of the pueblo, several houses smoldered. The sun broke above the eastern village walls. The morning warmed slowly. In the distance, a rooster crowed.

"Los Cumanchis?" Victoria whispered.

"I don't know," I said. On the far side of the trampled plaza, a few heavily armed Taoseños dressed in sheepskin coats chatted quietly by their breakfast fires. I picked Victoria up and struggled on. I staggered with her through the partly opened and unguarded zaguán gate of her house. Inside the walls, a small makeshift army of men and women armed with lances, muskets, rifles, and bows roamed pointlessly about. Bárbara alone grasped that Victoria needed help. She ran to me and helped carry her inside.

"¿Qué le pasó? What's wrong?"

"She is ill. No one was at home to help. I brought her here."

"Take her to her room," she directed. "I will tell don Manuel and señor Trent that you are here." The room was cold. I put her to bed while Bárbara lit a fire in the room's small corner fireplace.

Victoria sighed, "Gracias, querido, gracias. I am fine. Just tired and cold."

"Niños, I will bring you hot tea. Now you both must rest." Bárbara returned within a few minutes. She unbuttoned Victoria's coat and freed her trapped arms. I watched Victoria's exposed breasts and chest heaved as she gasped to breathe.

"Drink this, chica." Bárbara put a hot cup into Victoria's hands. Victoria dropped and shattered the cup. "Chica, the cup is broken," Bárbara scolded.

Victoria ignored us both and stared at her crucifix on the wall, her lips gently moving. "Y Su misericordia, His mercy is on those who fear," she mumbled. Her eyes grew wide and she clawed at her throat. She then slumped backwards into her blankets and closed her eyes. Bárbara put her hand on Victoria's forehead.

"Tomás, she is burning with the fiebre. How long has she been like this?"

"Since this morning I think."

"Chica, háblame," Bárbara sternly shook Victoria's shoulders. Victoria said nothing, but she re-opened her eyes and stared at her crucifix. She looked right through Bárbara and me. Soon, her heavy breathing slowed. Her head rolled back, and her eyes closed. In the garden people still chattered anxiously. I closed the heavy shutters and bolted them. I gently kissed Victoria's sweaty forehead.

"Joven," Bárbara whispered to me, "We must cool her down. Help me undress her."

I helped Bárbara take off the jacket loosely covering Victoria's shoulders. We pulled off her boots and sweat-soaked leather trousers. Victoria trembled but did not open her eyes or speak.

"Stay with her. I will go for cold water." Bárbara quickly left the room and soon returned with a basin of cool water and two worn cotton rags. We bathed Victoria from head to toe until her skin no longer burned. Exhausted, I sat down on the bed beside her. She did not move. Bárbara covered her with a thin wool Chimayo blanket.

"She needs to sleep now," Bárbara cautioned.

"Bueno," I whispered. "I am hungry and tired." I looked to Bárbara for comfort.

She whispered back, "Come with me. Hice pan y chocolate. I made fresh bread and chocolate por almuerzo." Breakfast, I thought, only breakfast. The day had already lasted an eternity and it was only breakfast.

I had not eaten since the afternoon before. I sat down at Bárbara's table. Doña soon dragged herself into the warm kitchen and sat down next to me, her leather pantalones and boots still caked in two-days-worth of black mud. Pale, tired, and her face streaked with trail dust and gunpowder, she peered through bloodshot and unfocused eyes. In her haste to bring Patricio home, she had not brought a change of clothes. She looked and smelled like a soldier who had been campaigning for days.

Bárbara studied the forlorn and bedraggled donseya. "Señorita, you buried the man you planned to marry. You have been up all night. This is too much for you. You must rest."

"I slept for a few hours yesterday before we buried Patricio."

"That is not enough for a woman who has suffered so many losses."

"¡Bárbara!" Doña was annoyed, "If I say I am fine, you must believe me."

"I will believe you when you have bathed and rested."

Doña toyed with her bread and chocolate. She half-smile vaguely in my direction. "Seigo rica pero no tengo nada.... sin amor, sin esposo." She whispered the words.

"This is what happens when a business arrangement fails," I said aloud to myself.

"Tomás, finish your food," Bárbara snapped at me. "I will take Doña María to find some clean clothing."

"He is right," Doña mumbled, staring blankly at her bread.

With an irritated glance at me, Bárbara pulled Doña out of her chair and ushered her out of the room. Along with Doña went the foul odor of death, trail grime, gunpowder, and sweaty horse. When Bárbara reappeared a short time later, she resumed mothering me.

"Tomás, niño, were the two of you awake all night?"

"We slept, but she started shaking. She shakes when she is anxious or nervous, but she has been so much better lately—until last night." I stopped speaking for a minute. Bárbara waited for me.

"Someone fired pistols not far from our house. She woke up, and she was shaking. I gave her tea and she dropped the cup just like she did yours, but she took the tea. She tried to take the tea, I mean. She was talking about Patricio. She confused me with him. She thought he was alive and she talked with him. Sometimes she talks in her sleep. She wanted to come home, so I brought her. She will be okay. I know she will. She is tired. She will be okay."

"Ella tiene calentura. I will look after her," Bárbara tried to reassure me. "She will be fine. Go find your father. He is on the roof watching los enemigos. Find him, then you must sleep."

"Bueno," was the only thing I could think to say.

I walked slowly up the opened stairs that Victoria and I had climbed so many times. On the roof, my father and señor Griego watched carefully across the plains. The Cumanchis appeared to be preparing to attack. Inside the village, two houses still smoldered, but the walls were well defended. One lone horseman rode toward the village. He addressed the men on the wall.

"You have killed a brother. We want an apology."

"There are no apologies today," señor Griego barked back. "My own son died yesterday, and your people refused to share my sorrow. You demanded the trade fair continue. I did not see my son before he was buried in the ground. You had no compassion for me. Then in the dark of night, like a coward, your kinsman robbed and burned two houses. I don't say this to insult you. I say it because it is true. The thief died. He paid with his life for his sins. Now you must leave."

The horseman rode back out of rifle range. In the distance, the captains discussed the situation. They waved, turned their backs to the village, and then abruptly rode into the Llano. They did not intend to compromise next year's trading opportunities over a thieving fool who had gotten himself killed. The Cumanchi party was not heard from again until news of their winter raids in Chihuahua arrived in late spring.

"We have had good fortune today," said a relieved señor Griego. "No one lived in the burned houses. The walls are still standing. The women will find the houses easy to replaster. The men will put up new roofs in time for winter." In the village's moment of great fortune, señor Griego briefly forgot the death of his own son.

Chapter 10: El Hacha de San Mateo—Wood that Cannot See nor Hear nor Walk (Rev. 9.20)

Thomas

On a bright chilly morning three days after Patricio's body arrived home, the entire village gathered to pray for his soul, but no one cried, not even Victoria. Two nights before, Patricio was buried without ceremony. There was no cura, no priest. There was no rezador to lead a prayer service. There was no velorio, no wake. No one sang, and no one played a flute, violin, or drum. Patricio's own father and mother were not even there. That night felt like it was years ago. Now, exhausted and struggling to stay awake, I leaned against the wall of la iglesia listening to Doña's sharp, angry voice.

"Hoy, today," she said, "We finally remember a Cabo in the government's service. We remember a Cabo that even el gobernador forgot. Two nights ago, we did not sing. We did not mourn. Today we will make up for it." She spoke briefly of her own mother's death. "Then too, there were no last rites, no mass, and no priest," she said. "My father has never forgiven the church or God for this. I cannot blame him. In the Llano, God waits to greet sinners for the first time at their deaths. He ignores them beforehand."

She spoke quietly and angrily, "¡Viva el Rey! We are here because of the king. Patricio died in his service. To live here is to die trapped in the king's service even though he is long gone. Bless him, for he left us on the Llano, and we can never go back."

Heavily armed aldeanos and Taoseño traders half-filled the church. They stood about in small groups gossiping and joking irreverently about the events of the last few days. A few expressed sadness for Doña and the Griego family, but most talked about escaping a Cumanchi attack. They half listened to Doña, but they cheered and hooted at her comments on the king.

Wearing her winter gamuza skirt and a sheepskin jacket, Victoria lay on the only church bench. Black ribbons dangled morosely from the tips of her long braids, and a black rebozo covered her head and hung loosely over her shoulders. She had slept yesterday morning and last night in her own bed. She remained quite weak, but her fever was gone.

"The Llano is our purgatory. We have lived here long enough for God to decide whether we belong in heaven." Señora Griego now spoke. She prayed that Patricio's soul would not stay much longer in purgatory. Señor Manuel and my father said nothing.

Finally, two Taoseños sang a sad stanza from an Alabado, a haunting Gregorian chant with Morisco influence.

> What a wearisome journey,
> Living is such a hard road!
> As God has determined,
> Patricio's earthly life is over,
> Now he begins a new life
> In eternity—
> Heaven, Hell, or Purgatory,
> Who can tell?
> His body and soul have flown.
> He leaves behind the pleasures and pains
> Of God's confusing world.

The chanting over, the lanceros of the village tramped through the small church in uniform to stand briefly on the grave now returned to hard-packed floor. They said their final goodbyes to the Cabo.

"He was a good man," they bowed their heads and agreed.

Outside the church, a few ciboleros fired their muskets to assure that evil spirits did not invade the church. Pascual carried Victoria out. Doña left last. Señor Griego did not take his eyes off her. To him, she was indeed the wife, son, daughter, and daughter-in-law he longed for, but would never have.

All November, Victoria sat alone in her secret room carving santos.   She refused to see anyone.   In her self-imposed solitary confinement, she carved row upon row of small santos--San Mateo's all. Each time she carved the saint, he grew smaller in comparison to his axe. Finally, she carved a full-sized wooden axe that had a handle in the likeness of San Mateo. A month after Patricio's death, Victoria bundled up the carvings and carried them to our cave above the frozen beaver ponds.

Victoria

"Mi corazón, mi hermano, mi hermano favorito está muerto." The sun set quickly behind the mountains. Set ablaze by the last light, the sky glowed an iridescent orange. In the east, the Llano disappeared into a cold, dark blue. Patricio had been dead a month. I stood at the edge of the cliff cerca de la cueva, cerca de nuestro casita, near the cave Tomás and I dug.

130

My clothing neatly folded at my feet, I trembled at the cliff's edge in the frigid winter air.

"Dios mío, eight long paces or less down—not far enough. Llano, you have betrayed me yet again," I raged. "You wish only to injure me, to break my back and leave me suffering. Kill me and get it done!" I pleaded.

From the night sky, the first few stars sparkled over the dark, empty, and indifferent plain. To the west, the somber gray silhouettes of clouds and mountains finally disappeared in the last cold light. With my chest painted red with ochre, I had become the dreaded bleeding and red-streaked Cristo hanging in the capilla.

I stood at the edge of the cliff and raged, "I am the blood-soaked Diana of the hunt. I am a target for an arrow or musket ball."

I tore at my chest, "¿Dónde están los indios bárbaros? ¡Róbenme! Steal me! Take revenge on me. I am naked for you to ravish and kill. Indios bárbaros, choose me. Bind my feet. Tie my hands. Throw me to the howling wolves. Let the wolves tear me apart. As a sign that I had lost a true love, I cut my breasts with the wooden axe

"Indios bárbaros, por favor I beg of you to put an arrow in my heart. Ahora, me llamo Dolores. ¿Quién conoce la Victoria de la Cruz? Patricio, why have you left me behind? Y la Virgen de los Dolores? Seigo como la Virgen. I am the Virgin, but where are the arrows for my heart, where are the arrows for my heart? Is my faith so weak?"

I stood above the frozen water with my bloody breasts bared waiting for death. The cold wind suddenly gripped my hair. I trembled. Murderers had their heads shaved. Common criminals are shaved, but I still had my hair.

"Dios, yo no seigo inocente. I am not innocent." I pulled at my hair. It was too thick. "I will burn this out."

I rolled the woven reed door from the face of the cave. With a branch, I swept out the dust. I held my chest, cried, and sobbed myself numb. With hidden flints, I started a fire in dried leaves and sticks. Shivering from the cold, I stacked the bundle of santos I brought with me on the fire. I placed San Mateo, the one that was all axe, in the middle of the flame. He soon burned like a martyr at the stake. I held him by his face and burned my braids off. I wanted to burn like my santos.

"None of us are innocent, none of us are innocent," I moaned. "Tomás" I shouted out as in a dream, "Pero, Tomás. Te quiero. ¿Dónde estás Tomás? Mi amor, mi amor. I love you." I lay on the floor bleeding, naked, and numb with cold preparing to sleep forever, but in my dream, I heard voices.

"Estoy aquí. Doña María está conmigo. Doña and I have come. We have looked for you everywhere. It is so dangerous. Los Cumanchis. You are here alone. I should have known. I should have known. We

131

should have come here first. Perdóname. Perdóname."

"¡Tu pelo! ¡Tus senos! ¿Qué pasa, qué pasa? Your hair!" Tomás cried. "You mourn as though a Cumanchi widow, but I have not died. In grief, you have been selfish!"

I heard the anger in his voice, but I was not sorry. My lips were dry and bleeding. My hair was gone. Estaba empelota. I was naked and my chest covered in red ochre and blood. Ashes burned my eyes and covered my face. Crying left me numb. The cold left me numb. Anger and despair left me numb. The smell of my own burned hair and blood turned my stomach. As Tomás touched me, I vomited. I deserved all of this, I was sure.

Tomás' face was so close to mine begging—pleading "Victoria, Victoria please, please speak to me. Get up. Get up." I did not. I could not. I wanted to lie on the dirt floor until I froze or bled to death, a rock rolled across the cave door, and all light extinguished forever.

Tomás and Doña dragged me half-dressed to the edge of the cliff.

"I should get help." Doña's frightened voice sounded very far way.

Tomás spoke. "We don't have time. She is blue with cold." He gave commands to Doña in a distant, alarmed voice. "Climb down first. I will lower her by her arms and you must catch her."

Gripping my wrists tightly, Tomás lowered me along the cliff's craggy, sharp face toward Doña. Soaked in blood and hanging like the terrifying Christ of the Llano, I dangled from the rocks until he dropped me into her waiting hands. She caught me, staggered, and then fell with me on top of her.

"¡Chingado!" She cursed. "¡Qué pendejada! She cursed again. "Su espalda está sangrando. Tomás, her back and legs were cut on the rocks. She is a bloody mess. ¡Maldita sea, Damn it!"

"Run for help," I vaguely heard him shout. I listened indifferently to his terror filled voice.

He wrapped me in my leather dress and picked me up. I cannot remember more. Pero Bárbara recordó, Bárbara remembered this nightmare. She later told me many times, always with tears, how Doña María ran up the path calling for help.

"She sounded like a rabid coyote. I did not know that she had such passion in her. The whole village was struck with terror." Bárbara feared they had found me dead.

"Ayúdalo. Ayúdalo. Help him," Doña screamed.

Bárbara remembered. "The night was filled with cries of pain and cries for help. We never heard her scream like that. When Patricio died she was silent, but with you, Victoria, her screams were those of a mother who has just lost her child."

"Tomás was struggling to carry you up the hill crying, '¡Ayúdame,

132

ayúdame! Victoria, Victoria!'" Mamá, papá, and Bárbara ran to help.

Bárbara remembered that I smelled, "like death—vomit, burned hair, no hair." She said that I was "naked, pale and blue, frozen, barely wrapped in my winter dress. Ashes and blood covered my face, back and legs. Red paint and blood covered my chest." She said that Tomás was soaked in my blood.

Bárbara said she carefully washed me and put me to bed. I cannot remember how many days I slept. I know that when I was awake Tomás was always there. I did not speak. I could not speak. I watched the low winter sun crawl across the sky casting frightening shadows on the walls. Shadow monsters, with axes and knifes, hacked their way through the latías in the ceiling. With each shift of the sun, evil faces with dreadful unspeakable names, crawled in and out of the white adobe plaster. Someone screamed in terror. It was me! I screamed until the light faded from the wall and the faces hid in the moonlight. I knew they hid only until sunrise. They would come for me day after day. They pulled the breath from my lungs and left me gasping. Soon enough, they attacked me in the dark. I screamed until my throat grew sore.

Bárbara rocked and held me. "Shh, shh," she whispered. Sometimes she sang, but my screaming did not stop until I collapsed in exhausted silence. Each day there were shadows and evil faces, and each day there was screaming until the darkness quenched the shadows. Tomás would pick me up and hold me. Each day he moved me more easily. "She has become a feather," I heard him say. I clenched his arm with all my might so that he would not leave, but my weak hands could no longer hold him. One day a priest arrived from Santa Fe.

"Puro calave, all skeleton," he said as he surveyed my body stretched out motionless on the bed. "She will starve to death soon." He anointed me with oil and now even Bárbara prayed.

It was advent. From that day until after Christmas, I calmly awaited my death. I even stopped eating small sips of my favorite bean soup.

"What did food matter so close to death?" my tired brain pondered. "If I did not eat, God would surely have mercy." I tried only to see the face of God. I stared at a half-carved San Mateo and the crucifix hanging on the wall.

Ah, Mateo's axe, I thought. I had no need to finish another. I would die under the axe as he had, but I did not die. What sin had I committed that I did not die, but lived in pain? Is a life of grief my punishment? My brain raced to find the answer, but none came.

I watched the spiders in the latías. I watched for the face of el Diablo. I looked for God and hoped for a quiet, merciful death. I turned to Tomás and begged, "Bury me in the church floor by my brother." Either I did not speak or he could no longer hear me. He is slipping away from me,

133

I thought. I looked into his eyes. I think they were his eyes. I looked into them and pleaded for mercy.

"Misericordia, Tomás, misericordia." Again, he did not hear me. I cried. He touched me. He wiped my eyes. Was I no longer speaking? Was I so confused that I only thought I spoke?

Every day, Bárbara put me in a chair by the window. I watched the garden fill with snow. I closed my eyes and dreamed of the flat whiteness stretching forever to the east. I drifted into the empty Llano crawling through snowdrifts toward the morning sun. I begged for death. In my snowy cold dream, I suffered from a horrible unquenchable thirst. I made no bargains with God in exchange for my life. Like the Cumanchis, God took what he wanted.

* * * * *

Thomas

Tía Ana stopped drinking wine. "I am numb enough without this," she said. "May God forgive me? I have lost more children than I can count. I do not want to lose another. But then this is not my choice." She poured the last flask of wine onto the stable floor. She resigned herself to her life on the Llano and stopped hiding in wine or sleep. She begged me to spend time with her.

"Sobrino, once I thought we would be amigos, good friends, y familia, you and I. Nevertheless, as you see I have not been a good aunt. It is time I make amends. God is not pleased with me." If she hoped I would speak, I failed her. She waited a few minutes then continued. "God does as he chooses, but perhaps this time, San Mateo will remember her."

"She is still alive," I said quietly.

"Sí, sí, Mateo will help. He knows her! She has carved him many times. He will rescue her!"

As far as Bárbara could tell, neither God nor Saint remembered Victoria.

"Tomás," Bárbara said. "Tomás, if she gets better, it will be because she chooses to. Stay here all you want, but do not think she will get better because of you. She has forgotten you. She is selfish." She directed her angry speech at Victoria hoping for a response, but Victoria's black eyes did not blink.

The three of us took turns sitting quietly by Victoria's bed or chair. Day after day, she did not speak. Every bone in her face soon stood out. Hair not burned in the fire soon fell out. On occasion, she suddenly sat on the bed's edge and moved her arms and legs as though swimming or walking. The wild motion dislodged the bloody dressings covering her breast wounds that refused to heal. Feeling guilt and anger, I finally hoped

134

for her death. I prayed for her death, and I prayed for her life.

I whispered into her ear, "Remember you are my wife, my only love. Wake up, please wake up."

Doña finally spoke to Bárbara sharing what was on many minds.

"She must get better soon. She is wasting the precious time of many people who want to live. Let the dead take care of themselves." She spoke bluntly and, from her perspective, religiously. From the moment of her mother's death, Doña understood that a person was alive or dead. She understood living was often heaven and hell and that one made choices. In life's battles, she neither expected nor granted mercy. She hoped, and even on occasion, prayed for love. She did not want to die alone. More importantly, she did not want to live alone. Still she did not grovel. She limited her mourning. She understood her duties. To Doña, Victoria's collapse after the death of Patricio was irrational and inexcusable. Victoria had one simple obligation. "She must pick herself up and make herself useful."

Many weeks after I carried Victoria up the hill, Mamá Paula called me away. She agreed with Doña, "Sometimes dying can waste the time of the living. There is no merit in learning patience at Victoria's deathbed. You must do something else. This is not healthy for you. Victoria is in God's hands and he will decide. You will soon be fifteen. Work with the men."

We walked slowly back through the pueblo to our house. "How does God assign the work of watching someone die?" I asked. "You are correct. I have lost track of time," I admitted.

"God charges those with the biggest hearts the task of holding the hands of the dying," she said solemnly. Mamá Paula mystified me. She denied the existence of God but sometimes prayed. She explained God's motivation better than any priest did.

"Mamá, what happened the night they brought Patricio's body home? Is it true a curse was put on the village?"

"Chico," she said, "First, there is no such thing as a curse. As to the night so many weeks ago, that excitement was nothing at all. The houses are repaired. The Cumanchis left for Texas and will not be back until spring." She did not mention that Victoria lay dying.

"Will Victoria ever walk again?" I asked.

Mamá Paula looked confused. "I don't know. No one is sure what is wrong with her. She seems to be dying from a broken heart."

"Pero, I love her."

"I know you love her. We all do. We will take care of her as best we can, but you must also take good care of yourself."

"Please, let me see her every day."

"You have been doing that, and I would never stop you, but you must remember that you are living. The living have chores and work to do if they wish to continue living."

I spent the afternoon in mamá Paula Teresa's garden picking through the frozen chile plants and pumpkins, stringing peppers and pumpkin slices into ristras, and hanging them to dry against the south wall. I worried that Victoria was punishing me. Did she still love me and care about me? It saddened me that she now chose to die. This was her choice, I knew. I could not imagine the pain her mother felt. She had lost her son and maybe would lose her daughter.

* * * * *

One cloudy day when I was done with chores, Doña María Josefa walked slowly up to our door leading her horse, her bow strapped to her back and her two rifles holstered on the sides of her horse. She wore her leather armor. The black ribbons in her braids were the sole indicators she remained in mourning. Perhaps she had been weeping and had not slept, for her eyes were red and she looked tired. Still, she looked younger without a chalked face and red lips. Worried, I ran up to her.

"Doña, you are not leaving us?"

"No, no. I have another request," she spoke sadly to Mamá Paula. "Señora Trent, ¿Puedo llevar a tu hijo a dar un paseo? Volveremos antes de que oscurezca. I would like to ride with Tomás. We will be back before dark."

"Señorita," mamá said gently, "that is his decision to make. Ask him."

Doña turned to me, "Would you care to ride into the Llano?" She knew my answer would be "yes." She handed me a leather pouch of gunpowder and lead. I was glad for a break from the eternal deathwatch. I saddled Viejo and took down my rifle.

"Gracias, Doña, gracias."

She replied, "Me llamo María. I am María."

I was surprised. "Pero," I said, "I was told that since you were a child you wanted to be called, 'Doña.'"

"For you and me that is a bad joke that has lasted long enough. Por favor, me llamó María."

"A bad joke? Doña *is* who you are!"

"Voy a cambiar. I am going to change. María is the person I want you to know. Doña is dying. When I am ready, I will let the others know this too."

At home with her father and servants, she still had the image of an iron-willed woman to protect. With me, she was María, a girl—a little older but still a girl. I pretended to protect her. She let me.

"Thank you friend, for taking care of me," she sighed, her body dropping with the weight of sadness.

136

"Semos amigos. Friends take care of each other," I assured her.

Sometimes the wilderness wore us down. Sometimes it fostered us. María's identity depended on it. She rode wildly into its heart with her rifle loaded to slay a deer or rabbit for dinner.

"El yermo mató a Patricio. Voy a matar al yermo. The wilderness killed my betrothed. I will kill it."

I rode wildly through the Llano with the woman who castrated horse thieves and the murderers of her genízaro slave. Now, she avenged Patricio's death by killing any creature that moved.

"As long as I have the money, there is no such thing as wasting powder and lead except for a miss," she assured me.

Soon we rode together every afternoon. María had enough money to buy shot and powder as she wished. Whatever her personal resources may have been, often times there was none available to buy. This did not stop her. She attacked the living creatures of the Llano with her bow and arrow. Dangling beneath the neck of her speeding horse, she easily fired off six to ten arrows in a minute. She brought down antelope and elk. She taught me well. I quickly learned to kill nearly as efficiently as she did. Still, I never matched María who could shoot off a deer or rabbit's ear and then, with her second rifle, drop the bolting and terrified animal completely.

Keeping to the business of killing, while avoiding the wasted emotions of anger and love, it turned out, did not mend a broken heart. One day María abruptly stopped riding. With pained, dark eyes, she squinted into the Llano then back at me. She broke and sobbed.

"¿Por qué Tomás, por qué? Look at me. Look at all of us. Victoria is dying and Patricio is dead. Y yo, yo seigo una asesina. I kill. And you Tomás, you hold the hand of a dying girl in the morning and then slay deer in the afternoon. You ride between the dying and the dead. I am sickened." She moaned and sobbed, then she cried out, "Me he convertido en una persona cruel. Perdóname, Dios, perdóname. Tomás, I have made you cruel too." A dam of pent-up anger and rage burst. She tried desperately to stem the flood of tears and stop her running nose, but could not. Overwhelmed by her complete loss of self-control, she succumbed further still and threw her bow at a small piñon tree. It stuck just out of her reach. She wailed in deepening frustration.

"María, María," I tried to calm her. "What is cruelty in the wilderness?" She made no effort to look at me. Shaking her head, she wiped her face on her sleeve, and stared blankly into the indifferent emptiness of the Llano.

"María, listen to me," I begged, "We ride and hunt, and people are fed. María, you are not cruel. Nevertheless, if indeed you are, it serves you well. Men approach you cautiously. By yourself, you have fed many families of the village this winter. I have heard the villagers say that God took Patricio and brought a huntress. They say God has given them life."

"¡Qué diablos!" María cursed, "God is a trader in lives! What makes Him think one life is more important than another?" Like a Cumanchi woman in mourning, she began beating her breasts with her fists. I watched and shuddered.

"Enough," I ordered with growing anger and frustration. "I forbid you to hurt yourself! You say you want to forget about pain. Now you injure yourself while Victoria is still bleeding from her own self-inflicted injuries. You have said so many times that love and anger waste one's spirit and your intended marriage to Patricio was simply business."

"Patricio is dead," she cut me off, "Business or no, I will now be alone, and your own love lies dying. Perhaps I have not hurt myself enough!" She shook her head at the sky and cried, "O Dios, ¿Por qué me has abandonado? God, why have you forsaken me?"

"Listen to yourself. Now, you sound like Victoria." I dismounted and pulled her from her saddle. She did not act like Victoria. Screaming wildly, she knocked me to the ground. I grabbed her leg and tripped her. Caught off guard, she fell hard. Her lips quivered and she clenched her fists. I reached to help her up. Rage-filled, she struck at me.

"¡No me toques! Don't touch me!" She grabbed my hands then refused to let me go. I closed my eyes and Victoria, tía Ana, my stepmother, and María, flashed before me. The Llano affected all of them differently. Now, the bravest of them slumped impossibly before me in the grass demanding to be left alone yet refusing to let go of my hands.

Unresolved grief is death, I thought. I tried to stand up. María pulled me down.

"María, you cannot control God!" I spoke to her too sharply. She squeezed my hand until my fingers felt like they would break. I pulled free of her and finally managed to stand.

She rose to her knees and wrapped her arms around my thighs begging, "Somebody, love me please. Por Dios, por favor!" I tried to pull her to her feet, but she held tightly to my legs. I dragged myself free, but she grabbed my belt and again pulled me to the ground.

She shook me and cried, "¡Maldito, maldito! Why don't you understand? Whatever I have said, I still need someone to love me! Patricio loved me!" She sobbed violently. "I did not love him, but he loved me. That would have been enough! That would have been enough!" Her voice was lost in sobs. She let go of me, hunched forward over her thighs, and beat her fists violently into the frozen grass. She prayed, "God, hear me. ¡Por favor! Seigo una pecadora. God, you know my sins." She did not pray to be forgiven. She did not want forgiveness. Her need for love blended tragically with her need for revenge. How does one avenge the loss of a "business partner" to a mystery infection? This she had to solve.

"Go home now!" She curtly dismissed me. "I will follow soon."

Several weeks before Christmas, Doña María Josefa's lonely father called her home. By then, her anger had worn out. Shortly after she left, I received a letter. It said simply:

Tomás,

In my moment of weakness, I dishonored my name and my family. Do not speak of my dishonor with anyone or me again. Gracias. God be with you until I see you in the spring. Take care of Victoria. I believe she will live.

Regards,

María

PS: Patricio's death freed me. I remain beholden to *no* man.

Chapter 11: She Sleeps (Matt. 9.24)

Thomas

Weeks had passed since the cottonwoods along the río faded from yellow to gray. Snow collected in the shadows of the trees and along the inner canyon walls. The tall, brown grass again snapped and crackled like dried bones. Amidst the chaos of death and illness, I had missed fall. The beauty of October and November slipped out of my hands and disappeared forever without my noticing. The foul, rust scent of dried blood and the leathery odor of decay and death were all that remained.

In mid-December, it snowed every day. The Llano grew into a treacherous winter serpent, hissing in the wind. Swirling columns of sweet piñon smoke, wafted across the snow-drifted village. Time stood still and time sped on. Victoria remained ill, and María had gone back to spend the worst part of the winter with her sickly father.

I am alone now, I will make the best of it, I thought. I read to Victoria every day. Tía Griego called me "jito." I would soon be fifteen, but I had become her "little son." When I visited Victoria, tía hugged me desperately as though she feared I might suddenly disappear. She said that I reminded her of a "better time" and that was "a good thing." I could not imagine what she meant by better time. For tía, I thought times had always been bad, but in the midst of tragedy, she began to smile and laugh.

"Sobrino, I have often wondered what it meant to be a good and faithful servant of God. You and Doña have taught me, each in your special way. You read for the living. To live, she fights and hunts. So you see, God is for the living. You are a servant for the living."

"Tía, I do not understand how I read for the living."

"Sobrino, the living take care of themselves, just as the dead care for themselves. I see now that caring for the living is our responsibility. We live in our realm and the dead live in theirs. We cannot care for them and they cannot care for us. So you see Sobriñito, we care for ourselves. But what do we do for those trapped between life and death?" She asked quietly. "That is the problem. That is the problem. We cannot die with them. They cannot live with us. So you see Victoria must now decide what she will do. We can only coax her so much. We can only tell her we love her so much. She must decide. Jito, you see, you are reading for me. Gracias, no one has ever done this before."

"You are welcome." Suddenly, I had no idea what I was doing. Perhaps, I was only reading to those living perpetually in purgatory.

Victoria grew thinner and thinner. When I held her head up, she only sipped tea and water. She was a skeleton wrapped in sheets, una mortaja, her shroud, ready for burial. When I read to her, she stared at me with intensity and yearning that shattered my heart. Her deep, black, and secretive eyes tore into my soul. We were the hunted and the hunter in the moment when both understand, who will live and who will die. I thought about how María tortured rabbits and deer before she killed them. Like Doña's prey, Victoria had her ear shot off. Toyed with and maimed, she awaited the hunter's fatal shot. Who would deliver it? Focusing on my mouth and face, she stared at me as long as she could—then she turned away. If she knew a Bible verse, sometimes her silent lips would move with mine as I read. She did not sob aloud, she did not make a sound, and she did not move, but frequently her eyes suddenly reddened and quietly overflowed. Her tears ended when she finally fell asleep. Each night now seemed it would be her last.

As Christmas neared, Bárbara now shook her head every time I visited. She still put Victoria in a chair by the window. Victoria still stared into the garden without speaking.

Bárbara spoke and thought aloud to me, "She will not see the holy child come this year. It will be a miracle if she ever sees him again unless there is a heaven. We must do something different. We must do something different." At first neither of us had any idea what different might be.

"Las Posadas begin tomorrow. It will be December 16. I have an idea. I must talk to señor Griego."

"Ah, Las Posadas, the story of Santa María y San José trying to find shelter at an inn. Victoria once said this was her favorite story. It reminded her that there is hope for children born in unhappy places like the Llano." Bárbara thought for a moment then added, "This will make her happy, I am sure. Talk with your tío."

I ran down the long familiar hallways past the chapel to the warm sitting room where señor Griego had his desk. A bright fire was burning in the corner fireplace.

"Señor, perdóname." Deep in thought, señor Griego was surprised. Fussing with his long braid, he turned to me.

"Qué te pasa, hombrecito."

"Señor tío, can we ask that Santa María and San José stop each night in Victoria's room during Las Posadas?"

"Sobrino, there may be others who wish to host the Holy Mother and her saintly husband." He crossed himself and quietly muttered that

San José was a fair and generous man. He turned again to me and said, "We cannot be unfair to others."

"Pero, señor, this is a special time. She needs everyone to visit her. She needs to hear the singing. She needs to have hope. We all need hope. Everyone will understand."

"Well, hombrecito, I do not plan this celebration. Come with me to see señor Armijo who does. If this pleases him, I will make sure we have vino, chocolate y bizcochitos para los peregrinos. You come with me. You will convince him this is the thing to do. Joven, put on your coat. We are going into the cold. It is snowing."

Señor Armijo and his family owned the next biggest house in the village. It stood at the southeast corner of the village wall. The house was a very large square with a placita or patio in the center. The only windows on the outside walls were just below the roofline and set for firing muskets. The door was barely five feet high and quite narrow. It was small enough to defend and just big enough to let the people in and out. Like our house, it was very dark in winter because there was no window glass and the high windows were always shuttered tightly against the cold.

Señor Armijo was a moderately religious man. He was renowned for arguing fine religious points whether he believed them or not. To assure good conversation and perhaps to badger the poor man, he provided bed and board to the itinerant priest who always mysteriously appeared before the Christmas Holidays.

Tío Griego knocked loudly. Señor Armijo opened the door without asking who was there. Smoking his pipe with the door slightly ajar, he had watched us walking down the path through the storm toward his house. Señor Griego introduced me to señor Armijo. It was a formality. We knew each other.

"¿Ah, qué quieres anglocito?" He spoke affectionately.

"Tengo una idea. Por favor, I need your help. Santa María y San José must come to Victoria. They must come every night. She must see the holy one." I ran everything together, but he understood.

"Bueno, bueno, chico. We will do it. Everyone will understand. We will all come to Victoria. We will come every night until Christmas Eve. Her room will be the inn. We will sing every night to make her smile," he laughed with satisfaction. "This is the least we can do."

"So, it is done!" exclaimed a surprised señor Griego. "Te lo agradecemos." He was clearly pleased.

"This is how the living help those trapped between life and death," I said. Señor Armijo squinted his eyes and looked at me mystified and, perhaps, tempted to engage in a theological debate but he said little.

"As you say."

"Gracias, señor, gracias." I grabbed tío Griego by the hand. "We will tell Victoria, we must tell her right away. She must be awake for the visits. We will tell her she must eat. We must tell her now," I insisted. Señor Griego cast a half-smile at señor Armijo.

"Amigo, compañero. I thought we would have time for coffee. However, it appears my nephew and I have much business to do. We are clearly in a hurry. Adiós, adiós."

I half dragged him back up the small hill toward his house.

"Sobrino, I hope this works. I hope we have Victoria back."

"We will tío, we will."

He began panting in the cold. "Niño, go ahead. You are too fast for this viejo." I ran ahead through the kitchen and past Bárbara without speaking. She muttered something about the wind and storm that just passed her by.

"Victoria de la Cruz, escúchame. Victoria, listen to me. It will soon be Christmas. Jesús expects you to eat and take care of yourself. María and José will come every night until you welcome them by eating with them." Victoria's eyes grew large. I wanted her to say something, anything. Her breasts barely moved with her shallow breathing. Her cracked and dried lips were silent. Tears slid down her checks, then abruptly stopped. She grew still as death. She stared into my soul and hid her own.

My efforts exhausted, I cried and could not stop. I looked into her eyes and pleaded with her, "Victoria you must say something. You must listen to me." She finally closed her eyes and shut me out. I brushed a few remnants of her hair back from her forehead. For the first time, I noticed that it was not only thin, but turning white. I traced her eyebrows and they too were turning white. I kissed her dry lips then moistened her mouth with a wet cotton cloth.

Defeated and sobbing, I ran from her room. I ran past Bárbara. I had no idea where I was going. Finally, I threw myself on the capilla floor. What would ever stop this pain? Gentle hands grabbed me from behind.

"Remember, we are doing something different. One storm for the day is enough, hombre. You must come to the kitchen and eat with me."

"Por Dios, Bárbara, what can I do? Nothing works. She is dead. Ella está muerta." I fell into Bárbara's arms. She held me until I could cry no more. She said nothing. She sat and rocked me until I was quiet, then she spoke.

"Hombrecito, ya basta. You came here with a plan. Tell me, what is it? We will make sure that it works."

"Bárbara, Bárbara, if María and José come every night, Victoria will be well. I just know she will, but now she says nothing. She cries sometimes, but she says nothing. She does not even move. Her hair is turning white. She is dying and she will not be alive to see María and José. She will not be alive for Christmas. She will not be alive. I don't know what to do."

"Querido, los padres do not know what to do. You are young. How can you do more? Still I think you have! I think you have done the most! I will tell Victoria today. She must live. I will tell her every day, todos los Dias, I will tell her. I will tell her that if she dies your heart will be as broken as hers is now. I will tell her she cannot hurt you or anyone anymore. This is what I will do. Entiendo, I know I will be like a hard person, but she must know the pain that she causes everyone must stop. I will tell her." Then she thought quietly for a moment. "Hombrecito, she has had all the time she has needed to die, but she has not died. If she does not have the courage to die, we must give her the courage to live. I will tell her this too. I will tell her she is a coward as her mother once was. I will tell her that her mother is now brave and that she alone is the coward. I will tell her that she has become the person who hides from life—she is now the person she most feared she would become. She must get up. This is what I will tell her." Bárbara smiled at her decision. She would end this suffering as soon as she could. Enough was enough.

Loco, loco. It was crazy. Lecturing a dying person was just crazy, but beginning that very day, Bárbara lectured and shamed Victoria in daily ritual. Señor and señora Griego said nothing. Everyone seemed to understand that this was the last hope—lecturing and Las Posadas. Which magic would work, we wondered?

December 16 came quickly. Every night there was singing and a loud knocking at the Griego's zaguán gate. Every night until Christmas Eve, Santa María y San José would enter Victoria's room followed by the entire Pueblo. Everyone sang. The children pulled on Victoria's bedspread. She would open her eyes. Some evenings she seemed to watch. Other evenings she would open her eyes and close them again. On Christmas Eve, farolitos, small fires, lighted the path for José y María. The singing was particularly robust and joyous. Victoria did not move. Her eyes never opened. She hardly took a breath. After the singing and revelry, everyone stopped in Bárbara's kitchen. All of us forgot Victoria for a little while. We sang and ate bizcochitos. Even the children drank wine.

I was happy for the first time since María left. I thought about her. I missed her. I looked forward to seeing her in the spring. I remembered María's soft naked body in last summer's early morning sunlight. Lost, I suddenly found myself reaching out to touch and smell her.

My trance abruptly ended when señor Armijo grabbed me by the shoulder and said, "Joven, you have done your best. She is in God's hands now. God will make the decision, but you must be proud that you tried." He went out into the cold night, "Feliz Navidad Tomás, Feliz Navidad y que tengas una vida feliz. La vida, it is all very short." He left singing.

The villagers were not concerned that Victoria slept through Christmas festivities. It was all God's will and what could one do in any case? Everyone said I had done my best. They too, felt they had also done their best. There was nothing left to do.

I felt good. I hoped that I had made a difference. Señora Griego smiled and sang for a few days too. She was happy. She accepted that everything that could be done had now been done. One day she announced, "If Victoria dies, she dies. I still have two sons left. I know a woman who lost all eight of her children before she died herself. There is much for which to be thankful."

After Christmas, I found myself spending more time at home. I still spent long parts of the day with Victoria, but mamá said she needed me home now. There was no real reason to have me home for it was cold and there was little work to do, but father was gone and she was lonely. In truth, I too was lonely and glad to spend more time at home. The warmth of our house and mamá's singing soothed me. My grieving was over. If Victoria died, we would both be relieved. We did not love Victoria less, but we had done all we could. We had cried since the last week of October. We had cried enough.

"Life does go on. This is either a brutal harsh truth or a loving glorious reality," María said in a letter that arrived shortly after the New Year. Although winter, she had been busy working with the men of the valley clearing acequias on the few warm days. On cold days, now most of the time, she stayed home with her infirm father.

"As you know, taking care of a sick person who does not want to live eats at one's soul, but father's death is just another death that will free me. I suppose I will be completely free one day whether I like it or not. Tengas cuidao de tu alma. Take care of your soul," she said. "I don't think God will."

Her letter noted that Felipe and Pascual had driven the Griego herds to pastures in the lower valley not far from her. "They come here to eat dinner from time to time. I miss riding on the Llano with you and I have not ridden much myself. Sometimes I ride with Perro. He is a good dog and makes the best company." When she could, she said, she also rode with Felipe. She got along fine with Felipe, but after Patricio's death, Pascual remained aloof. "He blames himself." She concluded, "I will come in March when Victoria is well enough to celebrate her birthday." María never wavered in her expectation that Victoria would survive her illness. I missed María and found myself resenting the time she spent with Felipe.

In late January, a mid-winter thaw set in. The weather warmed and the snow melted. Although I went less often to the Griego house, I came and went as though the house was mine. Tía Griego treated me like a son and a friend. Greeting me with tea, she would sit and talk with me by the large kitchen fireplace. She frequently asked me what I planned to do with my future. I had no idea. Before Christmas, if asked that question, I would have said, "Marry Victoria, build a house with her, plant an apple orchard, and raise sheep and goats." Now I sometimes wondered what it would be like to marry María, but I never admitted that.

"I will go to university in Boston," I said staring sadly at the floor.

"Sobrino, things change. I know this is a new plan. We are all making new plans these days," she smiled thoughtfully at me.

"I did not want anything to change," I said shuffling under her quiet gaze.

"But they did," she looked gently into my eyes. "I don't know who goes to university," she laughed, "But I know about Boston. A friend from Santa Fe married an Anglo and the two rode on horseback to live there. She wrote for a while, but it took too long to get letters. She stopped writing when she had children. She was happy there."

I stood up and paced about the room. "Victoria needs me."

"Bárbara is with Victoria. No te preocupes." Tired of small talk, I thanked her for tea and returned to Victoria's room.

Sometimes her room smelled the stale smell of impending death, but today the afternoon was warm. The windows were open. Lit by the low, warm winter sun shining through her window, Victoria looked so small and frail. The bright sun highlighted her sunken cheeks and outlined the bones of her near fleshless fingers. Her boney skull protruded from beneath her thin, fine white hair. She did not move.

"Her body is shocking to see," I said to Bárbara.

She understood how I felt and she now teased saying, "No semos buenos enfermeros. We are not good nurses." We laughed. We started calling Victoria "la Pelona, or baldy."

One day, when I entered the room, Bárbara hugged me.

"I know she is waiting for you. She is restless when you are not here." I began to read. Perhaps I read aloud for an hour or more. The sun set and a cold wind blew. I shuttered the windows and pulled the covers to Victoria's chin. I kissed her lips, lit a fire, and walked quietly out of her room.

"Te quiero," I whispered. She barely breathed, but she looked at me very carefully as though she wanted to say something. On the way to the kitchen, I passed señora Griego. She would now take her turn sitting with Victoria. In the kitchen, Bárbara was baking corn tortillas for the next day.

"Chico, stay and read to me too. What is this story of the crazy Anglo in the forest living with indios bárbaros?" The story touched her. She was the india. I read, and she asked questions.

"Chico ¿dónde está Nueva York?"

"It is far to the east of the continent," I told her. "Pero Bárbara, I don't really know anything about it except from this book." We learned together. "One day Bárbara, Victoria, you and I will go to New York!" I told her.

"Seigo una vieja, this will not happen," she laughed and added, "You are such a charming boy." The tortillas sizzled on the griddle on the coals. Bárbara handed one to me.

"Go back to her now."

I put the warm tortilla under Victoria's nose.

"Tengo hambre," said a very weak voice. "Do not call me pelóna. Estoy enojada. Have you no respect for the dying?"

"Only if they are dying," I whispered. "Are you coming back?"

"Sí, I am coming back. I am coming now. Help me eat."

Señora Griego ran from the other side of the room.

"Hija, gracias a Dios. Tomás call Bárbara. Have her bring weak tea and atole with goats' milk for Victoria. Apúrate, apúrate, Go, go, go!"

* * * * *

María's predictions were correct. By her fourteenth birthday, March 22, 1832, Victoria regained enough strength to celebrate. Señora Griego wanted to have a small birthday party, but Victoria refused. A birthday party would be too festive and Victoria refused to laugh or smile. Nevertheless, from her mother Victoria received a fine sheepskin coat—"for the mountains," said her mother. Bárbara and señora Griego had worked hard and in secret to make the coat. Victoria was completely surprised. María and Felipe arrived the day before Victoria's birthday for a week's stay. Both were anxious to see how she was doing.

On her birthday, Victoria asked to ride Francisco, but she was too weak. To placate and humor her, we went to the stable anyway. María and Felipe saddled Francisco. Victoria's hands trembled as she tried to put on her boots. She looked at me with wide exasperated eyes. I pulled them on for her. They were many sizes too big. In fact, nothing fit her. She bound her waist with leather straps to hold her clothing on.

Victoria could not mount Francisco without help. María, in old form, ordered, "Tomás, súbete en el caballo. Get on the horse and pull her up in front of you." I jumped into the saddle and pulled Victoria up while María pushed her bottom and laughed.

"¿Chica, dónde quedaron tus nalgas? Solo tienes huesos. You have no ass. You are bones. How will Tomás hold you?"

I blushed, but Victoria's answer surprised us all.

"¡Con mi pelo! My hair!"

María rolled her eyes, laughed nervously, and then swatted Francisco on his rump. Exhausted and trembling, Victoria fell against my chest as we rode into the plaza. With a furrowed brow and squinting eyes, María watched us and paced nervously by the gate.

"Take me back. I am too tired," Victoria sighed. María and I

148

helped her down and I carried her to her bed. "Tomás, stay a minute. I will sleep soon enough, but now you must hear me. I have been afraid all my life. I have wanted to live some place safe. I dreamed of Spain. I have loved you. Now I want more. Now, I want to be strong. I do not want to hide anymore. I want to be like María."

"She hides too. We all do," I reminded her quietly. Victoria did not answer. She had fallen asleep.

Chapter 12: 1832—A New Season

Thomas

The following spring and summer Victoria struggled to put on weight, to regain her strength, and to heal. Her progress was slow.

"Querido, I have been such a burden, but I beg of you to help me grow strong again. I promise to work hard every day. Punish me if I do not!"

"Punish you—you have punished yourself enough. Your breasts are scarred. Your hair is gone. You are skin and bones." Scowling, I shook my head and warned, "Regaining your strength and surviving will be punishment enough!"

She dropped her head and cried gently. Wisps of her thin silvery hair sparkled in the wind. I closed my eyes and pulled her to me. Holding her frail body and breathing deeply, I filled my nose and lungs with her scent until visions of who she once was came rushing back—long tallowed black braids, salty hips, cracked lips, and soft tongue.

"I will help you," I said. "Yo nunca te olvidaré."

On warm days in May, I took her swimming. The walk to the pond exhausted her. Swimming now frightened her. She did not trust herself.

"Hold me like I held you once," she begged.

I held her. "Kick," I ordered, "Kick harder!" She struggled to keep her emaciated body from sinking. The cold water exhausted her, and left her shivering violently and paralyzed in my arms.

"Put me in the sun," she begged.

Each naked rib stood out singly from her chest. Her hipbones protruded grotesquely from her back and from the front of her waist. The line of her spine was traceable from her shoulders to her hips. Her pelvic bones protruded beneath a thin cover of black pubic hair—the only body hair that had not turned gray. Knee bones dominated what once had been well-proportioned legs. What miracle had kept her alive?

By the end of May, definition and muscle crept back into her legs and hips. "Querido, see if you can grab my ass. Estoy comiendo como un cerdo. I am eating like a pig."

"I have seen you," I agreed. Still, only with a good imagination did she have a bottom to pinch.

At the beginning of June, she finally swam again on her own. She was thin but no longer repulsive. She sought assurance.

"Do I please you?" she asked hiding her scarred breasts with her hands.

"Muchísimo," I said. "Don't cover your breasts. I like to look at them."

Sobbing gently, she begged, "You must like them! You must like me! I need you to like me!"

"Querida, I know."

"Tomás, that is not an answer. How much do you like me? You must like me. I need you to like me!"

"I do. See," I said looking down between my legs. "You can see I like you. You are beautiful."

She smiled weakly. "Tomás, I will be a good lover. I will be well. My hair will grow, and I guess it will be gray, but I will be well. I will not let you down again. People will think I am la Llorona or a vieja, but I will be well. Just love me. Promise."

"Te lo prometo. I promise you." She fell asleep grasping the folds of my stomach. I cradled her head and massaged her frail belly.

She briefly awoke and looked up at me. "I know you nearly lost hope. I do not blame you. Lo siento mucho. Yo te haré feliz siempre, te lo prometo. I promise always to make you happy. I can see you like me. I am glad." With a pained face and sad eyes, she gazed into the distant Llano.

"Beloved, do not promise me anything except that you will live a long time. That will make me happy enough," I whispered into her ear.

"Sí, sí te quiero." She put her head back on my lap and slept.

* * * * *

By mid-June, Victoria had regained enough strength to ride for half an hour. Her hair grew back slowly in short tufted streaks of white and gray. It was a wild mix of short, curly, thin, and thick, but all white or gray. When the wind caught her frail silk hair, the few long thin strands that had not fallen out spun away from her head like silver spider webs in the sun. Her gray hair framed a young, tender, and serious face with dark black eyes that now only rarely smiled. Her face and eyes now frequently took on a dreamy faraway quality. Her eyebrows stayed white. She had the outline of woman's hips and breasts.

"Querido, my soul and heart are in your hands. It is not good to be alone. Tomás, do you love this old woman?"

"Victoria, do you love this little boy?"

"Oh, sí, sí, you know I do!"

"I have always loved you. When you were a very little girl of twelve, you married me. You said we would be married forever. Forever has not ended."

"Pero, what can I give you for this forever? I am gray now. I am not pretty."

"Querida, you have not yet asked me what I need. Your questions tell me that you want to be loved, but you assume you know what I need. You assume you have lost your beauty. Give me your life, our lives together. That is what I need."

"Ah, Tomás."

I pulled her head to me. "Your hair smells just like it always has. I can remember how sweaty and salty you smelled when I first met you."

She inhaled deeply. "Tomás, when I was ill, I knew when you entered the room by your smell. I liked when you were there." She grew thoughtful.

"Tomás, walk with me to the church. I must see Patricio. It is time. Tomás, por favor, take me to see Patricio. Take me to see him every day."

"Sí querida. Take my hand. We will walk to the church now."

We walked slowly down the stairs from the roof and out the zaguán toward the plaza. Inside the church gate, she fell to her knees. She carefully put small stones into her pocket. She crawled through the church door then toward the place in the floor where Patricio was buried. Her knees bled. I tried to lift her and make her walk, but she refused.

"¡Querido, no! This is something I must do."

"You are hurting yourself. I won't allow it."

"This is not about hurting myself. I will make it." She reached the smooth, packed floor that hid Patricio. She signaled that I should sit near her on the floor. She lay across the top of Patricio's grave for a very long time. She arose and placed the stones carefully on the floor that concealed his grave. Then she walked to the reredos and carefully examined them.

"These are in poor repair. Has your mother seen them?" I started to speak but she continued, "We must go. Regresamos mañana. We will come back tomorrow."

For the next two weeks, we made a daily trip to the church. Often trembling, she would lie across Patricio's grave. She said nothing and expected nothing of me. She arose, left her stones carefully on the floor, and then stopped to examine the altar screens. She stopped her pilgrimages near the end of June when the weather suddenly turned cold and rainy.

When the rain stopped in July, Victoria announced. "It is time for me to go visit my aunt. She has come to see me many times. I must return the favor."

"Let's go now." I jumped up and ran toward my house forgetting Victoria still did not run. She followed slowly with a confused look on her face.

"Tomás, you always run. It tires me to watch."

I ran back and picked her up. "I am carrying you home."

"Don't drop me, please." She grasped my neck.

"I won't."

Cradling her in my arms, I carried her home. I put her down by the door. She traced the latch and rough wood panels with both hands. She then turned to me and, traced my eyes and nose.

"I remember the first time we met," she said. She slowly entered the house as though for the first time. She stood still as her eyes adjusted to the darkened room. She shivered.

"Muchos días han pasado," she mused quietly. She walked to the large fireplace now cold and emptied of ash for the summer. She touched the floor where her teacup shattered. I started to speak. Mamá Paula stopped me with a wave of her hand and watched us carefully. Victoria finally spoke.

"Hola, tía Trent. As you see, I am now well." Victoria spoke stiffly.

"Indeed, you are looking much better."

"Then you agree that I am well. I need your help. I have examined the reredos in San Mateo many times. They are of a poor quality and very old. Do you know who carved them?" As an afterthought she added, "I know it was not you."

"Sobrina," my mother chuckled, "You are correct. I did not carve the reredos. I only carved the crucifix. The reredos had been there many years before I came. Tomás tells me that you have been examining them carefully for weeks. So as you know they are primitive and poorly done."

"Tía, indeed, they are poorly done. However, I am curious, how is it that the church is named for San Mateo when there is no likeness of San Mateo to be found anywhere near the altar? In fact, I cannot be sure who any of the saints carved on the screen are meant to be. Am I so ignorant? You must tell me more."

"Querida sobrina, if you wish to hear this story you will have to stay for lunch. I have missed you these many months. It is time for a visit."

We sat on a blanket in mother's garden surrounded by small bright white daisies growing amidst a tangle of onions. Mother seldom prayed, but today she said a simple prayer.

"Dios, estamos agradecidos por Victoria. God, we are grateful for

Victoria, amén."

"Amen," I said. Victoria blushed.

"I am not sure why anyone would be grateful for me," she said sadly looking down at the floor.

"Niñita, enough of this self-pity. Where are your manners? We thank God for you. The correct response from you is to say a kind 'gracias'"

Victoria started to speak about something else. Mother interrupted.

"I have not heard a 'thank you' yet."

"Gracias, tía, y perdóname. Thank you, I am sorry. I have been such a burden to everyone."

"Sobrina, you said that correctly, 'you have been'—what you have been, is now passed. We are all here safely now, so we go forward, and I think part of going forward has to do with the Church of San Mateo. Dear one, the church is not named for the Saint. The village is. The church was named after the village. No one has ever thought much about how to decorate the church or even make it a holy place. As you know, there is no priest here. Your mother has her own chapel. The church is neglected and forgotten until someone dies. Prayers and blessings were said for Patricio, your dear brother, but there has been no service of any kind there since. A few of the men and women re-plaster the building and repair the roof once a year. The floors are swept out twice a month and coated with buffalo blood and oil every year, but that is it. That is all. Sobrina, tell me when you yourself have heard mass there?"

Victoria thought quietly for a few minutes. "Maybe two times many years ago. When here, the priest always says mass for us in mamá's capilla."

Mother poured us each a glass of red wine, squinted her eyes, and then spoke thoughtfully, "Dear one, the Bishop in Durango has had so little concern for our souls that he has not helped us pay for a church or keep a priest in the parish. Worse, he has taxed us to build his big cathedral in Durango. So, the people do not have the money for a church. However, to be honest, they have never wanted a priest around, or the inquisition that comes with priests. When the governor sent the Franciscans home many, many years ago, our grandmothers and grandfathers celebrated, I am sure."

Victoria silently pondered for a moment. She then spoke with a quivering voice. "What you say then is that Church is not a holy place, but my brother is buried there."

"A place is as holy as you make it, querida. I think the church is as pleasing to God as any other place is. God created everything, and when done creating, he said that it 'all was good.' So you see, the church is good."

"So my brother is fine there?"

"He is fine wherever he is as long as he is in your heart, querida."

Victoria again thought quietly, "Tía, I wanted to re-carve the reredos for Patricio, but now I am not so sure."

"Jita, if this is what you decide to do, I will help. Winter is a good time to do such things." Mamá paused to dust a few old wood shavings from her dress. "If you wish to carve reredos, you must be willing to learn something about yourself. Last fall you spent time re-carving San Mateo until he became a weapon that you used to hurt yourself. Nine months have passed. What have you learned?"

Victoria sat still for a long time. "Perhaps I have learned nothing. I must come back to learn from you. This I know. I do not want to learn by falling down too many times. I know that I am a good woodcarver. Carving wood lightens my heart and keeps my hands still."

"So you will be a santera then? We will start working again this coming winter. Now you must grow strong. That is the task of anyone who has been ill, to grow strong."

Victoria stood to leave but suddenly stopped. She brushed her hands through her thin hair and furrowed her brow.

"Señora, I have a special favor to ask. ¿Ayúdame por favor?" She begged. "Tía, I need Tomás' help. Will you let him take me to see my brothers on the Río Mora? ¿Por favor?"

Mother looked at me, surprised by this request. Without thinking more, she said, "Sí, but, Victoria, will you be strong enough?"

"Yes, yes I am. I will be, I mean. Oh, gracias, gracias, gracias. We will be gone a week or two. Gracias. I will be strong when the time comes. I want to celebrate a velorio for Patricio on San Mateo's feast day. It will be a velorio and a vigil. We will give thanks for the life of Patricio and for mine. Each life has been a miracle."

"Sí, sí," was again my mother's simple response, but now she was smiling. "Sobrina," she said, "I said 'yes' too quickly, but I am glad I did. This is a very good idea."

"Y tía, I want to build a very small shrine. I will make a pile of stones to remember him. Can we do this?"

"When you say, 'we,' understand that I will not help you build a shrine. That is a job for you to do. How will you be ready for this adventura? You must be strong enough to ride for several days."

"Victoria, you are too weak to do this. You cannot go," I protested.

"In September, I will be fine. You will see," Victoria assured me.

"This is something she must do. She will be fine," Mamá agreed.

Chapter 13: Return to the Río Mora

Thomas

"Tomás, what does your mother wish me to learn about myself so that I will become a good carver?"

"Mamá is a philosopher and an artist. I am not sure that she wants you to learn anything. I think she asked if you had learned *something* in the last several months."

"What does she mean? I must understand."

Victoria read everything my mother gave her to read. She studied every book, and memorized every character. She studied the Bible. She carefully carved a new half-life sized statue of San Mateo. Mateo was no longer a weapon. His axe shrank to the point it was a mere decoration tucked into the rope belt of his robe. She raced to prove herself, to prove to me that my mother made the right decision in allowing us to journey to the mountains.

"I must grow stronger faster, I must," she anguished. "And, if our horses are to carry us into the mountains they need exercise. We must ride every day until the horses and I are stronger."

"Querida, we will ride and swim every day. I will help you, just as I have all along. You and the horses will be strong enough in September." I hid my doubts.

"Oh Tomás, you are so faithful. Gracias, gracias."

The next day Victoria rode about fifteen minutes without my support. She was pale and gasping. She clung to Francisco like a novice. He did not seem to notice his rider was in trouble. He was out of breath himself. Sensing that no one was giving him commands, Francisco turned around and took her slowly home. She did not stop him. In the stable, she managed to dismount without falling, and then she quickly sat on the stable floor. She looked at me and shook her head.

"Estoy cansada. I am tired," she whispered. "Help me up and put me to bed."

"Querida, I will help you, but I have something for you first."

"Tomás, espera, it will wait. I must lie down." She tried to pull off her riding boots, but could not. "I am helpless. Please, pull them off."

159

She dropped her head, turned away, and cried in frustration as I pulled them off by the heels.

"Please look at me," I begged. I brought two red and blue ribbons out of my saddlebags. "These are for you. Please. The ribbons are for your hair. Silver, red, and blue are beautiful together," I said. Annoyed and surprised, she pushed them away.

"But I am in mourning and can only wear black."

"You have mourned enough. The bright colors are perfect. Let me tie them in your hair. They will be beautiful."

"No, querido. I am tired. Quizás mañana."

I got up to leave. She looked at me and shook her head. "I have been rude to you. Lo siento. Forgive me. Carry me to bed and rest with me. I cannot make it without you."

Hurt by her sharp words, I carried her toward the house. Bárbara watched from the window. She quickly opened the door, then walked with me to Victoria's room to straighten the bed. Victoria had fallen asleep in my arms. I laid her down. She did not awaken. I lay down beside her, pressed my face into hers, and slept.

The next day Victoria rode to my house at eight. She wore the red and blue ribbons pinned to her shirt. "My hair is too short," she shrugged. "I brought fresh cornbread and honey. It is in the saddle bags." She sat quietly on old Francisco. "Querido, I cannot get down. I will fall."

I tied Francisco to a post. "Lift your right leg over the saddle and turn toward me."

"I can't. It is no use."

"Trust me then, and lean toward me until you fall off. I will catch you." She slowly leaned to her left until she fell into my arms.

"Hurry, put me on my feet before tía comes," she begged me. She trembled, but managed to collect enough energy to stand and carry her bread and honey.

"Tía, I have breakfast," she called. She quickly walked past me into the house and sat down before her strength failed her. Mother sat beside her and helped her slice the bread. The three of us ate quietly.

"This is very hard for you, but you can do it," mamá said.

"Today I will last an hour," Victoria promised.

After breakfast, we rode into the Llano. She swayed drunkenly in the saddle, but she refused to turn back or let me help her. Somehow, she made it home. Mamá waited for her.

"Chica, you must sleep. I know how much you feel the need to work, but now you must sleep." Mamá led Victoria to a bed she made for her in the shade. Victoria slumped into the soft blankets and fell instantly asleep.

The next morning, Victoria lasted less than half an hour, but she did not turn pale or look like she would fall off her horse. Francisco also managed to do more than amble along. When we returned, we walked to the pond to swim. Victoria undressed and just sat in the water.

With a weary voice she quietly asked, "Will I ever be able to ride again?" She looked at me for reassurance.

"You will ride again," I nodded.

In August, señor Griego and my father interrupted my hoeing in the fields. Señor Griego put his hand on my shoulder.

"Tomás, Victoria has chosen you to escort her to the Río Mora. This is a pilgrimage to the place where her brother died. She is convinced she must build a shrine of stones at the spot where he was injured. She is also grateful for her own life. And so, she promised she would build a shrine for San Mateo." He thought quietly for a moment and then continued, "This is what she must do. We keep our promises to God."

"We must keep our promises," I agreed, resuming my hoeing.

"You have been riding every day. She remains weak," he worried.

"We have a few more weeks before the end of the month," I said with the most confident voice I could muster.

"She will not be able to help you this time. You must be prepared to handle any danger by yourself." He watched me work for a few quite minutes. In the silence, the clanking of the hoe against the clay seemed louder than the warning bell on the wall.

"You have not fired a rifle or pistol since Doña left last winter." His voice startled me. "I have asked your father to spend time with you shooting."

"Yes," I agreed. "This is a good suggestion."

"I will provide a pack mule. You can take supplies to my sons. You will rest at Doña's." Señor Griego clearly intended to do everything he could to make his daughter's trip successful. Even if death awaited her, he would not stop her.

Father finally spoke. "Thomas, you have heard Bárbara and tía Ana talk of the bones in the Llano. Remember, señor and señora Griego have only one daughter. You are my only son. You both must come home."

"We will come back. I promise."

"When you return, consider marriage. You are both old enough." Father surprised me. Señor Griego said nothing. He waited to hear my response.

"Since last fall, she has changed so much I no longer recognize her."

Father turned to señor Griego, "Will she have my son?" he asked.

"Tomás is right. She has changed so much no one knows her. In truth, she no longer knows or trusts herself. Maybe she never did. Maybe it's my fault." Señor Griego's voice trailed off. After a moment he spoke again, "We will talk more of marriage later. I believe she still loves you

161

very much, but first things first. Are you prepared to protect yourselves? The dead do not marry."

"Sí, señor," I said too quickly.

"Thomas, can you do this?" Father asked.

"Yes, papá, yes. I am a man. I can do this."

"Of course you are a *man*!" He snapped. His furrowed face finished his unspoken thoughts, "and foolish!" He breathed heavily and then spoke softly, "You will leave at the beginning of September. Until then, you will practice loading and firing pistols and rifles every day. I will teach Victoria again too. She is weak now. Rifles are heavy." He shook his head. "She will marry you when you return, I am sure."

Marriage, as a reward for surviving the trip, was the furthest thing from my mind.

* * * * *

Thomas

Years later Bárbara would say she was the one who convinced our fathers that we could handle this trip. She told them, "God protected Victoria from death once. Surely, God will not toy with her and take her into the mountains to cruelly let her die. She and Tomás are old enough to marry. He can take care of her."

The days passed quickly. The horses grew stronger. Victoria now rode easily for an hour, but that remained her limit. The only way she would be strong enough was to wait another year before traveling, but Victoria was determined to leave by September.

Victoria carved a new San Mateo. She hid his face from me, but I could see his axe was now quite small. Dangling from San Mateo's belt, the axe looked more like a cross on a rosary than something dangerous.

The frenzied pace of readying for the trip, training rides, target practice, and carving left Victoria precariously worn out. Exhausted, she barely managed the walk to the beaver ponds where, instead of swimming, she slept every afternoon.

"Tomás," she begged, "do not tell anyone I am having so much trouble. I promise to be strong. I will make it, please do not tell."

"Querida, I promise."

I kept my promise. Only the ongoing presence of the Saint's hand explains how we later made it safely to the Río Mora, for when we left Victoria was not fit to travel. Fortunately, we travelled light. The most awkward and heaviest item was the carving of San Mateo. We took one pack mule and carried everything else on our horses. With a planned stay at Doña's, it would be at least a four-day ride to find Victoria's brothers. After an unduly cheerful goodbye from our families, we set out.

162

Victoria strapped her father's rifle over her shoulder. We both carried a brace of pistols in our belts. We rode cautiously. Neither of us spoke. I glanced at her frequently to assure she was still on her horse. She fooled everyone. She rode straight up in the saddle and sat at ease for more than an hour.

"Tomás, can you still see the village?" Victoria suddenly whispered in a quivering, desperate voice. I looked back. Small hills and trees completely screened the village from our view.

"It is gone now," I said

"The rifle and pistols are too heavy." She dismounted and leaned her head against her patient Francisco. She pulled her pistols from her belt, cleared them of powder and lead, and packed them in her saddlebags. She unstrapped her rifle from her shoulder and packed it carefully in the holster on her horse's flank. Panting heavily, she managed to pull herself back onto her horse and we trudged on. Soon, she stopped again.

"I am too hot. Forgive me." She pulled off her sweat-soaked shirt. "Now I must walk." She slowly plodded along, leading Francisco. The sun danced off her shoulders and the healing scars on her breasts. A wide-brimmed hat shaded her face and hid her short, gray hair. We did not make it to the Mora as planned. Exhausted and weak after riding and walking, Victoria finally sat down and cried.

"Querido, I am worthless. I cannot walk or ride."

"We must find a safe place to rest for the night. Can you make it to the small grove of trees up ahead?" I pointed to the trees on the near horizon where in better times we had stopped for lunch the year before.

"Tomás, I will rest a minute. Then we can start out." In the waning summer light, the green and vast expanse of empty Llano engulfed us. We sat quietly looking out across the top of the knee-high grass. To the west, the usual late afternoon clouds and thunderstorms gathered along the mountains. The distant storms quickly overpowered the sun and left us in shadows. I stood up.

"If we are not careful, the rain and wind will catch us in the wide-open. We will be wet and cold in a place where it is too dangerous to build a fire. Hurry, Victoria, you must hurry. We must make it into the trees before the storm hits. There is no more time to rest." She stood up and walked slowly toward the trees, but after ten minutes she began to stagger and weave.

"Querida, you must ride. Get on your horse," I ordered. I boosted her back onto tired Francisco and led the horses and mule onward, not for the hoped ten minutes, but for nearly an hour. Tired and exhausted, we finally made it into the safety of the trees as a light rain began to fall.

"Ándale, quickly, we must set up camp."

"It rained the last time we were here," Victoria quietly remembered. She staggered from her horse. She managed to unsaddle him, tie him to a tree, and unpack her sleeping gear and food. She lay down in the rain and immediately fell asleep. I covered her with oiled buffalo skins. Cold and miserable, I hobbled the horses and mule then slipped under the skins. Victoria woke up shivering and nuzzled against me as the rain poured down and the wind howled.

"We will make it to the Río Mora tomorrow," she whispered. "No te preocupes."

The waters of the Mora still lay more than two hours travel away.

"Victoria, we must make it to water tomorrow. This is too hard on the animals. When we get to the Mora, we will have to rest them and feed them for the day if we expect to make it to Doña's house."

"Mañana, mañana," she sighed, "San Mateo dice, 'No os preocupéis por vuestra vida, qué comeréis o qué beberéis. El mañana se resolverá por sí solo—Do not worry about tomorrow, what ye shall eat or ye shall drink. Tomorrow will take care of itself.'"

She brushed her trembling hands through my hair. "You are a good man," were her last words as she fell back to sleep with driving wind and rain pelting our makeshift shelter.

It took half the next day to eat, pack, and travel to the spot where the Mora emptied onto the Llano, the place where we both last saw Patricio alive. As she dismounted Francisco at the water's edge, Victoria shook. Her hands trembled, her legs buckled, and she fell forward splitting her upper lip as her face hit the ground.

"You are bleeding!" I tried to help her up. She covered her face with her hands.

"Que Dios me ayude. God help me. Querido, do not touch me. I will do this by myself." Hiding her bleeding face with one hand, she pushed herself up with the other.

"Victoria, your hands are shaking. Your face is dripping with blood and sweat. We should go back."

"No, no, Tomás, it is this place. It is Patricio." She carefully kept her lip covered. Blood oozed between her fingers and dripped down her hand. "Hobble the animals, then walk with me to the place where Patricio said, 'adiós.' I will be fine. I promise. I promise."

The horses and mule taken care of, we walked slowly through the meadows and the cottonwood bosque. Finally, tired and shaking uncontrollably, she dropped her hands revealing a mangled and gaping upper lip. Wretched in her bloodstained shirt, with her trembling hands, and gray hair, she made no further attempt to hide her injury.

"Tomás, this shaking will stop. I know it will!" She lisped awkwardly through her torn, swollen lip. We reached the spot where Patricio last spoke to us.

Victoria dropped to her knees and crossed herself. She reached toward the grass with her left arm and hand as though touching someone or something unseen.

"Estoy mejor ahora. Gracias a Dios. I am better now. Praise God." She crossed herself again and finally, she stood up. "Help me with my lip," she begged.

We walked to the water's edge and carefully rinsed it. She looked at her reflection.

"This should be sewn, but we have nothing." She shrugged her shoulders and sighed.

"It needs to be sewn," I agreed.

"I did not need this." Tears filled her eyes and she stomped her foot.

"We must go home."

"No, we cannot go home."

Eyes flashing wildly, she rolled up her handkerchief, pulled it tight across her lip, and tied it at the back of her head. I shook my head but said nothing. There was no point. She would not have listened.

Victoria whimpered as we set-up camp. To avoid discovery by indios enemigos, we did not make a fire. We prepared dried meats, hard bread and roasted corn. Victoria struggled to chew around her torn lip and bloody bandage. Moaning, she gave up. The wet and mild summer produced a second round of wild strawberries. I made them into a mash and fed them to her.

"It burns," she cried and pulled away.

In the west, the clouds burned gold and crimson. The sun flickered out. The chirping crickets in the cottonwoods multiplied from scattered soloists to an indistinguishable choral roar.

"Esposo," Victoria had not called me husband in months, "Esposo, according to el Cristo, the lilies of the field bloom and are attired in beauty pero no es la verdad. La verdad es horrible. Elk eat the lilies, and the sparrows grow cold, freeze, and die of hunger. Only those who do not observe the hawk eating the sparrows can think that God cares. ¿Qué piensas esposo? What do you think?" The deepening darkness hid our faces and thoughts.

She continued, "My heart has suffered enough. Mí hermano está muerto. My brother was young and he is dead. He was too young. Will God heal my heart if he cannot even protect the birds and the lilies?"

The final glow of twilight faded away. Along with the light, the last trace of the distant, blue mountains disappeared. Our world grew smaller and more uncertain.

"Esposo, do you still love me? Am I just a terrible sick girl that no one can ever love?" She questioned in a sad whisper. "Am I so weak and ugly with my gray hair—catorce años con pelo gris? ¡Qué barbaridad hombrecito!" In the darkness, I could not see her tears, but I heard her sob quietly, "Qué fea, qué fea! I am so ugly. Now my upper lip will be scarred. Please love me. Hombrecito, dime."

"Victoria, I have never stopped loving you."

"But I know I make you weary," she whispered.

"You do," I agreed gently.

I brushed the tears from her face and pulled her head to my chest.

"Once you could shake my head holding my braids in both your hands," she sobbed. Her running nose, tears, and blood stained my shirt. She gasped for breath, shuddered, and then sobbed again. In the middle of her overwhelming pain, I found myself staring into the immense sky and listening to the wind in the grass. There was noise everywhere, the stream and the woods sang. All of it was magnificent.

"Querida," I ruffled her scruffy hair, "We are not frail. We are not small. We are part of something big. You are the sparrow that did not freeze and fall from the tree. Let your hair grow long and it will make a beautiful silver braid. There is no shame in your short hair. People can see that you have been ill and that you are now growing strong again." I pressed my forehead into hers and kissed her nose.

"Victoria, our fathers want us to marry. You have called me husband for a long time. It seems so long ago, but once we spoke of marriage. I will marry you."

"You speak as though obligated." She started to say more but did not.

Neither speaking nor sleeping, we clung to each other in the vast, dark wilderness. Above us, the moon rose slowly then crawled across the sky. Time was both suspended and relentlessly moving toward dawn. Coyotes howled in the distance. The horses grew restless, but Victoria finally slept. For a moment, even her trembling stopped.

I could not sleep. I had spoken to Victoria of marrying. Did I think marrying her was simply an obligation? She called me husband, but in the end, she had not answered me. I thought of María. She had grown old so quickly. María must be twenty now. I remembered her dressing. I yearned for her. Would María ever find anyone in this empty place? Would she die alone? Victoria? Me? Would we die alone? My stepmother had not married until quite late, but she was happy. Reassured, I finally fell asleep.

When I awoke, the sun was already hot on my face. It was nearly 8 o'clock. Victoria still slept. For Victoria, sleeping on the hallowed ground where she last saw her brother was a blessing and miracle. In the wilderness, with the dangers of the Cumanchis, the Apache, and even the weather, she slept peacefully for the first time in months.

I slipped from our bed and looked for the horses. I tethered them closer to water and fresh grass. Victoria still slept. I picked more strawberries and then went to the water's edge to wash. Suddenly, a gray reflection rippled on the water. Victoria stood behind me. She was naked.

166

A broken-lipped smile fleetingly crossed her face. She pressed her lip and moaned. Holding her lip, she tried smiling again.

"María made you hard in this place." She was embarrassingly blunt. Suddenly, she knocked me into the water and then fell in after me.

"You have no obligations, no duties to me," she said hitting the water with her fists. "You have Doña." She was not angry. She was matter-of-fact. She slapped the water only to emphasize what she felt was the truth.

"I wish to marry you!" I shook my head at her. "I have never felt obligated."

"I keep hurting you," she sighed. "I am so sorry. ¿Que Dios me perdone?" Then she wondered aloud, "Why would God forgive me? The things that I said about Him last night." She slapped the water again with both hands.

"I forgive you and I don't think God cares what you said." I quickly crossed myself.

"Santa Teresa would say that God requires hard work, suffering and loving. Pero querido—how much? How much? He sufrido muncho. He sufrido muncho. I have suffered enough."

"You have suffered. As to what God wants, I have no idea."

She shivered in the cold water. "Please say it is safe to make a small fire and have something hot to drink!" She climbed onto the bank. Although frail and still quite thin, her scarred breasts had filled out, her pubic hair had grown thick and black, and the hair of her legs was now dark, long, and soft.

"Victoria, you are naked and beautiful." I found myself smiling with delight.

She smiled through her torn lip. She turned toward me and combed her pubic hair with her thin fingers.

"It is true. I still please you?" she questioned. Her eyes grew wide with relief.

"Yes, and, beloved, your hair is not all gray!" I laughed.

"¡Hombre!" For a moment, she forgot her painful lip. She splashed back into the water and tried to dunk me, but she tripped and slipped beneath the surface. I pulled her into my arms and carried her out of the water to a sunny spot in the grass. She sat quietly holding her lip and shivering.

"Una fogatita? A little fire?" she pleaded, squinting and tilting her head.

"We can make a fire for fifteen minutes. No smoke." I gathered small, dry twigs that would burn hot and fast. Naked and wounded, she squatted by the fire sipping hot mint tea made from plants that grew wild by the stream.

"Bárbara could be here. It smells like her kitchen," she sighed.

167

We sat in the sun, dipping hard bread in our hot tea and eating wild strawberries until the fire burned out. I waited for some sign from her that it was time to dress and leave. She arched her back, picked up a small stick, and drew faces in the ashes, but made no effort to dress or pack.

"Esposo, I am very troubled about God. Deer eat the lilies of the field. God does not care for them!" She frowned, lifted her breasts, and examined her scars, then mumbled as though I were not there, "¿Quién va a cuidar de mí? Who will care about me?"

I shook my head and stood up. "Bueno, querida. It is time for us to leave. I have no idea what God cares about."

She continued, "Tomás, we make this journey to remember Patricio. I must remember him because God did not." Lost, she stood and gazed into the bosque. A light breeze jostled her and she staggered. We dressed and packed up our camp.

"Esposo, help me with these." She pulled the red and blue ribbons and a shell comb from her saddle bags. "Put these in my hair."

I carefully tied the ribbons into the comb and pressed it into the side of her hair. The wind blew gently and the ribbons danced like sprites at the side of her head.

"Qué bonita. Come look at your reflection in the water."

She peered over my shoulder. "Completo," she said.

We let the horses drink one last time at the water's edge. We filled our clay canteens, mounted, and then rode slowly up the bank through the trees and out again into the Llano. Broken foothills and the wall of the high peaks of the Sangre De Cristos rose before us. Soon we would be in the mountains.

Chapter 14: By Fire Made Whole

Victoria

We rode slowly upward along the Indian trail. Cottonwoods gave way to pine forests. Tomás suddenly stopped, dismounted, and examined the trail.

"Fresh hoof prints and cerote, horse dung, just beginning to dry." He carefully studied the woods in front of us.

"Indios bárbaros. ¿Qué te parece? What do you think?" My heart pounded in my throat. I struggled to swallow.

"I don't know," he said.

"¡Maldita sea! Damn it. My hands are shaking too much to load my pistol."

Tomás turned to me laughing, "Querida, perdóname, we are about to be killed and you are making me laugh. I have never heard such language from you."

"Stop it. How can I load a pistol if you are laughing and I am shaking?" Cold sweat soaked my shirt and forehead. "Your laughter is a cruel distraction."

"Forget the pistol. Load your rifle first."

"Help me then." I started to jump from Francisco.

"Never mind querida. Stay on Francisco. Let's find a safe place. Follow me."

We rode wildly and dangerously through the thick forest until Tomás stopped at a large fallen tree and dismounted.

"Hide behind that log, now!" he ordered. "Remember the time on the río when we thought we were going to be kidnapped? Today is a day like that," he said with a stern tone tempered by a half-smile. He loaded both our rifles and pistols. "If we must fire these, you will have to reload yourself. Can you do that?" His voice was too sharp.

"No," I groaned, "Not if I am shaking. I cannot believe this luck." I shook my head at Tomás as I hid behind the log. He fell down beside me. We peered carefully into the thick trees. I pushed his sweaty hair from his face and eyes. I needed to touch him.

"Maybe our luck is good. We must find out." He scanned the

forest carefully for any sign we had been followed. "It is quiet," he whispered. "Let's hide here for awhile and see if anyone comes."

"I want to stay here for as long as we can. It is beautiful," I sighed in exhaustion, turned on my back, and watched the tops of the pine trees sway in the gentle wind. In the deep, comfortable grass, my heart slowed. For a moment, the whole world was the blue of sky and green of trees above me. I smiled and closed my eyes.

Thomas (Victoria)

New snow dusted the distant high peaks to the west. Steller's Jays darted in the trees, their wings as deep blue as the ribbons in Victoria's hair.

"Querida, I hear running water. Let's find the stream." I softly squeezed Victoria's shoulder to arouse her. "No one chased us," I said softly. "Listen!"

She shook her head, rubbed her eyes, and yawned deeply. She carefully turned over and peeked across the top of the log. "I will follow you," she whispered.

Only the occasional chirps of chickadees and the squabbling barks of squirrels disturbed the silence of the autumn woods. Nothing else moved. Relaxed, we inhaled the warm incense of pine and musty perfume of the nearby stream. The horses lead us through the forest toward the sound and smell of water. Viejo was completely at ease. Although I could not sense danger, I knew he could. He lazily followed his nose to the water.

At the stream's edge we unpacked the horses and the mule, took off their saddles, and tethered them in the grass. Our rifles placed next to us, we sat on the stream bank and dangled our feet in the water. In the far west, the afternoon clouds gathered along the highest mountains. Before we reached shelter for the night, the afternoon rains would come again.

"Bésame. Dime que me quieres. Kiss me. Tell me you love me," she squeezed my hand and whispered.

"Te quiero." I brushed my lips across her nose.

"That is nice." She smiled

She leaned against a fallen log. "Escúchame Tomás, te diré lo que me pasó. I will tell you what it was like to die. Te hablaré del dolor. I will tell you about my pain, but you must promise that you will not die before me. Tell me, you will always love me. I cannot stand to be alone. I cannot stand it." She was shaking fiercely and her voice rattled. "I do not want to live like Doña." I reached for her hand, but she gently pushed me away.

"Do not touch me now. Do not touch me. Just listen first, then kiss and hold me." She rushed every word through her chattering teeth,

170

but she grew calmer as she spoke. Nothing stopped the trembling in her hands. She stood up and I started to follow.

"Stay there." She unpacked her carving knife from her saddlebags, and then stooped to pick up a long piece of dried pine. She sat down and began to carve a face in the wood. Her trembling abruptly stopped.

"Promise me," she said, "that I may die first."

I closed my eyes and answered her. "¡Sí, sí, yo siempre te amaré! You may die first." It was a promise I intended to keep.

"Tomás, when Patricio died, I died too. At least part of my heart died, but I could see you. I heard you and I loved you. Remember the day in the tunnel? I said that I would always know you by your smell and touch even when I could not see you. When I could not see or hear anyone, I knew you were there. You have the smell of soft leather, of turpentine from your mother's wood chips, and of smoke from buffalo tallow. You smelled like your mamá, mi tía. I knew you were there. I knew she still carved. I saw your mother's house, and I could feel you in the dark. In my dreams, you slid naked over my arms and we swam together in our pond. I fought so hard to come back.

"I heard the rain on the roof, and I heard more rain. Llovía, todos los días llovía. It was so dark and it rained. Seguro era yo, I was crying. I could not tell the difference between tears and storms. I heard weeping. I looked down on a small child who wept. I was a gray woman looking down on the poor weeping child. I tried to console her. There was a chico. Pensé que eras tú. The boy read many books to the girl, but he never heard her speak.

"I watched her weep. It was como un velorio—like a vigil for a dead child. Her black eyes were big and always opened, but she did not see. He was so far away. She was so far away. Sometimes he would touch her. I was glad for her when he did this. But she did not move. From a place above her, I begged her to move, but she would not.

"Sometimes late at night, as I watched, ladrones y lloronas came out of the wooden ceiling. They attacked the girl with their fists. I watched her scream and scream. No one heard her but me. In the late afternoons, the evil shadows on the wall swallowed her. The winter days grew short. I feared the sun would sink away forever. She prayed it would come back. No one, not even Dios heard her. Los demonios crawled across her wall and onto her bed, but no one helped her. Shaking, she closed her eyes to hide, but she could not escape for they attacked her soul through dreams. I touched her. I touched you too, but you did not know. I cared about both of you, but neither of you saw me.

"A strange man from the Holy Book spoke to me. He told me of horrors yet to come, horrors that would attack the sleeping girl if I did not wake her up.

"'You must wake her up if you do not want to see her die,' he

171

ordered. But I could not awaken her. Tomás, you tried but could not awaken her. Santa María y San José llegaron but they could not awaken her. I knew she was dying. I saw her hair turn gray like mine. I saw her small body melt into the bed, but I could not wake her up. Suddenly there was Bárbara, la chiguata, the genízara slave. She ordered the girl to sit on the edge of the bed. She demanded that I re-enter the girl's body and sit on the edge of the bed. She sang and danced como una abuela matachina— she fought off death and ordered me to come down.

"'Sit down,' she called. 'Siéntate en la camalta. Put your arms around the girl and hold her. Embrace her.' She danced and called out mis pecados, my sins. 'You have hurt too many people. You have hurt the Anglo boy who loves you. Your mother talks as though you are already dead. Your father writes of your death in his diary. Ah, and Patricio, sí, Patricio está muy enojado. He is very angry. He wants you to live. Come down from there. Come down now and embrace your sister ahora, before I burn this room.'

"She made an offering to the spirits. She lit candles and sang a hymn to the virgin, 'Madre de los dolores, Madre de la tormenta, Hay dulce Madre.'

"She baked for me. 'Estoy haciendo el pan. Es tu favorito. I made your favorite bread.'

"She shook matracas, rattles, and sang in a high shrill voice. She knew where I was hiding. She grew angry. She had enough. She would not let me hide anymore. 'Come from the latías, or I will burn the roof.' She took a branch of dried pine, lit it, and came after me. I coughed in the smoke. 'Mañana is your last chance—come down and embrace the girl— duerme con ella en la camalta.' She filled the room with smoke, then left.

"I was more afraid of fire than death. You were reading. There was the child on the bed. I embraced her. She was cold and stiff. Her eyes were still closed. Her hair was so gray. She looked at me por un momento. She looked straight at me, straight into me as though I were her soul. I held her. We rocked and caressed each other until we again became one. Al fin, yo era la única chica en la sala. Finally, I was the only girl in the room.

"Suddenly, I could smell the bread baking. My arms were weak and stiff, but warm. I tried to bend my knees, but my bones and muscles creaked with pain from disuse. I hurt. My elbows and fingers hurt. My neck and head hurt. My jaw hurt. Everything hurt, but I was hungry, and I did not want to burn. You put bread under my nose. You brought me atole and tea.

"Angels came. They said, 'Pile stones and place a large cross in the meadow where Patricio was stricken.' They said, 'Build a chapel.'"

Victoria stood and stretched. Her short, silver hair sparkled in the wind. She pulled the red and blue ribbons from her hair, wove ribbons into a braid, and put the comb in the thin hair at the back of her head. She carefully placed her newly carved saint in the stream and watched it drift away.

"Seigo una inocente. I am innocent and chaste again. My braid is full and uncut. Y ahora, seigo una reina. Seigo una rica. I am a rich queen with silver," she said smiling. "I love you, and you have promised me that you will not die." We saddled and repacked the horses and mule.

"Victoria, te quiero. Adelante," I shouted and spurred Viejo forward.

"Una cosa más. One more thing." She stopped me. She thoughtfully sat in her saddle and put both hands on her cuera where it covered her breasts. "Mis senos, my breasts, I have hurt myself more than los indios enemigos. I have been foolish. I will never hurt myself or anyone like this ever again."

"I know it," I said with a new confidence.

She lay her head against Francisco's neck and let him lead the way. We found the trail and headed higher into the mountains. Suddenly we were in a wide valley with lush meadows, fields of grain, and scattered fortified farms spread haphazardly along the río. Two men operating irrigation sluices shouted and waved to us. We were safely off the Llano.

A sudden gust from the approaching thunderstorms set the barley rippling violently. We watched as a sheet of rain and fine sleet sped across the open fields toward us. The field hands ran to a small stone hut and waved for us to join them. Wet and cold, we pulled our horses and mule into a shed attached to the side of the hut. Calling from the open door, the men welcomed us in. Shivering, Victoria sat down by the fire. One of the men dropped mint leaves into a copper pot of boiling water to make hot tea.

"Gracias, gracias por el fuego. I am cold and tired." Victoria grimaced and looked at me trying to hide her exhaustion. "Do you know Doña María Josefa Chávez?" she asked. "She is expecting us." She sat quietly by the fire for a few minutes. Everyone waited for her to say more. Finally, she mused aloud, "I am so confused. So much has changed since I was here last. Barley grows everywhere."

"We have been prosperous," the tall man chuckled. He then introduced his partner and himself. "Qué tal, seigo Juan y mi amigo es Diego. When the rain stops, we will take you to the Chávez house.

"These are señor Chávez's fields. The Don is quite ill. We help when we can," Diego said shrugging his shoulders sadly. He added, "It is not enough."

The men looked carefully at Victoria. "You are the old woman disguised as a young girl," Juan said. "Your lip?" he added.

"No es nada, it is nothing." She covered the top of her mouth with her hand and smiled weakly.

Diego reflexively reached for her hair and caught himself. "Lo siento, I'm sorry. We have heard about your suffering, niña," he said, "and how the india drove the devils away."

Victoria's face turned pale. "It was the india and San Mateo." Her voice dropped off and her eyes narrowed with doubt. She quickly corrected herself, "And the grace of God!" She muttered and fell to her knees crossing herself.

"Señorita," Juan assured her, "we did not mean to offend you. We have heard stories of your miracle—how you were brought back to life. Señor Chávez told us these stories himself. He asked us to watch for you."

"I am not offended." She stiffly stood up and walked to the door to watch the rain.

"We will take you to see him and the donseya when the rain stops. Now both of you drink the tea and warm yourselves."

"Gracias. For the first time in three days of riding, we have shelter from the afternoon storms," I said with relief as sheets of rain and sleet pounded the roof.

Victoria returned, sat down on the floor, and curled-up comfortably by the fire. Suddenly animated, she drank her tea and chattered about her plans.

"We will build a new church and dedicate it to San Mateo," she said. "But I don't know how to build anything," she added with concern.

Juan reassured her, "You will have your church. Niña, I see no one has told you the Hermanos Penitentes will help build this shrine. We have been expecting you for several days."

"Sí, es la verdad," said Diego. "You are called a miracle here. Everyone knows your story. It is said you yourself have a special power to heal by carving santos."

"Her carvings healed her," I said forgetting the source of her scars.

"If that were only true," Victoria said pulling at her fingernails while she watched the rain.

"The truth is your presence. It is as they say, you are 'La Milagrosa,'" Juan said.

The sound of the storm faded. Chilled air perfumed with the scent of fresh wet pine and new mown grain wafted through the unshuttered windows. As the sun set, fog settled along the río.

"We must hurry. Doña will be worried," Diego warned. "It is a short walk. Juan will lead the mule. Señorita, you may ride or walk. It is up to you."

"I am rested. Let's walk."

"Cuidao," Diego warned. "The path will be muddy and slippery. Darkness will make it even more dangerous!"

174

The men led us into the dusk, across rain-drenched fields, toward a barely visible, fortified house surrounded by orchards and vineyards and protected by a low wall.

"Señor Chávez, he is mostly bedbound and talks about his coming death. His poor daughter will be left alone in the world," Juan lamented.

"She is not poor," Diego responded emphatically. "She has a good farm, and many flocks of sheep. She will not be hungry." Diego continued, "She owns genízaro slaves too. She will manage."

As the men chatted, Victoria staggered to a stop, grabbed my shoulder, and pleaded with me in a pained and desperate voice.

"Tomás, I cannot do this. I cannot stand up."

"We will get you on your horse." Juan steadied Francisco. I lifted her left foot into the stirrup and pushed her onto the saddle. Exhausted, she leaned forward, laid her head and chest against Francisco's neck, and closed her eyes.

Chapter 15: Two Women

Thomas

His hindquarters wagging along with his tail, Perro bounded out of the darkness to greet us. María followed immediately behind him.

"At last you are here. Tomorrow we would have come looking for you."

Undisturbed by María's sharp greeting, Victoria slept against Francisco's neck.

"Es una tonta. She is a fool," María mouthed looking at me and shaking her head.

She signaled to her genízara servant standing in the narrow doorway. The old woman darted to María's side.

"Gertrudis, make the señorita a bed. We are making the house into a hospital," María spoke loudly making no effort to hide her dismay.

"María, she is just tired," I whispered curtly.

"Tomás, you mean too weak," María pronounced in annoyance. "No one had the courage to keep her home." She snapped the heels of her boots together to emphasize her point.

"This trip will strengthen her," I said, caught off guard at María's anger.

"Or finally kill her," María answered. "Look at her face!"

Awakened by María's snapping boots and angry voice, Victoria spoke meekly from the dark.

"What is one more scar? My lip will heal. Doña, I will sleep and be ready to travel in the morning."

"Mañana. We shall see. Can you get off your horse?" María held Victoria's hand.

"Of course."

Pretending she was fine, Victoria dismounted with the last of her strength. María and I caught her and helped her through the narrow door.

Diego and Juan helped Gertrudis spread a pallet out on the floor for Victoria. All of us put her to bed, and she quickly fell asleep.

"We must be on our way," Juan called softly to María.

"Doña, be gentle with La Milagra." Diego gave María an officious

179

hug as the men went back into the moonless night. María and I walked them to the wall to bid them a final goodbye.

"Hace frio," María said shivering. "Summer is nearly gone."

"Sí," I agreed.

Returning to the house, she took my hand and whispered, "Joven, you have taken on such a burden. You both must stay here tomorrow and rest."

"*She* is tired." I said. I ignored María's comment about Victoria being a burden.

Gertrudis, María, and I unpacked the horses and sent them out to pasture.

"¿Estarán seguros? Who is guarding them?" I wanted to know.

"No one," Gertrudis responded with an evil giggle. "Doña's reputation protects the horses!"

She pulled out a small pouch of tobacco and rolled a cigarillo.

"This pouch is made from el escroto, the scrotum, de un indio bárbaro." Gertrudis chuckled and applauded Doña María, the protector of the valley.

"It is not something I am proud of, pero, tengo razón," María said, shrugging her shoulders.

"And, the horses are safe?" I confirmed. "Sí, es verdad, tienes tus motivos. You have your reasons."

Pouring tobacco smoke from mouth and both nostrils, Gertrudis led us to dinner. The main room of the house was now quite dark except for the dimly lit cooking area near the fireplace.

"Don't step on the sleeping girl," Gertrudis warned. She went directly to the large fireplace and pulled a pot of boiled, tender lamb with chili, beans, and onions from the coals. She carefully set the pot out in the middle of the floor.

"Make a circle and sit down any place that pleases you. Every place is just as comfortable as the next," she chuckled in a whisper that sounded like the low hiss of a rattlesnake.

"As you see, the Don is a lazy man. He has never bothered with a table. We eat like peasants. If only he had remarried." Gertrudis passed out tortillas and clay bowls.

"This is true," sighed María. She looked at me, shrugged her shoulders, nodded her head, and poured the wine.

"Still he is a wealthy man. What difference does a table make? There are only two of you and a servant who live here," I said.

"When papá was younger, he spent his time and effort on building his flocks and fields. He lost interest in the house after mamá died. The house is small with three rooms. Don Chávez and I have our own furnished rooms. This room is a workroom, kitchen, and sleeping space for guests."

In the dark, I could see that the room was poorly furnished except for an odd assortment of cooking utensils carefully stacked on wool rugs placed at the edges of the fireplace. María cared little about the house herself. She spent most of the year outside overseeing the operations of her father's estates. She needed only a place to sleep, to shelter her from bad weather, and a strong place of refuge in case of attack. The house served these functions admirably. The fact that everyone blamed her father for the house's inadequacies suited her. He was responsible for something.

Gertrudis soon disappeared to attend to señor Chávez. María got up, closed, and latched the heavy wooden shutters. She added wood to the fire, sat back down, and talked about the hardships of her life without a mother. Her father was an easy man, for he expected little of her and nothing of himself.

"Except for reading and the basics of shooting—father taught me to do those—everything else I have learned, I taught myself," she said with a combination of sadness, frustration, and pride. "Sometimes I am worn out." She added that they had enough wealth in sheep and wool to hire Juan and Diego to help the genízaros plant and tend the wheat and barley. The irrigated land always grew abundant crops even when her father largely ignored the fields. "We have the best grapes in the valley. I will manage when he dies. I manage without him now."

"Victoria has mostly managed without her mother," I said. "If it were not for Bárbara...."

"¿Te acuerdas de tu madre? Do you remember your mother?" she interrupted

"Mamá Paula drew a picture of her for me. Otherwise, I would not remember her."

"I don't remember my mother at all. I don't even have a picture."

We sat close to each other in the dark, staring into the fire.

"It is good that my father remarried." I brushed her shoulder. "We are happy."

She took a deep breath. "I am always exhausted," she sighed. She watched me carefully in the dark. She continued, "It is an easy day or day and a half journey to the Griego's camp if one is healthy but Victoria is not. She must rest a day here."

"She will not do that," I warned.

"She will, if you insist, and you will insist," María ordered firmly. She leaned against me and placed her hand on my shoulder to stand up. She smelled faintly of gamuza.

"Let's make your bed." She pulled bedding down from a log rail that extended the length of the main room. She did not place my bed near Victoria.

"Gertrudis sleeps on a pallet in father's room. He often needs her during the night. No one will bother you." She rubbed her cheek against

183

mine. "Buenas noches." I could not see her leave the room, but I knew she was gone.

The room turned pitch black when the fire burned out. I tried to sleep but I had nightmares of mutilated men, Spanish and Indio. María's genízaro shepherd lay naked and dead in the fields with his flesh, blistered by willow switches, peeling from his bones. Cumanchi men stared blankly into the Llano until hungry birds pecked their lidless eyes out.

Jolted awake and shaken, I desperately tried to remember where I was. I sat in the dark panting in fear until the smells of mutton, beans, and gamuza reassured me that I was safe in María's house. For a moment, visions of María and Victoria lit the frightening darkness and erased the horrible nightmares from my head. I compared the two women. Victoria is a woman scarred by passion, I thought. Her wild self-destructive acts directed against herself fascinated and terrified me. María was different.

María rode better than most men did. She was a better shot than many men were, and she had killed many indios enemigos. Maybe Victoria and María were right. The Llano took everything it touched. Feeling desperately alone, I shuddered in the cold, black night.

Then, I thought about María's hair. Everywhere it was thick and black. María was young. She was alive. For a moment, I pushed the broken images of Victoria from my mind. Comforted by memories of the cool morning wind blowing through María's hair as she dressed more than a year before, I finally fell back to sleep.

Victoria

Full daylight filled the room. I lay still in the quiet and empty house. A cool breeze blew in through the open shutters. "¿Qué horas son? What time is it?" I wondered. I felt stronger than I had in months. I crept out the door in rumpled slept-in clothes smelling like horse and sweat. I shivered in the chilly morning. I had missed dinner. My stomach hurt from hunger and my cut, swollen lip pulsed. Shielding my eyes with my hand, I squinted in the bright sun. Gertrudis sat by her horno baking bread.

"Come visit, child," she cheerily called out. We sat together warming by her oven. "La Doña rode off with Diego and Tomás just as the sun came up," she informed me. "She oversees the cutting of the wheat and barley. It ripens slowly here in the mountains."

"She works very hard," I agreed. I put my hands into my gray hair. "Delgada, gris y sucia, thin, gray and dirty, I am filthy like an old buffalo hunter. My stench will put out your fire."

"You make a good joke," she cackled. "Maybe you will put out the fire, but señorita, you are La Milagra. They say your purity puts out the fires of hell." She laughed some more. "Me, I am not superstitious. Follow me to the hot spring where you can bathe."

184

She led me across the trampled and barren ground surrounding the house to a warm sulfur spring that bubbled into a rock-lined pool.

"Aguas negras. It smells like rotten eggs, but it smells better than you and it is warm and clean!"

She helped me undress. "Gracias." I stepped into pool. "Está caliente!" I gasped.

"You will get used to it, now stand still." She pulled coarse, homemade soap from a rock ledge and scrubbed my back. "Turn around. Stop." Squinting, she carefully examined my breasts. "You have a widow's scars."

"No, the scars del hacha de San Mateo, Saint Matthew's Axe," I challenged her.

"If you say so," she shrugged. She grabbed my top lip and examined it.

"Cuidao, agüela. ¡Que me duele! Grandmother, that hurts!"

"When did you do this? It should have been sewn."

"Two nights ago."

"Soak your face in the hot water or like my mistress, you will soon have scars everywhere."

"What do you mean?"

"You love the same men. You mourn the same deaths. You each scar in your own ways."

"It is true. Patricio was my brother," I said, studying her carefully.

"And Tomás, he is also your brother?" She squinted carefully at me, assessing my face for any hint of response. Smiling toothlessly, she meant to be kind, but she frightened me. She threw my clothing over a low-lying tree limb and beat the dust out with a stick.

"La ropa, como la gente, necesita aire fresco. Clothing needs to be aired out," she said. "Stay in the water and care for your lip. I must see to the viejo."

"Bruja vieja. Hag," I muttered glaring at the back of her head as she walked up the path and into the house to check on señor Chávez. What does she know about Tomás, I wondered. I felt instant sadness and regret, not for fear of losing my beloved, but at my habitual lack of generosity. Tomás, Doña, and Gertrudis each helped me. I should have been grateful and thankful.

"Que Dios me perdone," I said aloud. I soaked all my scars in the healing waters until hunger and the smell of baking bread overcame me.

I stood at the edge of the pool until the sun dried me. Dressed and clean, my skin faintly smelling of sulfur, I walked up the path toward Gertrudis who had returned to her oven.

"Gracias por el baño. You have been kind to help me," I said determined to atone for my earlier angry thoughts. "Agüela, I am very hungry. What do you have for a girl with a broken lip?" I smiled at her.

"The bread is fresh, hot, and soft. I will soak it in milk and honey. This is what I feed to señor Chávez. It is very good and easy to chew."

"Put mashed raspberries in it and I will eat it. If I do not eat soon, I will faint from hunger, and who knows, maybe fall and split my bottom lip."

"I can sew a fresh cut," said Gertrudis joining me in a good laugh. She prepared my breakfast then sat silently by her fire watching me struggle to eat. My lip bled into my breakfast. "That will never heal," she finally said. "I *will* sew it." She stood up, stretched, and went inside. She returned with a sharpened bone needle and rough cotton thread.

She spoke matter-of-factly, "Esto va a doler como el infierno. This will hurt like hell." She looked at me and shrugged. "Quítate la blusa. Take your blouse back off. We don't want blood on it. Find a comfortable spot and lie down."

I removed my blouse and lay down as she ordered. She hovered briefly over me, and then suddenly jammed her needle through my lip. Before I recovered from the first stick, she jammed the needle through the other side. I fainted. When I awoke, two rough cotton stitches pulled my lip together.

"¡Maldita, maldita!" I lay on the ground bleeding and panting.

She gently held my hand and smiled. "Jita, I know you just bathed, but you must soak again in the sulfur spring. It will keep away an infection. Keep your lip under the water as long as you can."

I undressed and sat back in the hot water and howled in pain as the water hit my lip. I soaked until my lip was numb.

After the second bath, I asked Gertrudis to help me pack the mule and saddle my horse.

"Are you leaving alone, jita?" she worried.

"When Tomás comes back, I will be ready," I lisped.

"Doña said that you would stay here and rest a day."

"We will leave today."

"You are rested then?" Gertrudis asked.

"Agüela, you worry too much. I am fine."

After she helped me pack, I found my carving knife, picked out a strong piece of wood, and sat down in the sun near the horno.

"Agüela, it is hard work to care for someone day and night. How do you do it?"

"Niña," she said, "do you ask why I take care of the old man, or do you ask why so many people have taken care of you? If you want to know about me, I am an old slave. I take care of the old man, and his daughter takes care of me. I have no idea why so many people take care of you, but you know!"

"I think I know why, but I don't trust my answer."

She studied me quietly then said, "You must trust." A breeze came up and clouds scudded across the sun. She pulled her worn rebozo around herself. "Septiembre, it starts to get cold." She reached for her tobacco pouch, rolled a cigarillo, and lit it from the horno. For a while, we sat silently enjoying the warm fire. I concentrated on carving a face into the piece of firewood.

"Doña and Tomás are coming," called Gertrudis, jumping up and startling me.

"Gertrudis, this is yours." I handed her the carving. "I saved it from the fire."

"Gracias, señorita. You are kind. I will keep it to remind myself of the possibility of salvation." She stood and gave me a gentle hug. "You will take care of María," she almost begged with tears in her eyes.

"María?" I asked, and then answered myself. "Sí, you mean Doña, but why would I take care of her. She will be here with you." Gertrudis said nothing and quietly watched Doña and Tomás ride up.

"When Tomás is ready we will leave," I said and stood slowly to greet them. "My horse and mule are packed."

"You are packed?" Doña was puzzled. "I thought you would rest a day. I was wrong. Tomás was right." Doña turned and spoke to Gertrudis, "It seems we are leaving today. Get me a fresh horse and bring a mule of your choice. Feed Tomás." The prospect of leaving her father and traveling several days journey into the mountains delighted Doña.

"I didn't know that you were coming." I brushed my thin hair back with both hands and fought off a flash of disappointment. "But I am glad," I managed.

"I will stay until Patricio's wake," she announced. "Gertrudis will care for my father. El viejo me hace sentir cansada. The old man makes me tired."

Doña was matter-of-fact. She dashed into the house to pack. Gertrudis and I stood in the yard eyeing each other nervously.

"You will take care of her!" Gertrudis whispered urgently.

"Agüela, as you know, I cannot take care of myself," I said shaking my head in dismay.

Gertrudis directed Tomás to the fresh baked bread and then went to the pasture to retrieve Doña's favorite horse and best mule. Growing tired, I sat down on the wall to wait. Tomás finished his bread then helped Gertrudis pack.

When Doña came, she was dressed for a fiesta. She had carefully floured her face and reddened her lips with alegria. Her black hair was perfectly tied in two long braids at the back of her head and held in place with her best tortoise shell combs. She wore a light brown dress of carefully bleached gamuza. Its full skirt allowed her to sit comfortably in her saddle. Her blouse, made from white cotton, barely clung to her shoulders. Her breasts glared from her short sleeves every time she lifted her arms. Her concessions to practicality were her knee-high riding boots, her ever-present rifles, and her bow strapped across her back. She pulled a pack mule with a week's worth of supplies.

Dressed like a cibolero or lancero, I wore a cuera, leather pants, chaps, and heavy knee-high moccasins. I wore ribbons instead of braids. Tomás, who had been quiet since returning from his tour with Doña, looked us over with a smirk on his face.

"It appears one of you is hunting and the other attending a wedding," he laughed and added, "The huntress is not the one I would have expected."

"Hombrada, manly, the men call me that too often. Today, I will not be mistaken for a man," Doña snapped.

"Not while dangling your breasts before our eyes." My voice was too sharp. Gertrudis' words about sharing and scarring now seemed a warning, but Doña was attractive and I could not turn my eyes. My trembling came back. I bit my cut upper lip. The searing pain blanked out every distracting thought. I screamed.

Startled, Doña grew red and scowled. "¿Y ahora qué?" she barked.

"I bit my cut lip!" I whimpered.

"Oh!" Her scowl changed to a smile.

"Victoria, perdóname. I am tired of being treated like a man. I want someone to see me as a woman just for a moment. I hope I have not offended you."

"Doña, you have not. I am also sorry. Eres hermosa! You are beautiful." I re-bit my lip.

"If you do that again, you will ruin Gertrudis' fine work." She tilted her head and smiled. Lost in thought, we rode single file along a narrow path skirting the fields and then into the dense forest. To ride with Doña María Josefa was not part of my plan. Quizá esto explique por qué mis padres no estaban preocupados—perhaps this explained why my parents were not worried about the pilgrimage. They knew Doña María Josefa! They knew she would come along.

She took my brother. She knocked me down. I never thought we would be friends. Yet, suddenly I found her exciting and attractive. Her bow strap divided and accentuated her breasts perfectly. I wanted to touch her to see if she was real. My curiosity left me confused and distracted. I understood what drew Tomás to her. I laughed aloud. Startled by my laughter, and exasperated by my strange behavior, Doña and Tomás frowned at me.

"No es nada, it is nothing," I said too quickly. "I am alive and this is good!" I thought for a moment then stared right at Doña's chest and blurted, "¿Hombrada, Doña, hombrada? Why would anyone think you are manly when God gave you perfect breasts?"

Doña pulled up her shirt and held a breast in each hand.

"When God first made these, they were just for beauty. They were good." Annoyed, she pulled down her shirt and stared sadly into the forest. "What is wrong with beauty just for the sake of beauty? The punishment of bearing children wears women out, steals their beauty, and kills them. God made children to kill us. It is written."

Doña's deliberate display of her breasts and her anger caught me off guard. It had never occurred to me that God deliberately punished women.

"Perhaps God does punish us, but still you are perfectly made," I reassured her.

"Victoria, gracias. I am fickle. I complain because no one has noticed that I am a woman. Then I complain because I am a woman. I have been foolish."

"You are not foolish. It is not easy to be a woman here. In the past, I was jealous of you because of your beauty and your skills with a rifle. You seem made for this place but I know I am not. Be grateful for who you are. I am perfectly happy with you. If I could only say this for myself."

"We are both fickle then," she smiled happily at me. "We are co-conspirators in fickleness!"

For the rest of the morning, when I looked at Doña, all I saw was her breasts. At least, when riding, the bow strap kept her shirt on! Tomás did not seem to notice her. He suddenly stopped.

"Time to rest."

Doña sounded vaguely surprised. "So soon?" She turned and stared at me, then quickly agreed. "We must stop ahora. Victoria get down from your horse now."

"I am dizzy." Her command was all the permission I needed to slide from Francisco and abruptly fall down.

"Don't touch her," Tomás warned Doña, "she gets angry when I try to help."

I lay at the edge of the path looking up at the trees. With every breath, dust filled my nose. The grass looked tall and the ants big. In a mostly blue sky, thunderstorms formed along the far away peaks. I held my breath and listened to the distant thunder. I like rain, I thought, then closed my eyes and listened to them whispering.

Doña spoke quietly, "Tomás, you live with too much!"

"She is no more a burden to me than your father is to you."

"Too much in common," Doña whispered to Tomás as she leaned over me. She ran her fingers over my forehead and straightened my ribbons.

"No new visible scars," Tomás whispered in my ear. "You are lucky the ground is soft."

189

"Bien. Estoy tan cansada. I am so tired—leave me here." I squinted up at them.

"We can't leave you in the middle of the trail." He picked me up. Doña knew the woods. She led us to a safe place hidden in the forest.

"Tomás, we have not gone far. We can take her home."

"María, she wants to go on. We have a good start. We will stay here." He lay me down in soft grass and put his coat under my head.

María, he calls her María just like Gertrudis, I thought. The old woman wanted me to take care of Doña, but I am lying here on the ground. I shook my head and fell asleep.

I dreamed that the devil had come to take me back, and that Doña loved Tomás. She swam with him in our pond on the río. I watched them but felt no anger. Suddenly, I was an old gray woman dressed in a worn, white pinafore sitting on a high hillside staring into the meadows below. Gertrudis sat down beside me.

"You love the same men. You wear the same scars, " she warned.

Then Bárbara spoke.

"First, remember all knowledge comes from forgiving." With a pine branch, she splashed water on my face.

I awoke to the gentle patter of falling rain. It was dark. Tomás and Doña built a shelter over me, but occasional drops of water seeped through and splashed my face. A warm fire burned nearby. Freshly cleaned fish roasted on willow spits. Hot tea water boiled in a copper kettle. Snuggled together in oiled leather, Doña and Tomás chatted happily by the fire.

I smiled and thought, I have brought them together over and over again. Perhaps this is my purpose, my fate. Like the old lady in my dream, I watched them for a long time before I spoke.

"Estoy seca. Gracias. Did you both have a good day?" I asked.

"Chica, you are back," Doña called to me. "You were very tired and you nearly fell off your horse. You have slept the day away, but no matter. We are not in a hurry. No one will worry if we are half a day late when you were already two days late." She kindly did not mention that she had asked me to rest a day at her house.

I stared at her with the confusion that comes from sleeping too long and dreaming too much. "It is good to see you both," I said. It was the most important thing I could think to say.

Pushing against Tomás, she mused, "You slept a long time."

"I dreamt a beautiful dream of forgiveness."

"What dream would that be?" María wondered.

"I dreamed of Eden before knowledge. I dreamed you found a good man." I studied Doña carefully. Neither she nor Tomás made any effort to move.

"You have become a mystic," she replied. "Come join us in the rain." She made a place for me between them.

Wrapped between the two, I gazed into the yellow and orange fire. Tomás and Doña cared about each other. They had no choice. They supported each other after the death of my brother and my illness the year before. Love is always good, I thought, no matter where or how it starts. I studied them both carefully.

"I would not be here without you. I am ashamed. I have made life hard for both of you."

"No, you are the one who led us here, and life is always hard," Doña reassured me.

Smokey and wet, we ate fresh trout and soggy corn bread with wine.

"Gracias a Dios for this feast," I prayed. The fire steamed and flickered.

"Soon it will snow. So, you see this rain is a good thing," Doña laughed, "It is not snow." She carefully got up and piled as much dry wood on the fire as she could find. In spite of the drizzle, the fire roared to life. She passed around her wine skins and began to sing.

"This is a song for Patricio. This is a song for his beautiful sister, Victoria, and her lover, Tomás." Making the lyrics up, she sang a song in the style of a Saeta. She sang a song of the lonely and solitary gypsy. Her voice trilled and broke.

I mourn the pains of life, but praise God
for my own life is blessed.
Giii-iitaaanos, semos giii-iitaaanos, en el campo pobre.
Tenemos vino. Tenemos pan.
Nos tenemos los unos a los otros.
We have wine, bread, and each other!
We have enough.

Tomás clapped and cheered her on. She stomped her feet and swirled. Her full leather dress fanned the flames. The rain suddenly stopped and the stars came out.

"María, you have chased the clouds away!" Tomás cheered.

"Now it will get really cold," Doña moaned.

I studied Doña and Tomás carefully. They traded barbs, small jokes, and affectionate glances. They touched each other without noticing or thinking. She had chased his clouds away many times.

"Tomás, Doña, thank you for this special night." We dried out by the roaring fire, and then made our bed.

"Sleep in the middle," Doña ordered. She curled against my right side and Tomás rested against my left. They fell right to sleep. Even after wine, I lay wide-awake. I watched the fire until it completely died away.

They let me come between them, I thought as coyotes howled and barked in the distance. No, no, I connected them!

* * * * *

For the second day in a row, I awoke alone and shivering with the cold. Doña, already dressed in leather trousers, shirt, and jacket, talked quietly with Tomás while boiling tea over a small fire. I sneezed. She glanced over at me.

"You are awake." She smiled, then ordered me out of my blankets, "Wash your face and hands and come eat. We cannot be late again today." She chuckled and added gently, "because of you."

"I promise that I will not make us late again today," I assured her. We ate breakfast, saddled our horses, and packed the mules. We rode higher into the mountains.

Thomas

The second day, without the complications of a dress, María Josefa rode with the agility and strength of a seasoned Cumanchi warrior. Her strong thigh muscles rippled through her leather riding pants. She was the relentless María who tracked down horse thieves. She was the María who shot off ears. Doña María Josefa was the curative tonic Victoria needed. María demanded life from herself, from everyone and everything she knew. She challenged Victoria to ride hard all morning. Trembling and sometimes wobbling in her saddle, Victoria rose to the challenge.

Shortly after noon, we stopped to rest near several small beaver ponds. Victoria was the first off her horse and the first to have her horse hobbled. Returning to her mischievous self of two years before, she stripped and splashed into the cold water challenging Doña and me to join her. María did not hesitate. She quickly pulled off her clothes and splashed into the water. Victoria jumped on her back and dragged her down. María pulled herself from Victoria's grip and with mock horror begged me to help her.

"Caballero, puede usted ver que seigo una damisela en apuros. ¡Ayúdeme! Oh knight, help this doncella."

"The water is too cold," I shouted back. I stood on the bank watching the two women who were so alike and yet so different.

"Pero, por favor, señor you must help me," María begged as Victoria wrapped her legs around her waist and clung to her back attempting to drag her under the water again.

"Not today señorita. I must watch the horses and mules." Tired, I sat down on the bank, pulled dried buffalo and hard bread from my pack, and chewed them slowly. I watched María and Victoria splashing. They had not been this happy in months.

"You must come into the water," Victoria pleaded impatiently.

"I will not come between you," I told her.

"You will never come between us," she insisted. "Por favor swim with us," she pouted.

"The two of you do well enough without me." I watched them a while longer then stood up impatiently and paced on the bank. We were hopelessly behind schedule, and the two of them were playing.

Suddenly, Victoria climbed out of the water shouting, "Semos indios bárbaros." She painted her face and chest with mud. She threw her clothes in her saddlebags, and tied the red and blue ribbons in her short, wet hair. Encuerada, naked, she jumped on her horse, and charged onto the trail.

"What are you doing?" I shouted after her.

"Riding my horse!" Victoria shouted back as she disappeared into the forest.

Laughing, María pulled on her leather and challenged, "Siga a la dama encuerada. Follow the naked lady. The one who captures her will have a fine slave." María pulled her mule up behind her, spurred her horse, and dashed onto the trail. I chased after her.

"María, I hope no one meets her on the trail."

"It would be the first time in years."

In the distance, Victoria darted through the trees singing. Francisco sensed his rider's joy, and he ran for her until he could run no more.

"She will pay with saddle sores and sun-blistered skin," I commented as though commenting mattered. With two mules in tow, María and I did not even try to keep up.

"One tired horse is one too many. She and Francisco will tire. We will find them soon enough," María reassured me.

We stopped at a cold stream to water the animals then pressed on toward the shepherds' camp. Thirty minutes later, we caught up to a fully dressed and washed girl with short gray hair and brightly colored ribbons, walking leisurely and munching carefully on dried corn bread. Francisco followed behind, playfully pushing her along with his nose. Victoria held out her arm signaling we were not to speak. We dismounted and walked quietly behind her. We walked on for another hour before she said a little prayer.

"Proclama mi alma la grandeza del Señor. My soul glorifies the Lord. Gracias por Doña y Tomás, y por la vida. Amén." She smiled, crossed herself, and then stretched her arms upwards toward the sky.

"Doña, you are a good and true friend." She pulled Doña to her in a gentle embrace. "¡Nada, nada, podrá cambiar eso!" She released Doña and grasped my hand.

193

"I will marry you."

Before I could answer, we walked out of the forest into a large grassy valley filled with Churra sheep. Dazzling sunflowers swayed heavily in the light wind. Overwhelmed by the sea of sheep, snowy mountains, green pasture, and sharp blue sky, Victoria abruptly stopped and clapped her hands.

"I made it, la mocosa, the shepherd's camp!" Smiling from head to toe she turned to me, "Querido, even Salomón in all his glory was not arrayed thus." She held her arms open and turned around slowly, embracing the flowers, the grass, the sky, and the mountains. She smiled and her eyes filled with tears. "Querido, sunflowers are like our love. They always come back. They are always bright. They reflect what is best in us. They know the sun is a simple blessing and are grateful for it. With each season of blossoms, we know we have loved for another year."

All traces of sentimentality suddenly evaporated into a wide, impish grin. "These souls *think* they are safe in heaven!" She pointed to the peaceful herd, jumped onto Francisco, and rode screaming like one possessed into the middle of more than a thousand sheep. The peaceful souls scattered, and a breach opened in their midst like the parting in the Red Sea. She spurred Francisco through the opening toward the camp on the north side of the meadow.

As Victoria cleared the way, María cheered and laughed aloud, "Es un milagro. Vamos, Tomás."

"Hermanos, we are finally here," Victoria shouted above the din of barking dogs doing their best to regain control of the bleating, scattered sea of wool. Alarmed and shirtless, her brothers scurried toward us with their muskets at the ready.

* * * * *

I had not seen Pascual since he brought Patricio's body home. I had met Felipe briefly the spring before. Felipe loved his independent mountain life and seldom came to San Mateo. He was tall. His hair was deep red and tied in a single braid. His eyes were green like his mother's.

"Tomás, we will roast a fatted lamb in honor of the returned prodigal sister and your first visit," announced Pascual. Pascual looked out across the meadow again filled with peacefully grazing sheep. "We will find a fat carnero with short horns. Follow me." We walked into the middle of the herd. Pascual quickly grabbed a plump lamb. "This one was born in February or March I think. Life can be short even for a lamb," he shrugged sadly, "especially for one that enjoys eating too much."

Pascual held the lamb by its front feet and lifted him from the ground into an upright position. He carried the unhappy and struggling animal into the woods away from the other sheep.

194

"I don't want to scare the other sheep. We must respect them. Hermana has scared them enough for one day," he whispered.

He transferred the lamb's back feet into his right hand, pulled out his pistol, and shot the lamb at the base of his budding horns. He quickly inserted his knife through the lamb's throat just below the jaw and under the ears. The tip of the knife jutted through to the other side. He pushed the knife forward, slicing through the lamb's carotid arteries. He twisted the head toward the lamb's back, and then cut the spine. He quickly cut away the tongue and removed the head. He hung the lamb by its hind legs to a tree. Its blood poured onto the ground as the sheep dogs with wagging tails gathered to lap it up.

Victoria suddenly appeared clad only in a leather loincloth. She carried the belduque given to me by Patricio.

"I will finish butchering the lamb. Pascual, show me what to do."

"La encuerada está loca. Wild women are the reason the priests complain," Felipe sighed shaking his head in dismay. "The itinerant priest complained of such behavior the last time he was in the valley. He said that los indios behave better than the Spaniards. He meant the civilized indios of the Pueblos."

"Personally, I see no reason why she should bloody and ruin her riding pants and leather shirt to satisfy a priest in Santa Fe. The reason we live on the Llano is because there are no priests," María scolded him with a hearty laugh. "Pascual, show her how to butcher the lamb. Imagine, the daughter of a sheep rancher about to marry, and she has never butchered a lamb!"

"If we are done worrying about priests, I will show you what to do," Pascual smiled at Victoria. "The greatest theological truth for me is my empty stomach."

He saw her scarred breasts for the first time. His face reddened and he trembled. He touched her torn lip. La criatura desnuda standing unashamed before him, reopened every nightmare, every terror, every raw pain, and wound of the last year. Suddenly, sobbing uncontrollably, he pulled her into his arms.

"I am *sorry* we didn't take better care of Patricio. We haven't taken good care of you either. Perhaps we are not a good family."

Felipe, María, and I watched nervously. María looked as though she might speak. Felipe and I touched her shoulders. The three of us remained quiet.

"We are a good family. What could you have done for Patricio? ¡Nada! As for me, you will teach me to butcher a lamb. You will make sure that I don't cut myself. I have plenty of scars." Victoria put her hands on his shoulders then stepped back and wiped away his tears.

With Pascual's help, she pulled the lamb's front legs toward her and cut the skin and wool down one leg and around the neck. They repeated the process with the other leg, and then removed the skin and hoofs. They cut out the organs, then cleaned and rinsed the carcass in boiling water brought by Felipe and María.

Pascual carefully set aside the animal's brains to boil and mash. "Tomorrow, we will use this to tan the lamb's hide."

When done, Pascual and Victoria walked quietly to the stream and washed away the lamb's blood, but neither could quite rinse away the sad odor of Patricio's death.

María and Felipe simmered the lamb in a large kettle of wild herbs, fresh onions, and dried chili. Steeped and partially cooked, they skewered the lamb with a large scrub oak pike and placed it over the fire to roast. María brought out her father's red wine. We pulled up chunks of wood and stones for chairs and soon sat down to dinner.

Pascual spoke gently to Victoria. "You have come to make a memorial and celebrate velorios for our brother, for yourself, and for your saint. Los Hermanos Penitentes heard about your wish for a monument. They have agreed to build a church. They have come for many weeks to make adobe bricks. Pascual and I've been helping them. There are enough to build a small chapel at the north end of the meadow. We have also cut trees for vigas y latías. Todos los materiales están ahí. Los hombres regresarán mañana para ayudarte. They will come tomorrow to help." He paused, "This is not just for you. People are slowly coming into the valley. There is need for a church."

Victoria carefully listened as her brother surprised her with the enlarged plan.

"I had no idea." She looked at me as though I had kept a secret from her.

Felipe spoke again. "One of the men who is coming is a santero from Truchas. This winter, he will help you carve the bultos, reredos, retablos, and church doors si quieres. Several families there weave. If you are interested, they will teach you to use a loom. You will need to live in Truchas for the winter." He added with a laugh, "You will have to stay dressed like a lady. ¿Qué te parece?"

"Pascual, this is unexpected. Tía Paula is my teacher and helper. She taught me how to carve and read," she paused and looked at me. "Tío Trent, he spoke to papá about marriage to Tomás. I told papá, 'yes.'"

"You said 'yes' to your father? Today you said that you would marry me, but this is the first time I've heard that you said 'yes' to your father!" I shook my head in excited confusion. I felt everyone staring at me. María appeared sad, but not surprised. Later she reminded me, "Last winter I said she would be well."

Victoria had no intention to go to Truchas. Still, her eyes had widened with the possibility. She stepped back, looked at me, and repeated her plans to her brother.

"Pascual, I intend to marry Tomás this fall."

"You must go if this is something you wish to do. Don't waste an opportunity. Still, I will miss you very much." I could not hide my sadness at the prospect she would be gone all winter.

"Tomás, you stood beside me for the last two years. I will only go if you go with me as my husband."

"How would that work?" I looked at her carefully. "We have no money. We would be poor and hungry. But please, you must talk this new plan over with your father."

Following Victoria to Truchas while she carved reredos and learned to weave seemed foolish. Still, if she wanted to go, her family had the money to send her, but I was not so fortunate. It was time for me to learn a skill so that I could make my own way. Perhaps I could work as Mr. Griego's secretary—did he need a secretary? I had been lost in thought for some time, when María kicked my foot. I nearly dropped my plate into the fire.

"My father and I sell wool to the weavers in Truchas. You could work for us," María offered.

"There is too much to think about right now. Victoria and I must discuss this alone. Unless, of course…of course she has decided to go in any case," I said.

"I will not leave without you. This is too important. We must talk by ourselves." Victoria turned and stared intently, the ribbons in her gray hair danced in the wind.

"I didn't come here to discuss living in Truchas. I have no interest in weaving," she said sharply. She changed the subject.

"Mañana we will start the chapel. Los Hermanos are right. There is need for a church in the valley. It will be a living memorial. Some days I am not so sure that God cares about us. Nevertheless, we build churches and worship Him because we feel better afterwards."

Felipe crossed himself and cast a look of alarm at Pascual. "Victoria, you will bring evil upon us if you do not watch your words. You spend too much time with the genízara Bárbara. She teaches blasphemy."

Victoria defended Bárbara. "God is not worried about her words, I am sure. It is the work of her manos y corazon that God cares about."

María stood and paced around the fire.

"Maybe a church will stop the devil, but will it stop the Cumanchis?" She spoke to no one and everyone. She spoke to everyone's fears.

Beyond the fire, a ring of darkness fully settled in. The coyotes and wolves stopped howling. Only María's sharp voice and the crackling of a dim pine fire interrupted the stillness. The thick forest near the meadow's edge disappeared in the darkness.

"So do we think God is up there?" María asked pointing vaguely at the sky. "Or maybe just at the north end of the meadow?" María thought quietly again before speaking. "Patricio was to marry me. God took him. In the end, God takes everything."

María and Victoria's irreverent talk made Felipe increasingly nervous. Shuffling from foot to foot in the Griego family tradition, he spoke. "We should sleep soon. Tomorrow will be a very hard day. The hut is small but everyone will fit on the floor. The fire will be warm. It is safe."

"No, es mejor debajo del cielo," said María reflecting what Victoria and I were thinking. "Better under the sky than in a crowded hut." She grabbed Felipe's hand. "Felipe, come walk with me to get water." The two sang as they disappeared into the dark.

"Sleep at the corner of the stone corral on the south side of the hut. El corral es seguro. Es como una fortaleza. It is a fort. The grass is soft and comfortable for sleeping," Pascual suggested.

"We should have set up camp in the daylight," I said as we felt our way back to the corral in the dark.

Victoria responded softly, "We found each other in the dark and we have found our way over and over again in the dark."

By touch and smell, we pulled out our buffalo robes, shook them, and spread them on the soft grass. We loaded pistols and rifles and placed them carefully within reach. We sat on the edge of our buffalo robe bed and listened to Doña and Felipe laughing and singing in the distance. Victoria's faint scent wafted over me. The heat from her body told me where she was. I pressed into her.

"Ella es más como una hermana para él que yo. She is more like a sister to him than I am," Victoria mused.

"¿Hermanos o novios? Lovers or family?" I asked.

"Hermanos. They are like family. Felipe is mostly a hermit. They dance and sing together," whispered Victoria, "but she only loves us."

"What do you mean she loves *us*?"

"Querido, wake up! Look how she watches you."

"You have seen how she watches me?" I asked. "Does she watch you in the same way?"

"Sí, she does. She watches us like a mother tecolote. Her eyes are big and her ears are wide. Her talons are sharp. She does not hide that she watches. She forgives my jealousy and my anger. She catches us in her full soft wings. She has always taken care of us." She continued softly, "We are the children she will not have, and we are the children she never was. When she takes care of us, she takes care of her dreams. Gertrudis asked me to watch over her, but I am too weak. Por favor, watch over her as you have me."

"Watch over her?" I asked. "How? As you say, she takes care of

198

us."

"Watch over her. Watch and pray." She insisted softly. She sighed deeply and put her head on my shoulder. "We have seen many night skies together. Each one is better than the last," she whispered.

"There is no night sky without you." I gently assured her. I peered into the darkness. "Victoria, if you are to be a great santera, you must go to Truchas without me. Perhaps while you are gone, I can work as a clerk in your father's trading business. I can speak and write good English and Spanish. We will marry when you return."

"Because of illness, I left you last winter but did not mean to. I can never lose sight of you again. I can't!" Victoria's voice shook. She let her tired body slump slowly into the blankets. She gently grasped my hand and softly begged, "Marry me. That is all I want."

"I will. I will."

María and Felipe suddenly appeared above the stone wall. Felipe wished Doña goodnight and then silently vanished into the darkness. When she could no longer hear his footsteps, María bumped against my arm and mumbled so that only I could hear, "He is only a brother."

"I know," I said.

"Doña, come to bed. I am cold. The three of us will sleep together like we did last night." Victoria's exhausted voice evaporated into the moonless dark. She said no more. Her arms and legs spasmed and jerked, and then she relaxed into the stillness of sleep.

"Good friends keep each other warm," María mused in a hushed voice.

We undressed and lay down with Victoria between us. María reached over Victoria's head, touched my shoulder, and whispered, "Why are we here?" She did not expect an answer. I could not explain it in any case. We drifted off to sleep.

A noise awoke me just before midnight. Low clouds hid the stars. In the meadow, the sheep bleated nervously. Victoria shook and moaned in her sleep, but did not awaken. Shirtless, María knelt over me, urgently pressing my shoulder. She silently pulled me up, then bent and carefully tucked the blankets back around Victoria.

"Get dressed," she whispered. "Hurry!" She pointed repeatedly toward the forest. She pulled on her leather trousers, cuera, leather jacket, and boots, and picked up her rifles and bow. Without speaking, I followed María's instructions. When dressed, I leaned down and gently kissed Victoria's forehead. The taste of her cool, salty skin clung briefly to my lips.

María darted into the cold, dripping woods. With my rifle in hand, I followed closely behind. Two practiced hunters speaking only with hand signals, we drifted noiselessly through the starless night. After twenty or thirty minutes, María suddenly stopped near the camino de herradura that crossed the mountains to Taos and Santa Fe. From the deep gloom to the south came the nervous, heavy sniffing of horses and unintelligible, muted voices of riders.

María dropped behind a row of fallen logs near the road and cautiously unstrapped both rifles and laid them out ready for use. I huddled beside her, my heart pounding in my throat. ¡Indios enemigos! Cumanchis headed by on the road to Taos. Straining in the darkness, I barely could see the outlines of their packhorses and mules.

When they were well past I nervously asked in a soft voice, "How did you know they were here?"

"I always listen," she responded with hushed confidence.

We followed them half a league through the forest until it was clear they had no intention of attacking our camp or stealing sheep.

"I hope that Los Hermanos and the Cumanchis do not meet on the road," I worried.

"The Hermanos are many and travel only in daylight. They will be safe. The Cumanchis are the ones who will be in danger if they don't clear the road by dawn. They know this. That is why they are hurrying through the dark."

We hid in the brush near the road without speaking for another half hour. I nodded off. María awakened me with a gentle squeeze of my leg.

"Vamos. Time to go."

I followed her as she picked her way carefully through the blackness back to camp. The darkness was as complete as the escape tunnel from Victoria's secret room. Reflexively I reached out for María, my hand landed gently on her back. She said nothing. I slid my hand into her leather trousers and grasped her belt. Moving as one, we skirted fallen logs and wild rose brambles as we found our way back through the cold night. María abruptly stopped and I ran into her. The moment seemed so familiar, were it not for the danger, I would have laughed. She stood still. Warmth radiated from her body. She turned slowly toward me. I started to move my hand from her belt. She stopped me.

"Don't move it," she begged. She carefully turned toward me. My hand slid across her hip, over the soft skin of her belly, and stopped at the front of her trousers. My fingertips just touched her pubic hair.

"Sometimes I am so tired of the wilderness. I want someone to hold me and to care about me. My father cares in his own hopeless way, but he is very old and very ill. Maybe he died while we were gone." She was matter-of-fact. "It is comforting to have people in my bed. Victoria moves violently in her sleep, but still, it is good not to be alone." She pressed her chest into mine, pushed my hand deeper into her trousers, kissed me, and then regained control of herself.

"Dios mío, perdóname, perdóname."

"Shh." I pressed my lips against her ear. She slid her hands inside my leather jacket. She was not ill, tormented nor trembling, but calm and comforting. We held each other until a faint dawn light glowed on the eastern horizon and crimson reflecting from the sky unmasked her face. I ran my fingertips across her rough lips, and then cupped her face in my hands.

"I know you even when I cannot see you. I know you as a hunter knows the deer he hunts."

"We know each other," she said. "*We* know!" She emphasized placing her hands briefly over mine.

Soon we were walking again. We arrived back in camp as the sun topped the trees on the east side of the meadow. Victoria still slept huddled in her robes. Smoke curled from the shepherd's hut. Felipe and Pascual had fired the horno to bake bread. Felipe arched his back, stretched, and scowled as we approached.

"Were you hunting?" With narrow, suspicious eyes, he carefully examined both of us.

"Para los indios bárbaros. We heard horses in the night and went to see," María replied.

"Why didn't you awaken me, Doña? I should have come with you. Instead you take a boy."

Her black eyes glowered. "There are only men and women in these woods. He is a good shot. I taught him myself."

"Still, you should have called me."

"Señor Felipe, I'm under no obligation to report to you or anyone!" María's voice briefly shook with anger.

"Los caballos, our horses?" Felipe panicked.

"Fool, the horses are where they belong. Not because of anything you have done, but because I was watching. I was awake."

Felipe chuckled nervously. The horses grazed quietly at the north end of the meadow. María dropped to her haunches, leaned on her rifle, and rubbed her hands over the fire.

"What about Los Hermanos? Are they coming today?" she asked casually.

Felipe replied, "They planned to leave at dawn." Felipe patted her head and turned away. "Call me next time. Bueno, breakfast, atole, sheep's milk and honey." As a second thought he added, "Everyone carries arms today."

"No te preocupes, I am always armed. You insult me," María scowled. "The next time I will call you if I feel like it, and today I will carry a knife in my teeth. All this to please you!" María dropped her head, curled her lips, and clenched her teeth. She pointed her finger at Felipe, cocked her thumb, and fired. Doña María would never call Felipe for help. Felipe knew that.

She smirked at me and muttered, "He worries like a brother. He pats me on the head and treats me like his dog or horse. We have known each other since we were little. He is a terrible shot. He could not hit a tethered deer at five paces. Why would I call him to help me?"

I shrugged, "Why would you?"

Chapter 16: Nuestra Señora de los Milagros

Thomas

In mid-afternoon, the men of the penitente brotherhood arrived. A few brought their wives. They led an impressive pack train of mules and horses carrying food and equipment. They had clearly committed to the hard work of completing the church in a short week's time. The Hermano Mayor established the ground rules in his opening greeting to Victoria.

"Ave María Purísima!"

"Sin pecado concebida. María, born without sin." She responded.

He asked for a cup of mint tea. Victoria anticipated his request. She had a heavy clay mug poured and waiting for him.

"Your health is good except for your lip," he commented.

"It is healing," Victoria blushed.

"It will leave a scar. Better to live and collect scars," he mused.

"Tengo munchas cicatrices. I have many scars," Victoria nodded in agreement.

"El tiempo es breve," he warned. Refreshed by his hot drink, he led his pack mule carrying his tools to the proposed building site. Victoria, Felipe, Pascual, and I followed him. María hung back. "Too much religion. Too many rules," she explained later.

El Mayor pulled some grass and chewed it. He surveyed the suggested building site. Then he spoke thoughtfully.

"Demasiado cerca del arroyo. La tierra estará siempre mojada." It was too close to the stream, prone to flooding, and not a safe place to build. He walked out of the meadow and up a short hill.

"Las rocas sobre la colina serán una base más sólida. We must follow the teaching of el Cristo and build on the rock. This is a church for the valley." He examined the hillside carefully. From time to time, he dug small holes to confirm the placement of the bedrock.

I carefully watched Victoria. She struggled to control the fine tremors in her hands. In desperation, she bit her fingers and hid her mouth with her hand. She looked at me with quiet frustration. Her eyes watered, then she abruptly turned away.

The Mayor paced off a relatively flat spot on the hill. He marked the front and rear of the church to correspond to heavy boulders in the ground that would serve as footings.

"Hay que cavar una trinchera del doble del ancho de las paredes para sentar las bases de las piedras." He carefully paced out the lines of the footings that were to be double the width of the walls. He was not a master builder, but he was an intelligent one. He built many small churches and chapels over the years. No church he built had ever collapsed or washed away in a rainstorm because of thoughtless construction near a small stream or arroyo. El Mayor stared briefly into the afternoon sun.

"Victoria, esta iglesia es tu idea. Está hecha en la tierra de tus padres con el dinero de tus padres. Pero va a ser una iglesia para el pueblo. Tu familia es muy generosa. Pero Dios ha sido misericordioso con ustedes. This church is your idea, built on the land of your family, with the money of your family. You are very generous. God has been merciful to you."

"Señor, es la verdad. The fact that I am alive is a miracle. Gracias a Dios." Victoria crossed herself.

El Mayor continued, "God does not look for us to remember the past, but to go forth with grace and thanks. Los muertos cuidan a los muertos, pero nosotros estamos vivos. The dead care for the dead, but we are alive. To name the church San Patricio, in honor of you brother, is to remember the past. The church must be built in your brother's honor but the people who worship here should look forward with thanks. The church should be called 'Nuestra Señora de los Milagros, Our Lady of Miracles.'"

"Sí, sí, señor, es una buena idea. Yes, yes, a good idea. We will call the church, 'Nuestra Señora de los Milagros.'" Victoria accepted the name change without question or dispute.

"What matters is that I will always have two places to remember Patricio. The village church where he lived in winter and the mountain church where he was a shepherd in summer. Whatever the names of the places, it does not matter. I will never forget him. That is all that matters. In truth, el Mayor is right. Patricio is gone. I knew that last night when I butchered the lamb. It is time to move forward."

Victoria was glad to be alive. For this moment, rejoicing was all that God demanded of anyone. "Naming the church, 'Nuestra Señora de los Milagros' captures the essence of joy, don't you think?"

"It captures your essence," I said.

"These people are here to help me. That is a profound joy indeed." She looked at me with her impenetrable eyes.

"Querida, they are here to help you, but they are also here to help themselves. They have come because you inspire them. You are the one who chose to live. They know this. They understand miracles and they know God's grace."

"These people are kind, but they don't understand that I first wanted to die. They would not approve of me if they knew this. This time, I lived because I chose to. Next time I may not have a choice."

"Death usually comes when we do not have a choice, but you dismiss the miracle of your life so carelessly." María walked up with a rifle in both hands and one strapped to her back. "So you see, jita, it is a miracle, you chose life, and here you are. This church is a grand celebration of your birth. Find joy in this. Now, we have solved this problem of miracles," María ended the conversation and turned to me.

"Tomás, with the permission of your lady we shall find a nice deer for tonight's dinner. I think we'll soon be tired of mutton. Here is your rifle."

"Victoria, with your permission?" I asked.

"Doña, take care of Tomás. I know you love him as he loves you, and I love you both." Before either of us could speak, she turned and walked away. "I must help build a church. Bring back a large deer." She called over her shoulder, and then sang happily as she walked back to the building site. The ribbons at the back of her head blew wildly in the breeze.

Across the meadow, the men and women cleared the ground for the new church. María and I walked into the trees. Moving as one had become second nature to us, but today María nervously tripped over her own shoes. Victoria's parting comments had left her as shaken and confused as they had me. When the noise from camp faded away and the forest enveloped us, she regained focus. The wilderness calmed and strengthened her. Always the huntress, she knew the woods and guided me through them with hand signals. We quickly came to the edge of a clearing filled with beaver ponds.

"Deer come here to drink," she whispered carefully scanning the forest.

She checked the direction of the wind and her powder, and then crouched behind a large log to wait. Worried about Victoria's comments, I awkwardly avoided sitting too close to María and settled down behind a log a few feet away. Fidgeting, she glanced at me. She said nothing, but her haunted eyes and stressed face told me she understood why I kept my distance. Thirty minutes crawled by in tense silence.

Four deer approached. Focusing only on the deer, María and I were suddenly shoulder-to-shoulder. On some unheard and unseen cue, we carefully cocked our rifles with one soft click. The deer stood still. Pop! Pop! Two deer fell. Panic stricken, the others ran wildly into the woods. María gently touched my shoulder then handed me the rifle she had just fired. With the loaded rifle at the ready, she crept cautiously towards the backs of the two deer lying in the meadow. She examined each one carefully from two-rifle length distance. Neither was breathing. It was safe to approach them.

"How did you know which one I would shoot?" She asked.

I laughed, "The biggest. I chose the lightest one for us to carry."

Annoyed, she offered, "We'll clean yours first then."

"My honest answer isn't what you wished to hear. Perhaps you wish to clean them both while I head back to camp!" I snapped at her.

"¡Estás muy enojado! You are angry. I have insulted you. I did shoot the biggest one." She began to cry. "Victoria is right. I love you. I am so sorry. I am so sorry!"

She stood in the middle of the forest like a little lost girl begging someone to take her home. Utterly confused and unable to move, we stared at each other until she spoke again.

"I am so sorry I spoke inappropriately. This is not my character. Forgive me." For the third time, she asked me to forget something she did or said.

"María, there is nothing to forgive and I won't forget," I paused, "Let's clean your deer first."

She smiled half-heartedly, put down her rifle, and folded her leather jacket.

"Neither you nor the priest will need to worry about my behavior. I will ruin my shirt and leather trousers before I tarnish *your* reputation." She pulled out her knife and walked to the deer I had shot. "Help me turn this animal on its back."

I said nothing and pulled off my coat. We rolled the deer over. While I pulled hard on the bottom legs, María cut a line down the deer's center, around its udder to its pelvis. She opened the abdomen and reached in to pull the intestines and organs free. We then turned the deer on its side and poured the organs out. We cleaned the second deer in the same way. Finally, we cut off their heads to lessen their weight, and then hung them up to drain.

Exhausted and covered with blood, María stood up and arched her back.

"You are a sloppy butcher. This is something you and Victoria have in common." I teased her gently.

"If that is all we had in common it would still be too much. Pero, hay más, we have Patricio, we have you, and above all we are the lonely tares left in the Llano to burn. All we ever dreamed and hoped for is to be brought, like wheat, safely into the master's barn." She dropped her head and forgetting the condition of her hands, pushed them across her face smearing herself with blood and gore.

"I will help you wash." I gently picked her up and carried her to the water's edge. I set her down. "You are precious," was all I could think to say. She bent down to splash the cold water on her arms and face.

"It is too cold," she gasped and hurriedly finished. Her teeth chattering, she knelt beside the water.

206

"I will not forget what you said to me today," I promised her as I leaned into the water to clean my hands.

"You have forgiven me then?" she asked hopefully.

"There is nothing to forgive." I took her hand. She tightly clasped my fingers. Hand-in-hand, we walked slowly back to collect our rifles and jackets. We tied both deer to a dried aspen pole, and struggled with them back to camp. A young woman ran up to examine the smallest doe.

"The fur is so soft," she said carefully touching it as though it was still alive.

"I will help you skin them. The hides are yours. It is my gift," María offered.

The deer skinning done, the other women prepared the venison for dinner. The Hermano Mayor supplied red wine. Everyone gathered around the fire, to sing, drink, dance, and tell stories.

As the fires died out, the Mayor posted watches. We had never taken this precaution, but we did not complain that someone else now did. The others camped on the new floor of the church surrounded and protected by piles of brush and trees cleared away earlier in the day.

In the corral, we climbed beneath our warm buffalo robes, and watched the night sky. Victoria put her head on my shoulder. María rested her head on Victoria's breasts. Victoria counted falling stars and occasional distant lightning flashes.

"My dreams haunt me," Victoria whispered. "¿Te acuerdas de tus sueños? Do you remember your dreams?"

"I often dream that I have been left alone on the Llano to die." I said. I tried to forget the gruesome dream of mutilated men I had while at María's.

"That is my dream too, that I am left to die alone on the Llano. I dream this over and over," whispered Victoria. "Gertrudis would say these dreams are some of my scars."

"I have had such dreams too, but I don't give in to them," María mused softly.

"There is nothing wrong with me then?" Victoria sighed with relief as she drifted to sleep.

María nuzzled into Victoria. She studied me carefully in the darkness.

"Gracias por un día perfecto. Nunca lo olvidaré. I will not forget it," she whispered.

Soon Victoria and María breathed softly in the unison of contented sleep. I listened to the distant, muted rush of the stream, and the hushed flapping of an owl's wings.

The next day, the work of building began in earnest. The men and women quickly dug a trench down to solid rock, then heavy stone footings were laid on top of the granite rocks embedded in the hillside. Adobes, stacked since early spring, were laid after the footings were completed. The adobe walls went up quickly.

Chapter 17: Velorios y La Misa de Cabo de Año

Victoria

The church construction was almost done. Months of careful planning by the penitentes and the work of my brothers made it all look easy. The adobe bricks quickly became walls. Heavy timbers became lintels to frame windows and doors. Vigas y latías turned into a flat roof with a gentle slope and canales to drain the water. Women plastered the inside and outside with mud and whitewashed the interior in yeso. Through the construction, the Mayor kept me at his side.

"You are the real boss here," he said. "I am glad you chose to speak through me. The work has gone well. I hope this brings you brief happiness."

"Happiness is always brief, señor. I cannot thank you enough, and I am pleased with the name you chose. It is fitting."

"We have many bricks left over, enough to make a small tower. Maybe one day your father will find a bell."

"Gracias, Mayor, gracias. You have done so much more than I ever could have. I came intending to build a pile of stones and to place a cross on top of it. Instead, we have a church. I never thought this would happen."

"We have two miracles then," he replied, gently crossing himself. "You are alive and there is a new church. God must be pleased."

Thomas

According to the Mayor's plan, we completed the work on September 20, the eve of San Mateo's feast day. The labor done, everyone ate, sang, and danced until dawn. On the morning of the feast day, the church was open for use, but not blessed or consecrated since no priest was available. The Hermano Mayor serving as a resador began the morning with a prayer of thanks for the rising sun.

"Thank you God, for our brother sun.
He warms the day and strengthens everyone." He continued:

"God of mercy, you chose San Mateo, a tax collector, to share the dignity of the apostles. Mateo was a common man, a man despised for his occupation and station in life. We are not despised, but our station is lowly. Our country forgets us, but Mateo does not. San Mateo, the patronal saint of Victoria De La Cruz Griego y Lucero, returned her soul to us. She walks with us. She remains a servant and helper to all who live in her village. Victoria reminds us that all life is miraculous. Ave María, bless us San Mateo, bless us Jesús, Gracias a Dios, Amén."

The Mayor paused then concluded. "This new church is now called, 'Nuestra Señora de los Milagros, Our Lady of Miracles.' We are very few people, and Santa María never fails us. We are also indebted to San Mateo. He will have a special place in the Church.

"It is right to celebrate a mass on the first anniversary of a person's death. That day is still about a month way, but we are gathered here now, all of us. There will not be a priest in a month and there is not a priest now, so we celebrate Patricio's life anyway. Patricio was a good man, a good son, and a good brother He was the Governor's best soldier. He would have been a good husband and father. That is all we need to say of his life, and that we miss him. To say more is unnecessary. It is time to move on."

With that, he signaled the special procession to begin. A shrill flute and deep drum led out. The men carried the cloaked carving of San Mateo into the church and placed it on a large stone on the floor that served as a temporary altar. When the cover was pulled back, everyone gasped in surprise then grew silent. San Mateo, with detailed face, hands, and feet and with a very small axe that could injure neither him nor anyone else, stood solemnly in front of us. I had not seen the finished work myself. With everyone else, I reflexively crossed myself.

The Hermano Mayor continued, "We now see the third miracle. This carving nears perfection."

"A lot of money was spent on this santo, there are so many poor," an older woman spoke disapprovingly.

"Silencio señora, the santera who carved this memorial stands among you." At first, no one spoke, but then everyone chattered in amazement.

The Mayor stopped them. "This is the work of Victoria de La Cruz. We have this fine statue and a person with the talent to make many more. This is a blessed day. We are truly grateful, amén."

The Mayor then led the group in songs of praise to thank San Mateo for his role in saving Victoria's life. Patricio was again eulogized. The moment was bittersweet. An unstoppable cycle of hurt and pain, of endless hardships and deaths, marred the year since Patricio's death. Victoria and María held hands and cried quietly for Patricio one last time. The prayers and songs concluded, a lock of Patricio's hair was buried in

210

the church floor and the burial spot marked with small pebbles in the shape of a cross.

The velorios done, the Hermano Mayor announced a two-day holiday. "It is time for the competitions. Today we play games. Tonight we feast and dance. Tomorrow we rest and the next day we depart."

"Tomás," María called me to her, "cuñao, we will make the games. I will buy two Griego lambs to give to the winner. Come with me." Thinking aloud, she picked up a shovel and walked into the middle of the meadow.

"We have no chickens here. We must find a substitute."

"Chickens?" I asked.

"Sí, sí, chickens. Watch." She found a sturdy, thin piece of dried scrub oak and buried it in the ground leaving a small portion exposed. "This is the chickens head," she said.

"This tree is our target." She marched three hundred paces across the meadow to a tree with a large X carved into its bark. She pulled a piece of old cloth from her pocket and tied it to the tree just above the X.

"Follow me. I will tell you the rules. You must pull the stake from the ground, secure it to your horse, and then from beneath the horse's neck or belly, shoot an arrow into the middle of the target. The first one to do all this wins the sheep. If I do this, you will kiss me since I cannot win my own sheep."

"Then we will both be disappointed," I laughed, "You have made an impossible task."

"We shall see." She confidently led me back to the breakfast fire.

"Ahora, los juegos. The games," she announced. "The winner will take two lambs home from the Griego herd. I will pay for the lambs." Without mentioning a kiss, she repeated the instructions she had given to me to everyone else. She concluded, "I will be last. The game ends when I pull the stake and hit the target or someone before me does. If I pull the stake, and hit the target first, no one will get a lamb. I will get nothing no matter who wins." She looked at me briefly with a squint and the slightest smirk, and then quickly turned away before anyone noticed. "If there is a tie, those who tied will play until there is a clear winner. ¿Preguntas? No? Men and women, prepare your horses. The Hermano Mayor and señorita Victoria are the judges. Their decision is final."

The young woman who helped skin the deer was the only woman who joined in the competition. Everyone wagered on the game. Heavy bets were placed on Doña and a young lancero named Miguel.

I had never pulled the stake or chicken before, but I was good with the bow. I carefully cinched a rope around Viejo's neck to steady me while I fired. He stomped the ground in excitement. He knew that the placement of the rope meant a competition or battle.

211

As I prepared Viejo, Victoria slipped up behind me and whispered, "He is a good horse. I think he will win for us, don't you?"

"He has done this before, but I have not."

"Then querido, trust him. Let him do what he does best. Let him run without your guidance. He will take good care of you."

She pulled a blue ribbon from her hair and tied it to the saddle.

"Querido, you are my knight. If you are to marry me, we must have sheep. This is to be my dowry." She kissed me and ran to stand by the Hermano Mayor. The other young women teased her.

"Victoria, you have a favorito. Don't cheat for him."

She shouted back, "I am a gray-haired old woman. What would that young man care about me?" Chuckling, the Hermano put his hands on hips.

"Señoritas, if this old woman cheats, I will have to spank her like a child." Everyone joined the Hermano Mayor and laughed at his new joke. Feigning indignation, Victoria curtseyed to her friends and to the Hermano.

A pistol popped. It was Doña. "There are ten riders. We will draw lots for the first three riders. They will then determine who goes next. I will go last."

Miguel lost the draw. The others placed him in the ninth spot fearing that if he rode first he would win before they even had a chance to play. I was chosen to go fourth. It was an advantage to be an Anglo. Everyone assumed that I could not ride.

"As soon as the first rider has fired an arrow, the second rider must start out. Go!" María yelled.

The first rider spurred his horse toward the stake. He bent down to pull it from the ground. It did not budge. The rider did not let go of the stake soon enough and was pulled from his horse. He jumped up immediately, but his nose was bleeding. The next rider, the señorita, experienced a similar fate. At full gallop, she transferred her full body to one stirrup, bent down to grab the stake, but found herself quickly jerked from her horse by the apparently immovable wood.

The Hermano stopped the competition and went to see if the stake was too deep. He carefully stepped over the fallen rider and tested the stake. It was easily movable.

"Señorita, if I touch you, you are disqualified. ¿Estás bien? Will you be okay?"

The dazed young woman struggled to her feet.

"Señor, I will win this on my next turn!" She proclaimed slurring her speech and wobbling drunkenly.

"As you say," he shrugged. "This is a dangerous game. Buena suerte."

As she staggered off the course leading her horse behind her, the next rider came barreling for the stake. He easily pulled it but quickly overran the target without firing his bow. It was my turn. I missed pulling the stake, but easily hit the target. One by one, each rider failed to accomplish the assigned tasks. Finally, it was Miguel's turn. He quickly pulled the stake. His arrow hit the target dead center, but the stake fell from his horse disqualifying him.

With her mouth full of arrows, Doña María Josefa mounted and spurred her horse to the stake faster than any previous rider. Unconcerned with the possibility of injury, she deftly hooked her left foot through the rope around her horse's neck and slid below his belly. She pulled the stake with both hands, and then without slowing, she tucked it safely under the saddle horn with one hand while, with the other, she un-slung her bow. Galloping on at breakneck speed, she fired her arrows. Her bravura performance ended, she trotted back to us smiling. We all ran to check the target. She had hit it twice. The competition was over. Everyone except Miguel was relieved by her quick victory. No one else wanted to ride the course again.

Victoria ran to me pretending to be horribly disappointed, "You have lost my dowry. We will never marry!"

"Victoria, I will give you all the sheep you need to marry this man," María teased. She then called everyone to her, "Oye, today two brave fools fell from their horses—I will give them each a lamb. It has been a good day. No one was seriously injured."

María discretely pulled me aside, smiled, and whispered, "You owe me a kiss. I promise to collect."

Chapter 18: The Duel

Victoria

Late on the afternoon of the velorio, Diego and Juan brought the sad, but expected news that Doña's father died. The news of his death was not all, however. Upon finding the house defended by a dead man and his old slave, the Cumanchis pillaged it.

"Had I known, I would have killed them several nights ago." Doña raged. "I must return home at once. Tomás, you are coming with me." Doña gave orders and expected that everyone would follow them.

"Victoria, es tu iglesia, es tu monumento. You must stay here. You will not be alone. Your brothers will be here. My men will come to escort you back in the next week or so. Tomás is very good with a rifle and bow. He is coming with us. We leave in an hour."

Tomás frowned and gave me a curious, confused look. Felipe and Pascual agreed with Doña's plan.

Felipe spoke. "Hermana, this is your dream. It is now the dream of many. You must stay and discuss the completion of the reredos. This is your work. You will become, no, no, you have become the new santera. Pascual and I must watch the flocks. We will watch after you. You will be safe."

Felipe turned to Tomás. "Tomás, Doña insists that you can shoot. I have to trust her. I have also seen you with a bow. I will give you my extra rifle. You each will have two rifles and two shots. Que nuestro Señor los acompañe." He went into the hut and returned shortly with his rifle.

"Felipe, I want to go," I stomped my foot in anger. "Felipe, I am not a child!"

His face turned deep red and he refused to look at me. "Then do not act like one. Victoria, you have responsibilities here."

Stung by his harshness, I stepped backwards and tripped on a large rock. Doña grabbed my jacket and quickly steadied me.

"Victoria, when you are done with the work here, I will send Juan and Tomás to bring you back," Doña reassured me.

"Adiós, Doña. You must take care of Tomás."

215

"No te preocupes. I *will* take care of him."

"Tomás, you must take care of the señorita that you and Gertrudis alone call María. I promised Gertrudis. O, Dios mío, Gertrudis may be dead."

Tomás kissed me, and then mounted Viejo. "Querida, te quiero. You are my only love. I will take care of María. We will find Gertrudis, I promise you." He leaned down from his horse to touch my gray hair.

"Sí, lo sé. I know. Be careful. I never wanted to lose sight of you again, yet I am."

With darkness only a few hours off, Doña and Tomás accompanied by Juan and Diego rode quickly southeast and out of the meadow. It took us a day and a half to ride the distance from Mora. They intended to make it in one night.

The next few days went by quickly. Two days after Tomás and Doña left, the Hermanos packed up the camp and loaded their mules. Before he left, the Hermano Mayor begged me to come to Truchas for the winter.

"Señorita, your carving is very good. Come to Truchas to finish the reredos. There are many carvers in Truchas who are very good, but you have much to teach them. Consider spending the winter with us. There is a poor viuda there who could use the company and the money of a boarder."

"Tía Paula will help me with the reredos when I am safe at home in San Mateo." I studied him carefully. I felt my face redden. He provided so much and I was turning down his request that I help his village. "Señor Mayor, I cannot teach anyone to carve santos. I am young and not very good. I will disappoint everyone." Pushing up mounds of dirt and pine needles with my feet I added quietly, "I wish to marry."

"Señorita, you are good enough. You know more about carving than anyone in Truchas! I believe that you have a Christian obligation to share your knowledge."

"Pero," I paused shaking my head, "I plan to marry Tomás. I would like to wait to make a final decision until I speak with him again."

The Mayor ignored my marriage plans. "Senorita, think about this. Your father would forgive you for not going home now. He would understand this since Truchas is a hard ride from San Mateo. Before the snows are too deep, he will come again across the mountains to trade. He could bring your things when he does."

"¡Perdóneme! Pero señor, I cannot make this decision without my beloved. I cannot."

"Señorita, you will lose much in marriage. You must teach. In return, the santeros and carvers will help you finish your church."

"Señor, I am growing old too quickly. Many young women marry by twelve and fourteen years. I am fourteen and have the hair of a very old woman. I wish to marry. Tía Paula will help me with the carving. I will marry her son, and then work with her to complete the church furnishings."

"Your good friend Doña is not yet married. Perhaps you should wait until she marries."

"She is not happy, but señor, you flatter me with your insistence." I curled my healing upper lip, half-smiling at his efforts.

He shrugged. "Next summer you will come then? Do not forget. We have much to learn from you. Next summer," he insisted. "¡Tienes que prometerme! Promise!"

"You flatter this frail old woman," I said meekly. "If Tomás agrees, we will come. That is all I can promise."

"¡Niñita!" he corrected me gruffly. "If you come, we will arrange a house for you. Please come." He held out his arms. I stepped into his fatherly embrace. He patted my back with his strong hands. "Un milagro, gracias a dios." He stepped back and marked the sign of the cross on my forehead. He saluted me, walked quietly to his horse, and mounted.

The Hermanos, their wives, their packhorses, and their mules soon disappeared into the forest. Alone, my brothers and I stared at the hollow shell of a new church sitting on a hill overlooking a meadow of grazing sheep.

"We built a ghost church," Felipe mused to Pascual. "It is an empty building guarding a vast wilderness."

"Felipe, you are wrong. I am sure," I tried hard to cover my disappointment. "In time we will furnish it with paintings and carvings. Perhaps one day it will even have window glass."

"Someday, someplace, the wilderness ends," Pascual encouraged me. "I believe it will be here."

The cottonwoods along the stream shimmered with a hint of yellow. On the slopes high above the hut, the flickering gold of aspen mingled with the varied greens and blues of pine and spruce. I walked slowly through the sheep, and then climbed the hill where the church now overlooked the meadow. The church completely and dramatically changed the fall landscape. Its presence pushed the boundaries of civilization further into the wilderness. The building was small. Still, on its hill it towered over everything else. It smelled new and fresh, but it remained haunting in its emptiness. There were no parishioners to come and go to mass, and no feet to wear a path to the door. I remembered the dream at Doña's in which I stood on a hill watching tortured humanity below. The church took that burden away from me. It would do the watching.

Exhausted, I wandered into the holy place created at my insistence and sat on the floor. No benches, no altar screen, not even a crucifix, I thought. The sole furnishing was the carving of San Mateo.

"How will I ever finish this?" I shouted, surprising myself. "There is too much to be done. It is impossible!" My voice echoed off the barren, freshly whitewashed walls. A single candle left by the Mayor flickered as though trembling in response to my despair.

The walls were an empty canvas, white like lilies. Lilies, lilies, I suddenly remembered, they neither toil nor spin. I had nearly forgotten all that had been accomplished since the beginning of September. The Mayor was correct. Memorials are built for the future, but in this moment I could not know or grasp what future my memorial would address. If building the church suddenly seemed foolish, it was because in my own human arrogance and vanity, I could not imagine it ever being used in this dangerous place.

"Patricio, forgive my stupidity, la vanidad!" I moaned, "Que Dios me perdone."

Alone in the darkness, I pondered my life and my worth. I was a woodcarver, a maker of holy statues, but had I lost Tomás even as we discussed marriage? He had always been there for me, but I had not been there for him or anyone for the last year. Without him, my life was as empty as the newly completed church. Exhausted, I knelt down on the floor in horror, clasped my trembling hands, leaned against the cool wall, and rocked myself to sleep.

Thomas

The winds change quickly on the frontier. I knew this the first time I saw a fire on the Llano. One day I was helping build a church. The next day I was riding with María, not to Mora, but to Taos to confront a small band of enemigos Cumanchis who had looted her dead father's house. We headed southeast out of the shepherd's camp. When well out of sight of the camp, María veered northwest and revealed her changed plans. María knew the mountain trails well. She led us quickly through the darkness toward Taos.

"Do not talk, just listen for danger," she ordered. A weak half-moon occasionally lit the forest path, but mostly we rode quietly through unrelenting, deep shadows. At midnight, we dismounted. María led us off the trail and up the middle of a stream for half a mile. She took us deep enough into the woods to hide us from casual riders. At daylight, if someone wanted to find us, he would have to decide whether to go upstream or downstream.

We quietly unpacked our exhausted horses and tethered them. We transformed our saddle blankets and saddles into beds. We posted no guards. Juan and Diego, fearless and clearly comfortable outdoors went to sleep immediately. The morning before, they had no idea they would spend their next fourteen hours on a horse. They too understood the wilderness took them where it wished.

After the others fell asleep, María moved her blankets to my side.

She whispered, "Victoria won't mind." She went to sleep with one hand on her rifle and her other hand on my leg.

María awakened us early. Furrowing her brow and squinting at us she thought aloud, "Los indios regresarán por este camino. We will stop them and take back anything they may have stolen."

"Eso es peligroso. ¿Estás loca?" Juan protested. "They probably sold everything in Taos."

María challenged, "Is it too dangerous for ten sheep apiece?"

"I am bought easily. It is a good fight too. I am with you," affirmed Diego.

"Well, I have no wife. If I were to own sheep, I might persuade someone to marry me, perhaps you Donseya," Juan laughed, "But of course, all the wealth in the world did not help your father with a wife."

"You flatter me and insult my dead father at the same time, señor," María placed her hand across her forehead in mock pain. "I will not marry you, but I promise to help you find a wife."

"Good enough! You are a gentlewoman."

"María, Juan and Diego may be satisfied with sheep, but I want to live, and I don't have a place to keep sheep, and I soon hope to marry," I objected.

"Of course you do not need sheep or a wife, and I did not offer them to you. I will think about this carefully," she said. "I will think about what it will be. I will pay you well." With everyone committed to staying, María laid out her plan.

"The Cumanchis must stop here for water. We will wait for them."

Doña put on her leather armor and tucked two pistols into her belt. She carried her bow and full quiver on her back. Armed with two rifles each, bread, and water for sustenance, we set our ambush along the trail. The truth was that no one was sure los Cumanchis would return by the same road. For María it would be a miracle if they did. The rest of us thought it would be a miracle if they did not.

"We will wait a day," María promised, "If los Cumanchis do not appear by sunset, we head home."

Within an hour after our arrival, María's miracle occurred. A small party of los Cumanchis appeared on the trail.

"Wait here, I will speak to them first." She jumped from behind her rock and walked directly toward the capitán carrying one rifle, her other rifle and bow strapped over her shoulder. She aimed her first rifle. Crack! The shot reverberated through the woods. The capitán's ear flew off. Before any of los indios could respond, she aimed her second rifle.

"¿Quién robó mi casa? Who is the guilty one?" She aimed her rifle at the leader. He held the side of his head where his ear once was. She demanded, "Tell me who is responsible, ahora!"

Ignoring her threats, everyone but the capitán slowly plodded by her. From the hillside, we saw that the riders were covered with the telltale heavy rash of smallpox. Matters of honor were not at the moment their business. Outraged by so many ignoring her, María's face and neck grew red with a rage I had never seen in her. She turned her full fury to the chief.

"¿Quién robó mi casa?" She screamed again aiming her rifle. The chief knew and understood matters of honor and revenge. He understood this was personal and she was acting alone. We watched silently from our hiding places hoping she would not be killed or injured.

"You have dishonored my father's house. You have desecrated a dead man. You took my dead father's things. ¡Te voy a matar!"

"You, with the reputation for stealing dead men's spirits and sight, worry that we took a few possessions, a few simple things, from the house of a man who had the rare privilege to die in his own bed and at the end of his time. Señorita, usted se llevó mi oreja. Eso es suficiente. You have my ear, that is enough. We are both even for now."

"You have taken my reputation. You have stolen my spirit," she challenged, her voice only slightly more controlled.

"Doña," he called her by her title and reputation. "Your anger damages your spirit. Your anger blinds you. Tenemos viruela. Vamos a volver al Llano a morir. My friends and family have smallpox. I am taking them home to the Llano to die."

Blood streamed down his right cheek. He made no effort to stop it, but rode quietly by with his back erect and head high. María kept him in her rifle sites. After they disappeared into the forest, she fell to her knees frantically crossing herself.

"Gracias a Dios, I have escaped death twice in one day. They had smallpox! I have forgotten my own lessons. He is right. My anger blinded me. I did not see the pox until he warned me."

We followed her back up the stream to the horses. No one spoke. We rode slowly through the forests to avoid overtaking the Cumanchis who would soon be dying beside the road. Unless we could by-pass them or stay out of their sight, we would never get back to María's ranch.

We tracked them at a safe distance into the late afternoon. When it began to rain, the Cumanchis pulled off the trail and into the trees to rest. Hidden by the heavy rain and gray mist, we slipped into the woods and safely detoured undetected around their camp. Back on the trail, María ordered that we pick up the pace for the next several hours. The rain soon stopped. We pushed the horses until they were exhausted. Just before dark, we made it to the place where we camped on the way up the valley weeks before.

"Let's stop for a few minutes, then we can lead the horses for an hour or so to let them rest further," María suggested.

We watched the road nervously. In the end, except for the horses, there was no rest, just tiring wariness. Soon, we led the horses back onto the path and walked. After walking for an hour, Juan and Diego approached Doña.

"Our trail splits off just ahead. We can make it home tonight. We are closer than your ranch. Permit us to leave. The indios are dying. You should be safe."

María agreed and dismissed them, reminding them she would keep her promise about the sheep. "Gracias y los borregos son suyos."

Diego and Juan mounted their horses and disappeared quietly into darkness.

"Tomás, we can make it to my ranch, but it will be at dawn, or we can move off the trail into the forest and sleep. It is up to you."

The two of us shivered on alone in the silent, cold woods. A miserable freezing drizzle mixed with the first snow made the path treacherous. Riding on was now more dangerous than wise.

"I am tired. You know the safe places to hide in the woods," I whispered.

María again waited until we came to a stream to leave the trail. The stream's gurgling masked the splashing of the horse's steps.

"It is too dark to see the muddy water kicked up by the horses," María whispered. "The snow will cover our foot prints. Dios mío, we are safe." She was clearly relieved.

We dismounted and led our horses up the middle of the cold stream until the trail disappeared a long, safe way behind us.

"María, we will freeze to death if we cannot find a place to build a fire." I cautioned with chattering teeth.

"It is too dangerous. Pero, we will not freeze." The water grew suddenly warmer.

María led her horse out of the water into the middle of a defensible circle of fallen logs that seemed familiar to her. I followed. We unsaddled the horses and staked them in the center of a small grassy area beginning to fill with snow.

"We must be as quiet as possible. Noise travels far in the darkness," she worried, but the snow grew heavier and muted every sound. There was nothing but the hiss of snow falling through the trees. Nothing moved. In a thicket of heavy brush, we built a shelter.

"We can build a small fire here," she whispered more out of habit than need.

"If attacked and killed tonight, our bodies will never be found. Worse, we might be tortured. We will die helpless to save ourselves. We will manage without a fire." I found myself worrying like señora Griego.

"Cálmate, calm down." María put her arms around me in the dark and spoke with a strong and sure voice. "Aquí estoy. I am here."

"I hope that is enough." I pulled her tightly around me until she fully enveloped me like a warm cape. Neither of us spoke. We embraced but listened intently for the slightest noise in the dark. The thick, falling snow soon muzzled the sound of the gurgling stream and muted the wind in the pines. The silence was so complete that I thought I heard her heart beating. Perhaps, it was my own anxious heart.

"Our hearts are racing!" I tried to laugh but could not.

She carefully pulled away from me without releasing my hands. In the darkness, she motioned with her head that I was to follow her. She led me back to the stream. The snow briefly relented. The water steamed in the dark.

"There is a hot spring here. It will warm us. We may not need a fire," she spoke softly. She undressed herself, then undressed me and pulled me into the water. She unbraided her hair and let it fall thickly below her waist.

"You will help me fix it tomorrow, but now I am tired of the dirt and horse smell." She repeatedly dunked her head into the hot bubbling water at the spot where it tumbled into the cold stream.

"Have you been here before?" I asked.

"Many times," was all she said.

In the hot water, my numb toes quickly recovered from the walk through the freezing stream. I lay carefully at the bottom of the heated pool, leaving only my nose exposed to the cold. So much of what was important in my life happened around scarce, precious water. My thoughts drifted to Victoria. The hot, gurgling water brought forth memories of the many days we spent together swimming and left me struggling with loneliness.

"You are warm now," María half-commented, half-questioned. She pushed against me. She draped her hair around me, and then pulled herself on top of me. I trembled in the warm water. She pushed her breasts against me as she had many nights ago. Now, her cuera did not hide her. Her breasts were unscarred and her skin soft and smooth. My mind drifted back to the day more than a year ago when, unashamed, María dressed in the early morning light while Victoria and I watched. I remembered that María looked frail, yet strong like a big cat. Now, I had to feel all of her. I needed to touch María with my fingertips the same way Victoria first touched me. I needed to lock her smell, her soft skin, the texture of her lips, and the taste of her breath in my memory just as Victoria and I had once locked each other in our memories. I touched her breasts and buttocks. I ran my fingers up and down her back and across her lips and face until I was sure that nothing would ever take her away from me.

"¿Te gustan mis senos?" She asked. "I said I would pay you for helping me." She pressed my hands firmly into her unscarred breasts and

222

then between her legs. She reminded me that I owed her a kiss. She pulled me out of the water into the cold night and carefully dried me.

"I will keep you warm tonight. I will not let you marry Victoria without ever having known another woman. There is no need for you to feel guilt. I think she expects it."

Tangled in each other and wrapped in every warm blanket we had, we fell asleep. We slept until the heat of the mid-morning sun penetrated our bed and skins. Sweating, María awoke and clasped me to her as though she never planned to let go. She pressed her damp forehead into mine.

"It is warm enough to get up." She smiled, her rubbed her nose against mine. She pulled slowly away from me. I watched her stand. Her long hair fell to her hips. She stretched, and her thin ribs rippled. She looked down at me and smiled. She spoke with a mischievous grin.

"Señor, ayúdeme. Mister, you must help me with this hair. It comforted you all night and now it needs attention! It is warm enough. See, the snow has already melted." She sat on a log just high enough to keep her hair from trailing in the grass and pine needles.

"Which hair kept me warm?" I laughed.

"All of it. Aquí está mi peine." She gave me a large toothed comb. "Start at the bottom."

"Esto tomará todo el día." I carefully combed her pubic hair and the soft hair of her legs.

"We have all day." She smiled and closed her eyes. "I have paid all my debts. Now, you may braid my hair or you may chose to cut it since you know I am not a virgin. It is up to you." She teased, pressing her head into my chest.

"I will cut it. It will be easier." I looked for the belduque. A look of concern shot across her face.

"Lie down and hold still," I ordered. Grabbing her head with alarm, she did what I asked. With a quick slash, I collected a locket of pubic hair, held it to the wind, and let it drift away like dandelion seeds.

"It is done," I chuckled. She let out a big sigh of relief.

"Sit up." She did. "María, I like giving you orders. You follow them very well."

She smiled. "Sometimes it is good to have someone to tell you what to do."

I helped her braid her hair.

"Braid it carefully. Without Gertrudis to help, it will have to last a long time," she warned.

In half an hour, I was done. She stood and pressed her chest against me. Then she pushed me away, looking me up and down. Her eyes were black and wide. She laughed and danced childlike.

"¡Qué hermoso! Tomás, ¡Qué hermoso! You can dress now.

223

Today is a fiesta day!" She packed away her leather armor and pulled on her trousers and favorite low cut blouse.

"It is time to ride. We will be home before dinner." María happily sang as she saddled her horse and we found our way back to the trail. She stopped and looked back into the woods one last time. With a smile and sigh, she gently touched my arm, "This is my favorite place." She spurred her horse, and we raced home.

Within sight of María's ranch, the Cumanchi capitán ambushed us.

"Señorito, joven, quédese allí," he pointed to the large yellowing cottonwood tree. "Wait there," he ordered, signaling to me.

"María, what does he intend to do?"

Before María could speak, the Cumanchi shouted, "My friends and family lie dead on the other side of the hill. I alone am not infected with la viruela. You insulted my dead family and me. You," he pointed at María matter-of-factly, "I will kill you, or you will kill me. It makes no difference."

"María," I begged, "let's go home."

"I cannot. He has come for my ear. I owe him the opportunity to take it. Honor demands I respect his request. Do as he asks!"

"¡María! ¿Por favor?"

"If you do not intend to do as he asks, then, querido, do as I ask." She reached over and pulled the reins from my hands. She signaled the Cumanchi capitán to wait. She led my horse to the tree, and tied it. She called up the trail.

"Mi amigo es honorable. Él no va a interferir. He is honorable. He will not interfere." She turned to me, "I have made a promise you must keep. I trust you. Do not interfere, but you must come when I call you. You must first fire your rifle, and then ride like the wind." She turned, loosened her bow, and pulled five arrows from her quiver. She charged. I did not have time to look. I dismounted and untied my horse as fast as I could. I jumped back into the saddle as the Cumanchi capitán fell dead just in front of me.

María screamed, "Ahora, ahora now, ride, ride." I fired my rifle and spurred Viejo as he had not been spurred since his younger days. With his nostrils flaring and panic in his eyes, he charged after María. In full flight, we dashed across the fields. We rode our sweaty horses into the walls of the ranch. No one pursued us. My rifle shot gave the alarm to others nearby.

Safe inside the low walls of her ranch, María staggered from her horse. She grimaced at me with a pale, pained face. A carefully aimed arrow protruded from her lower abdomen. She leaned against her horse with blood and urine trickling from her wounds. She wailed in anger.

"I am done with my life. ¡Ave María! Perdóname por mis pecados." She collapsed to her knees, pulling desperately at the arrow embedded just below her belt buckle.

"¡Dios mío, me muero. God have mercy." She looked at me with the complete surprise of a person who until that minute believed she was indestructible.

"¡Ayúdame! ¿Por favor?" she howled in pain.

"Cuidao, do not pull the arrow." I ran to her and quickly cut away her leather pants. The tail feathers of an arrow fired at close range and constructed with a deadly jagged head protruded from the softest part of her right abdomen between her pubic bone and her belly button. Covered with broken skin, blood, and guts, the point poked from a flap of torn skin to the left of her spine. The arrow had pierced her bladder and intestines. She looked at me with complete surprise, but she fully understood that she would die. She could not believe they had actually killed each other. I carefully carried her into her father's ransacked house. Her blood gently oozed onto my shirt and coat. She smelled faintly of a freshly gutted and butchered lamb. On her bed, she shook her head repeatedly in disbelief.

"Tomás, you must never tell Victoria about last night, that I loved you." She corrected herself, "That I love you. God has punished me. That's all that matters. Promise me that she will never know so long as she lives. Promise."

"Te lo prometo, I promise."

"Hold me," she sobbed.

I held her until Diego and Juan arrived. Soon, others also came. In the wrecked house, someone lit a fire. Diego and Juan studied the arrow wound. Juan crossed himself.

"Dios tenga misericordia. I am killed by an angry, strong man," Doña María shook her head violently. Juan confirmed what she knew. She had been killed, but her death would last for several painful days.

Diego called for warm water and a knife.

"Perdóname Doña, no puedo proteger tu modestia," Juan apologized.

"I am not worried about modesty. Who has not seen a butchered animal? I worry about honor. Did I kill the enemy of my father?"

"María, he was not the enemy of your father. He was your enemy, and he fell dead at my feet," I assured her.

"Bueno, he was an enemy. That's all that matters." She closed her eyes.

Diego cut away the remainder of her trousers and shirt. He carefully removed the arrow point from her back then slowly pulled the arrow from the abdomen by its feathers. A woman from a nearby ranch helped. She dug through the overturned furnishings until she found a clay jug of turpentine. She mixed it with water and pushed the neck of the jug deep into the wound to wash out the bowel and bladder contents as best she could. María whimpered from time to time but otherwise said nothing.

Shaking her head in disbelief, she looked at me with the eyes of a tormented sinner.

"Muchacho," the woman called. "Help me clean la Doña and change her bed. The wound must drain better." The woman carefully turned María onto her side and probed the wound. Turpentine, water, blood, and urine drained into the already fouled bedding. We washed her and covered the wounds. We changed her bed. The scent of gutted animal and turpentine filled the room.

I called to Diego, "Por favor, traiga a Victoria, Felipe y Pascual. Hurry, bring them here."

"He needs many horses to make this in one day. María, he will take your best," Juan informed her.

Shaking her head in disbelief, she whispered a soft, "Sí, sí." Then she asked, "Where is Gertrudis?"

"She has not been seen since the Cumanchis came." The woman said. "Dead?" she guessed.

"Oh," María moaned.

To reach the shepherd's camp, Diego rode a long, hard day from dawn to midnight with a string of three horses. Victoria and Felipe returned on exhausted horses near midnight of the second day. Pascual stayed behind to guard the sheep. Expecting their late arrival, I kept watch and heated water for tea. Dozing off, I awakened suddenly from the commotion of horses and excited voices in the yard. Victoria flew through the door and ran to me.

"¿Qué pasó?" She demanded.

"Victoria, María groans in pain and she runs a fever. I am not sure how long she will last. The good thing is that she is not bleeding."

Victoria looked at me in disbelief. "Querido, tell me from the beginning what happened. Diego said she was injured. He did not tell me how. He said it would be up to you."

"Victoria, she dueled with the Cumanchi capitán. She killed him, but as you will soon see, he also killed her." I told Victoria about the ear and final duel on the road.

"La arrogancia y la vanidad. She has killed herself," Victoria was furious. "I love this woman as I love you. What did you do to stop this stupidity?"

"Not enough," I said, bowing my head to hide my tears.

* * * * *

Before she died, María recited her will in front of Diego, Juan, Felipe, and Victoria. I carefully wrote down her words.

"Tomás, keep 50 sheep, and 5 rams to start a new herd. I give twenty sheep and five rams to Victoria. I give my wheat fields, orchards,

226

vineyards, and house with all its contents equally to Victoria y Tomás. To you, Victoria, I give 250 pesos to take to the Hermano Mayor to have him pray for me and to pray for my father's soul. To Felipe, I give my silver beaded rosary as a token of sisterly love. Divide the rest of my sheep, more than a thousand, between Diego and Juan. If the number is not even, slaughter the extra one for my funeral dinner."

Her will completed, she called me to her side and dismissed everyone else. With burning, dry, pale hands, she reached for me. Her foul breath smelled of newly plowed and manured earth. Black blood flecked her dry, cracked lips and tongue. With a cotton cloth, I pressed water into her dying mouth. The dark odor of rotten, decaying flesh soaked into her bedding and seeped into every crevice of her room. The same sickly incense from the night she and Pascual brought Patricio home drifted in the air.

"Tomás, I do not intend to confess before I die. If anyone ever asks if I did so, you will say that I made my last confessions to you and that, as required, you are keeping my secrets. This is all I confess. I confess that I loved you from the first time I saw you. You were a child and I never could be one. I love you now. You are the only one I have ever loved with all my heart. Gracias por todo, hombre." She sighed deeply. Mustering her last energy, she desperately pleaded with me, "Acuérdate de mí, mi cabello, mis senos y mis labios. Seigo la última. Seigo la última. I am the last. Consérvame en tus quimeras y tus sueños."

She shook her head, "Gracias por todo. ¡Basta con el deber! All my debts are paid." Her "gracias por todo" encompassed every possible meaning of the word grace—a passionate thanks for the few minutes and hours we spent together as well as her gratitude for my assurances she would not be forgotten.

"Basta, basta. Call all my friends!" She was done. She spoke her final confession and her own absolution. She rightly counted on me to forever hide her sins—our sins—and keep her name alive because of them. She knew I would not forget her.

She died with all of us gathered around her bed. She was the last of her family. She was the last niña. She was la única Doña. To me she was María. She never visited the fresh grave of her father. We buried her beneath the floor of Nuestra Señora de los Milagros. We buried the dead Cumanchi warrior beside her. Victoria insisted on it. She prayed a simple prayer for both of them.

"Dios, los dos eran tontos. God, they were each the last of their line. They were foolish and brave, but you made them both. Now finally, you must take care of them. Amén."

At the church door, Victoria grabbed my shoulder. "This is for you." She gave me a newly made pine box with delicate hand-carved hearts. It contained María's braids. The ones I had braided myself. The ones María hoped would last. I cradled the box and sobbed.

Victoria kissed me gently with her broken lip. "María gave these to you a long time ago," she whispered.

Victoria

In a short few days, Tomás and I returned for the second time to Doña's hacienda from Nuestra Señora de los Milagros. Doña's house was now ours, but I was no longer sure if Tomás and I would marry. So much had changed. I walked alone into the forest behind Doña's empty house.

"I am alive, but I am not made to live," I said aloud. "How can I endure?" I followed a small stream deeper into the woods. I pulled off my tewas. Carrying them in one hand, I waded into the cold water. The rocks cut my feet. I did not care. I walked in the freezing water until past noon.

"Death always follows me," I spoke to the trees. "Is death my fault? Was this all my fault?" The trees kept their opinions to themselves. The people standing at Doña's deathbed were not surprised by any of what had happened. It was just God's will.

I remembered Bárbara did not blame her god, or any god for a tragedy. "Death stalks those who are born," she said. "If you are not a good lover, it is because you fear death too much. Overcome the fear of death so you can love."

I sat down by a clear, quiet pool bathed in the warm fall sun. October approached too quickly. Yellow aspens dotted the hillsides. Several days before it had snowed, but the snow had melted away except for a fresh glaze of white covering the high mountains.

"What is today?" I asked. I answered myself, "I have no idea."

"When did we leave San Mateo? How many days ago?" Again, I answered myself, "I have no idea."

"It is about the 26th day of September." I barely heard my own words above the hissing stream.

"So much has happened. Sometimes life feels like dangerous little snippets and episodes connected by safe periods of boredom." The silent, somber trees towered over me refusing to answer.

"My lip," I spoke to my reflection on the water. "My lip is healed with a scar and strange wrinkled shape." I pressed my tongue against the inside of my upper lip. The skin was now hard and tough, not like a lip at all. "And my short, gray hair? God has clothed his handmaiden in scars!" I moaned. "¡Munchas, munchas cicatrices!" I shook my fist at the forest. The trees kept silent.

Exhausted, I undressed and tried to beat the dust and smell of death from my clothing one last time. I stepped into the cold water and scrubbed myself with wet sand to remove the foul smell of death permanently tattooed into my skin and hair like a curse.

"Shall this bad perfume be my raiment?" I shivered from cold and despair.

"Maybe it is the warmth of the sun that I need." I stood to face the sun. A soft warm breeze danced across my nipples and brushed my pubic hair. I thought about Doña and Tomás.

"She called for Tomás with her last breath," I shouted and clenched my fists. She had been glad to see Felipe and me, but she looked at Tomás and shook her head, her hair, and her eyes in disbelief. Her lips mouthed her disbelief. Once before I caught her secretly shaking her head at him. I noticed! This time, she did not hide her thoughts. She only spoke to Tomás. "Basta, Basta" I heard her say. Only Tomás called her "María." I knew why. María was more than business. María loved!

"Where do I go now? Where do I go now when everyone is dead?" Finally, I understood pobre Mamá. I forgave her. I forgave everyone. I understood that knowledge comes with forgiving. The scent of death is also the perfume of life. The death of a loved one is crushing and freeing. The Llano buries *only* the dead, but Tomás and I were alive. Last year, I lay down in la cueva to die, but the Llano threw me back. I tried to give Tomás away, but God sent him back. Lo que sea se verá.

"I will tell tía what I have learned," I told the water and the trees. I dressed and walked quietly back to Doña's house, our house now. From the edge of the forest, I stopped to watch Tomás pacing and pulling at his coat. He had grown a short, scruffy beard. I remembered we were niños once, but that was a long time ago. He ran toward me and embraced me.

"Everyone is dead," he said.

"No querido, we are alive. The church of San Mateo needs a new altar screen. Nuestra Señora de los Milagros must be finished. We will return to San Mateo to gather our things, we will marry, and come back here to live just as María asked."

Epilogue

Josefa's notes and letters related that her grandmother, Victoria de la Cruz, was a romantic who ran to the window with little girl enthusiasm to watch the far-away trains. With her slightly trembling hands and brightly colored ribbons flowing from her long gray hair, she waved to trainmen in the distance. Even though she knew she could not be seen, she ran to the window at the sound of every whistle until the week before her death on Easter in 1891.

Getting Victoria to speak was difficult for Josefa. The easier task was prying a story from Thomas. Perhaps the death of his beloved led him to tell her story, but he also told Doña María's too. Long nights of storytelling kept his love for both of them alive.

Thomas died in December of 1891. He sleeps eternally beside Victoria in a now abandoned cemetery somewhere near Cimarron. The markers, made of hand-carved wood, have long since decayed away. The cemetery and its nameless graves are identifiable in the otherwise flat and empty prairie only by the sunken ground that reveals the collapsed wooden caskets. Victoria, Doña, and Thomas' memories are preserved only in our family history and lore. Like everything and everyone else, the Llano devoured them, leaving behind only scraps of paper, an old carved box, and a thick set of braids.

Made in the USA
San Bernardino, CA
26 October 2013